Critical Praise for *The Dewey Decimal System*

"*The Dewey Decimal System* is ~~a winningly tight, concise and~~ high-impact book, a violent, ~~exhilarating odyssey that pitches~~ its protagonist through a gratu "

~~D0029628~~

"*The Dewey Decimal System* is ~~proof positive that the private~~ detective will remain a serious and seriously enjoyable literary archetype."

—*PopMatters*

"Larson's voice is note-perfect in this tour-de-force. When called for, his clipped, brisk prose expands to the lyrical, adeptly singing the praises of beautiful women, cockroaches, and rubble. Reading *The Dewey Decimal System* transports you to another world, and although that world is a grim one, you'll be sorry to leave it. Let's hope that this book isn't a one-off, that poor damaged Dewey will return to lead us through the ruins on another near-future adventure."   —*Mystery Scene Magazine*

"*The Dewey Decimal System* is clever, inventive, lovingly satiric, and easily one of the most notable debuts of the year."

Bookgasm

"Like *Motherless Brooklyn* dosed with Charlie Huston, Nathan Larson's delirious and haunting *The Dewey Decimal System* tips its hat, smartly, to everything from Philip K. Dick's dystopias to Chester Himes's grand guignol Harlem novels, while also managing to be utterly fresh, inventive, and affecting all on its own."
—Megan Abbott, author of *The End of Everything*

"The perfect blend of dystopia and the hard-boiled shamus. It's great to know that there are still debut novels coming through the pipe that can knock me on my ass. With *The Dewey Decimal System*, Nathan Larson has announced his arrival with style and clarity. I'll be first in line for his second novel, and his twentieth."
—Victor Gischler, author of *The Pistol Poets*

"Nathan Larson's Dewey Decimal is a combination like no other—in a dystopian landscape, he's discursive, loves dissing fools, dissecting language and violence, and has a hell of a system. He's like Walter Mosley's sometime L.A. hit man Mouse, but with Chester Himes and Jerome Charyn threaded in. This novel is a love song to New York's streets and boroughs and people, even when they're decimated, and Larson's 'postracial' character, a mutt for all times, is someone I'd follow over and over again through whatever secret paths he finds in this world."
—Susan Straight, author of *A Million Nightingales*

"*The Dewey Decimal System* is a brilliant and compelling read, and Dewey is a unique protagonist: tough, resilient, smart . . . and, well, nuts—but in the best possible way. We should all be so crazy."
—Robert Ferrigno, author of *Heart of the Assassin*

"A nameless investigator dogs New York streets made even meaner by a series of near-future calamities. [Larson's] dystopia is bound to win fans . . ."   —*Kirkus Reviews*

THE
NERVOUS SYSTEM

THE
NERVOUS SYSTEM

A NOVEL BY
Nathan Larson

Published by Akashic Books
©2012 Nathan Larson

ISBN-13: 978-1-61775-079-3
Library of Congress Control Number: 2011960946

Akashic Books
PO Box 1456
New York, NY 10009
info@akashicbooks.com
www.akashicbooks.com

To my family, with love

Moment I cut through the nylon cord I'm up running, and hell no, I don't look back, slam through the stairwell exit, the bike chain still fast around one wrist, sprinting like I never thought possible, certain it's too late, that the Boogie Oogie Man will chase me down, burn me, fuck me, and kill me like he did those other kids, got no reason to think otherwise, too terrified to feel shame as I piss my Jordaches, taking the damp stairs three at a time, barely maintaining my footing, flat dirty-white Keds providing little traction, hear the man now come crashing out of his "art studio" two floors up, shrieking, I think of the Young Skulls colors I am leaving behind, that the beating I'll take from my brothers as a result of this loss is on balance worth it if I survive the moment, I'm four floors up in the semidarkness, moving, and can hear bass through the stairwell walls, bass from what must be a big-ass sound system, I can make out Zulu Nation, Black Spades, and Glory Stompers tags, poop both human and dog, rats of various sizes scattering as I skid down the stairs, behind and above me the echo of heavy footfalls and choppy breath, dude howling to himself in a language I don't understand, cannot believe that I am almost at the ground floor, take the last set of stairs in one leap, nearly fall on my ass, smelling gasoline and paint fumes, smash through the metal fire door into the hot loud night, block party in effect on Crotona Avenue, party really bumping and it's Memorial Day or Veteran's Day with dense throngs laughing and fighting and dancing with forties and red and blue plastic cups, nothing can be heard over the bass, it's the Commodores or some shit, I'm pushing through this wall of skin and sweat, smelling cheese and corn and burning pork fat with folks smacking me as I pass, I knock over an improvised grill, white coals and uncooked burgers go tumbling, trying to make my way toward East Tremont, I see the barricade and the black-and-whites and the cops, 41st Precinct so they might recognize me, but fuck it, pressing forward, so afraid, gotta tell them the Boogie Oogie is no urban legend, look back to see a big figure come through that fire door, put my head down to haul it but oh God I'm grabbed from both sides, arms tight in the grip of two grinning kids I went to school with, two Junior Reapers, screaming at them, "Boogie Man!" but the bass is too loud and I catch a fist with a roll of quarters on the chin, then another, then another, and my legs buckle and I slide to the concrete, positive now of two simple facts: the monsters are real, and no one, no one can save you from them. Not the cops. Not your friends. Not your mom. And certainly not your drunk-ass dad, who these days can barely scare up the energy to smack your mom down like he used to.

So rather than keep on running from monsters, I became one. Flipped the script on it, went on the urban offensive. Learned to hunt, rather than be hunted. Got handy with the necessary tools: fists, teeth, knives, and in time came the guns, progressively more sophisticated. Which served me well in the Marines, in future locales in every corner of this planet, both populous and barren, and still later in my service for an unnamed branch of the U.S. military, where I helped put the "black" in the term "black-ops."

And eventually as an inmate in military hospitals and facilities in Washington, D.C., where I truly learned about fear and survival. It was in these hospitals that I was robbed of my identity. Made incomplete. And it was there that my body and mind were restructured to suit even darker purposes.

With the collapse of the empire I had once served, militarized mashups like myself were made irrelevant.

So in the end, there was nothing left to do but drift home to the ruins of the city of my birth. And live on the outside, as a scavenger. As a monster.

Five hundred feet above the toxic East River, I clock a figure caterpillaring its way up one of three remaining suspension cables on the wreckage of the Brooklyn Bridge.

Moves a bit, stops. Maybe twenty feet from the very top.

Through these binoculars, of mid-twentieth-century vintage, I can't determine if the dude is sporting any kind of safety harness. All I can make out are orange coveralls and a bare head.

Don't see a work crew, it's apparent this guy is kicking it solo. Clutching at the heavy wire with thighs and elbows, flesh rubbed raw, no doubt.

It's a windy day too. The windows of this office on the nineteenth floor at 100 Centre Street rustle and thump.

I'm thinking, okay, dude can take no more. High diver. Another jumper.

And yeah, sure, from the dark, dominant side of my dome come these observations: here's yet another quitter, a weak bitch taking the easy out. Natural selection in effect.

One less mouth with which to compete for shitty food. One less set of lungs to battle for whatever oxygen remains in the blighted purple cloud that squats on Manhattan island and its lesser boroughs.

Not the kindest outlook but it's about survival up in

here. You either make it happen for yourself or you fade out.

But fuck it. I'm just procrastinating.

Don't need to see how this shakes out with the climber. I've seen bodies tossed, jump, and fall from great heights before. And it's always less interesting than one imagines.

Drop the binoculars on the crappy industrial carpet.

No more digressions. Came here, to the former district attorney's corner office, to make double positive my tracks were covered. Not perv-peep on the suicidal neighbors.

Pull off the surgical gloves, lob them at the overflowing trash bin. Messy messy.

Produce a bottle of Purell™, squirt a bit in my left palm, and rub vigorously, scanning the room. The office appears exactly as it did on my last visit.

And my former boss, DA Daniel Rosenblatt, has been dead for, what, six weeks?

I should know. I shot the man myself.

Unhygienic elements abound. Like there, on the desk. Half a submarine sandwich, peppered with mold, a sad bit of pickle. Balled-up napkins, wax paper bearing the word *Subway*.

Get the shivers. Think, motherfucker: poor air circulation, floating spore colonies. Readjust my procedure mask to securely cover my nose and mouth.

But it's not the filth that bothers me most, cause for filth I'm more than properly equipped. It's the chaos, the disorder. The lack of methodology. My System abhors disorder.

And of course this makes my task here all the more difficult. See now: I've come to expunge myself from the official books. If indeed there ever were "books" as such.

Spent half a year in the dead DA's employ. Partook in activities I don't want to discuss. With anybody, including a possible successor. If he or she is a goodie-two-shoes, they'll wanna sully up old Rosenblatt's posthumous reputation. And mine too, by association. Should my name be anywhere in this room.

Judge not. The shit was a living. And it kept me in pills, pistachios, and Purell™. The three Ps essential to my continued well-being.

Donning a new set of gloves, I exhale.

Start with the filing cabinet nearest to me, planning to work my way clockwise around the room, and then dive into the stacks of loose folders and papers.

Fucking tedious, y'all.

See, DA Rosenblatt was an enthusiastic dirt-digger. Guess that's how he held his office. In the final analysis it was this tendency that got him dead. Had he kept his substantial nose out of the dogshit, well . . .

Maybe forty-five minutes of solid rummaging crawl by, and I've learned:

—Former NYC comptroller dug she-men. Like a lot, like all the time. I actually don't get what the problem is there. His dime.

—Former comptroller Ray Stevens has or had a revolving stash of six- to ten-year-old Dominican/South/Central American girls in the basement of his Hamptons hideaway, shackled to metal rings in the floor, if I read the photos correct. I dig what the issue is there.

—Former mayor is in business with Russian/Chinese/Ukrainian crime outfits, and collects his pound of flesh from each and every construction firm in town. Shockeroo! I recognize some names in there, particularly the Ukrainians.

—Current state senator (representing the 15th Congressional District, just a touch over from the territory of my childhood) sired a child with a certain Korean hooker, who was then, most conveniently, found dismembered (along with the kid) in a barrel of kimchi. This led to the quote-unquote 32nd Street Massacre, which the NYPD has always claimed was triggered by their well-intentioned if clumsy attempts to quell a Korean turf war.

Et-fuckin-cetera.

All flavorful stuff, none of it the least bit surprising or useful, unless I wanted in on the blackmail game.

Ha. A slow horse if ever there was one, blackmail, in these times. Not much of a racket. Nobody around to preserve your good name for.

After the large-scale destruction wrought upon New York City last February (known as the "Valentine's Occurrence"), the town stands at about one-tenth capacity. And since elections have been suspended, those in power can simply kick back and hang in. Who's gonna say different?

No, the blackmail thing just isn't my bag. Plus, I dig life too much, so I mind my own.

Yawn, stretch.

All these goddamn documents, but I'm no wiser with respect to my own status, and I'm in need of a piss break. Handy that the office has an en-suite half bath.

Mirror, mirror. Wringing my hands with rubbing alcohol over the sink, I spy a thin dark-skinned male of mixed piedigree, in a hat, tasteful dark brown suit, knitted charcoal tie. Maybe midforties, though that's hard to say, given that those of us who survived this far now possess that dried-up look of the malnourished yoga obsessive. Or a late-stage HIV sufferer. The blue surgical mask perhaps clashes, but it isn't an accessory; it's for my own protection.

Lean in for a closer inspection of my mug. My nose won't ever be exactly the same, and the amateur stitch job on my cheekbone has left behind a jerky swipe of discoloration. Lower the mask. The scab on my lips is constantly cracking, even now, so it remains practically an open wound.

If you observed me walking, you'd see that I have a fairly pronounced limp, and favor my left leg. You would too if you'd had your kneecap blown off.

Otherwise, I like to imagine I cut a dashing figure. Even the limp bestows a certain casual elegance. See me on the street, perhaps taking in the virulent air, you'd reckon I got a style all my own and tony places to be. Exclusive spots way out of your league.

Add the rubber gloves, the face mask, I reckon it lends a whiff of the mysterious. That is, yo, I like to think so.

Flip the lens and I present as just another black vagrant, rough-sleeper a couple inches from death, overdressed in bespoke kit. Stone crazy in SARS gear.

All in all I must say I've done okay for a bookish (if violent, as my environment dictated) ghetto child of the South Bronx. Survivor of wars domestic and foreign.

Check my left breast: the Beretta under my jacket helps fill out the sunken cavity where my heart used to be. The Sig Sauer achieves the same effect on my right side.

Symmetry. That's the System working for me, people. Watch and learn.

I pop a pill, get a smidge misty. Reminisce on it: Jew Rosenblatt used to keep my pill supply flowing, part of our quid pro quo. Now I get my shit from a military doctor in exchange for "protection," which is pretty hazily defined. I think the guy is under the misimpression that I'm CIA or mobbed up—or both. What's the difference anymore? And who's to say he's wrong?

Regard the late DA's papers and dig in again. My third pair of gloves. I hit the loose piles.

Driving me nuts is the lack of any perceivable pattern or methodology. I like logical processes. I *live* logical processes.

See, Decimal is my handle. Dewey Decimal.

The dead DA dubbed me thus. In reference to my life's work: getting the gargantuan collection of books organized back at my crib, the Main Branch of the New York Public Library.

It's not my real name, this should be no surprise. My Christian moniker, and much of my past—most of this is information I don't have access to. Can't recall. Not like I try that hard. I'm man enough to admit it: from what little I do know, I'm afraid of what I might find, and see no reason to fixate on that which is done.

And yet here I stand, waxing full nostalgic now.

On a lot of levels, Rosenblatt understood my methods. Sure. For as much as he used me, for all the dirty business I did at his behest, the DA gave me context, and a connection to the outside world. Sure, he was a white man. A Jew. Sure, he was a crooked ambulance-chasing attorney turned opportunist politician.

Was a sad part of me that recognized a sad part of him, and vice versa. A kind of color-blind, sicko kinship founded on mutual need.

After my active military service, and my subsequent escape from the torture labs at the National Institutes of Health near Washington, D.C., Rosenblatt was one guy willing to throw me the kind of work that played to some of my less savory strengths.

No questions asked. Not that I had answers, or wanted them.

Naturally, none of this was on my mind as I hefted Rosenblatt's corpse over the lip of one of the many open fire pits that appeared across the city after the Valentine's Occurrence, usually reserved for industrial garbage but equally well suited for the disposal of bodies.

In the end, it came down to him or me, with a woman caught in the middle. Faced with this kind of moral conundrum, the outcome is a no-brainer for your humble narrator.

Lest you've already diagnosed me as a hopeless psychopath, irredeemable, I do have a Code. Which sets me apart from the bulk of the animals in this town and elsewhere.

Shake off this digression. Focus. I sigh, hunker down again over this train wreck of documents.

Another hour of this noise creeps by. My bad knee giving me deep grief, lower back barking, yeah, I'm more or less convinced there's no paper trail with respect to yours truly.

It's entirely possible. Rosenblatt never paid me in cash as such. Not like I ever got any W2s. I was taken care of in other ways, like the pills. It was a unique arrangement, very much in groove with our brave new environment.

Empty the file cabinets, deposit their contents on the floor with everything else. I can never be positive I'm not mentioned anywhere given this impossible fucking mess. This is a serious concern.

Fact in mind, I withdraw a bottle of Grey Goose vodka from the lower left-hand desk drawer, and a couple of loose Cohiba Coronos Especiales. Look around, yeah, here's that cigar clipper. With the man's engraved initials. Jackass.

I've been organizing the papers a bit as I go along. Can't help it, really. Force of habit.

Almost as an afterthought I nudge a box of aforementioned files, the tabloid-y shit on the big operators, toward the exit. Remember tabloids? Remember newspapers? A quaint thought.

Yeah, I know what I said about the blackmail racket not being what it once was. But hey now: you never know when spicy intel like this might serve some future purpose. Make a good bartering tool—but would never want to deal in this firsthand, are you crazy?

Place the set of folders out in the hall, empty and silent this late Sunday afternoon. Not that one would notice, and not that Monday will look much different. Wonder if anyone works up in this building, period. Anymore.

Douse the place in spirits, around in a circle twice.

Take a final look about. Out the window, the great Woolworth Building visible due northeast, about to be outdone (again) once they wrap up that new Freedom Tower piece of shit.

Frisk myself, locate a book of matches, reading: *Millennium Hotel*. Gives me a little zing. Obviously I haven't been smoking much lately.

There in the doorway, I take a moment to scrub those paws good with the Purell™, and kit-up with a fresh mask and set of gloves.

Lower my face mask, clip the tip off a Cohiba. Jam it between my split lips and spark a match. With the flame applied I rotate the cigar, getting a nice even cherry going.

Flick the match back into the office, it hits a stack of documents, whoosh, manila and paper go up in hot blue, the flame charges right, chasing its tail.

The room blossoms fire.

I kick the door shut, pick up the box, and head toward the elevators, huff-puffing on the expensive cigar. Trying not to inhale.

Waiting for the alarm, the sprinklers, cops, movement, something, anything. Doesn't happen.

Because like most of everything and everybody in this ghost town, like my knee, like my head, like my heart: everything is broken, and barely there.

Cause I'm afraid of what I might have done.

Memory, it's said, is either cruel or kind depending on who you're talking to.

In my case I can't say it's not cruel, as I'm only allowed a peek at a pile of fragmented snapshots. It's rerun material, rotating past my mind's eye with agonizing sameness, over and over ad infinitum.

And on the other hand, I can't say memory is not kind, because if the images I am shown mean what I think they mean, I'm better off never knowing the whole story.

Yeah, I am afraid of what I might have done, and what might have been done to me. And I am forever stuck between gears, with the clutch grinding uselessly. Grinding itself down.

So with nowhere to land, and to get myself through the goddamn day, I've adopted a System of behavior. Adherence to it is the last shred of structure I have available in an otherwise chaotic maze.

Yeah, I'm afraid of what I might've done.

Limping up the marble stairs that lead to the Main Branch, I shift the box of files to one arm and tap the southern-most lion's stone ass.

That's System protocol: a tap on my way out, and a tap on the way in. Balance, people.

Twin monster cats, keeping vigil over my home here at 42nd and Fifth Avenue. Again: balance.

I take a moment to groove on it all, applying Purell™ as I do so. Clean of hand is clear of mind.

Just made that shit up. I mouth the words, repeat it to myself.

By some miracle, the beaux arts façade of the library remains as magnificent as ever, pretty much unblemished. In the darker hours, such as this Sunday evening in mid-September, automated floodlights illuminate the building. Even now. One or two have burned out, and I wonder how long the surviving lights have yet to live. I will mourn them, believe me.

I look south. You could roll a skull down Fifth Avenue. Absolutely zero traffic. Dead quiet, with the exception of a distant industrial hubbub, a construction site to the east, the night-crew going at it.

Get itchy around crowds. That's where true believers go to blow themselves up, right to the dead center of a nice crowd.

This is why today's New York City couldn't be a better spot for a cat like me.

In this sense the town is much improved. I should know, I'm the original native son.

The air? The air is getting steadily worse, if that's possible. Or at least that's my perception. The Stench, which has been brutal since February 14, is now actively *visible*: a jaundiced haze of burnt plastic, burning oil, and smoldering trash. Hard to go more than five blocks without feeling a tightening in the chest, shortness of breath. Comes off the water, out of the ground. It rains from the rancid sky. Gets in the eyes and nostrils as well, glassy little particles and fat snowflakes of ash.

I can see it in the floodlights, a slow-moving yellow fog. Shiny bits wink at me like glitter.

You can learn to live with anything. That's the real.

Upstairs in the grand hall known as the Reading Room, I shove the box of documents beneath the bench nearest the corner where I keep my shit.

Make positive nobody else is around. Funny. Ever since that drama with the Ukrainians went down nearly two months back, I haven't seen a soul up in here. Usually there would be at least one or two ghosts looking to flop. Maybe it's cause the weather's holding steady, a touch chilly but not particularly cold yet. Maybe word spread that folks got themselves killed in these rooms. No matter. Happy to be on my lonesome.

Strip down to my boxers, shrugging off my shoulder holster, which stinks of sweat. Stow the guns. Carefully hang up my suit on a plastic Century 21 hanger.

Consider doing a little work.

Man, just when I reckon I'm getting somewhere, I discover a whole new cache of books in the twisty underground cathedral that houses the library's collection. Sets me back freaking weeks.

As much sense as the decimal system resonates with me, as much as I dig its logic, there are difficult days; I will not lie.

Coming up on seven months, and I am at classification number 004: "Data Processing and Computer Science." This can be found within subheading 000, known as "Computer Science, Information, and General Works."

Now Melvil Dewey, the father of this ingenious methodology, and its subsequent editors could not have possibly known how many volumes would come to fall under the heading "Computer Science." It's seemingly infinite. Might just take the rest of my natural life to log everything in this sub-subheading.

Check it: a good analogy is the U.S. Constitution. Essentially suspended, per Amendment 30. The one after the close-the-borders amendment, number 29. Championed, I should add, by husband-and-wife Senators Clarence Howard and Kathleen Koch.

Look at the Second Amendment. Think about all these frothing delusionals, running around hopped-up on meth and/or religion, armed to the freaking gills—I'm talking *before* 2/14. All bets are off now.

As a kid in the Bronx, I saw close to a hundred situations in which shit went south just cause some stupid fuck had a heater and an inferiority/Napoleon complex.

The founding slaveholders couldn't have foreseen how our culture, our diseased urban centers, would devolve.

My proposal? Gun ownership should only be awarded to citizens like me, who will generally keep the peace, and will only ever bust a cap in a motherfucker if said motherfucker really deserves it. It's about wisdom and character. Knowing when to stay thy hand.

Sure, there are no more licenses—for anything. But there's just as many guns, if not more so. And all this mental jawing on my part is for naught now, being as we are all so much closer to the end of history. Assuming we haven't staggered over that line already.

But let's accentuate the positive.

Strip off the shrink-wrap and pull on a brand-new hospital gown. Consider my larger task.

Naw, fuck it. It's been a busy Sunday. I'll bunk down early so I might get the jump on the morning.

Unfurl my bedroll. As I do this, my eyes are drawn to the box I pulled out of Rosenblatt's office. A couple outstanding issues nibble at my chest.

One: Did I miss anything? Could Rosenblatt have been holding a document stash somewhere in his apartment, aside from the material I know I destroyed weeks ago when I offed the man? What could I have passed over, unawares? Did the DA keep duplicates—perhaps at yet a third location, unknown to me?

Two: Was this the wise move, grabbing these files? Realize having this stuff around makes me twitchy. Blame my pack-rat instinct. Perhaps I don't need the headache this kind of stanky material could generate.

These concerns bounce around my brain like pissy wasps, and I'm at a loss as to how to silence them for good. I take a temporary measure.

Making a promise to deep-six this gear at the first opportunity, I fetch the box, carry it over to the dumbwaiter, stick it in, and send it downstairs. Press the button to open the bottom of the lift, dump the box, recall the dumbwaiter, and jam the thing by removing the control faceplate, and the buttons with it. This I stash with the rest of my gear.

Close the door to the cubby, a wood contraption with fake book spines. I've gotten a lot more careful of late, used to just leave my things out in the open.

Kill the power to the building and grab my flashlight next to the fuse box. Purell™ up, pull on a fresh pair of gloves, and raise my mask. Settle in with a copy of *Experiencing Totalitarianism*, in the original Latvian. Happy with how my Latvian is coming together. I must have absorbed some along the way during this recent period of action.

See, I can read and speak an unknown number of languages. Not cause I'm some kind of linguistic genius. It's cause the government stuck something in my head that allows me to do this. Sound batshit crazy? Indeed it might be.

But dig it, as this is a solid fact: I am constantly surprising myself with a total command of new and unexpected languages. Languages I've never heard of. I don't know the extent of it, this "gift," this unearned ability.

But apparently Latvian wasn't written into the master code, cause I'm struggling with it a tad.

Get hung up on the sentence, "As the Fourth Panzer division crossed the border . . ." Not sure of the Latvian word for "division," perhaps they mean "battalion" or "regiment," trying to recall the difference in terminology, this thought-stutter like a skip in an old LP record, and gradually sleep takes me.

A loud crack jerks me out of the only goddamn dream I ever have. The one where somebody who looks and feels a lot like me murders my wife and child.

I roll sideways, pop open my camouflaged cubbyhole, and root around in there for a couple seconds. Withdraw my guns and come to a squatting position. Wide awake now. Listening to my blood. Listening to the dark.

Another snap, down the hall. And a third.

My pistachio shells. Laid out on the stairwell. Somebody tramping on 'em. Means visiting hours start now, like it or not.

I raise the Beretta and the Sig.

Can't see shit. I hear my flashlight, which fell off my chest as I popped up, rolling toward the back of the room. Somewhere amongst my gear I have those night-vision goggles, but I can't go foraging for them now.

I have that CZ-99 as well, it occurs to me, but I've never fired it, so best to stick to the known.

There, in the hallway, thin shafts of light. Getting steadily brighter, less diffuse.

The lights round the corner into my room, four slivers dancing vertically, making jerky sweeps. Just under these, moving in tandem with the light, red lasers cast pinpricks on bookshelves, tabletops.

Tactical weaponry. Customized, expensive. I experience something like envy, but just for a sec. Mostly cause for all my lone-wolf posturing, I do miss being part of a posse. Pack animals, after all.

I grin, nasty. No problem. Aim just north of the beams, take two of them out, one of the remaining two will panic and do something stupid. Positively no sweat.

Cock both guns.

And a metal object is pressed into the back of my head.

"Drop 'em, shitbird." Scratchy-voiced male behind my right ear.

Hell, I do it. If these people were skilled enough to get in here, get *behind* me, me sleeping like a baby lamb? Strictly pro shit, and I do not want to play cute.

"On your stomach, go."

A boot in my back and the floor meets my face. Thinking: goddamn. Mental flab. Going soft. Events should not be rolling out in this manner.

"Subject is disarmed. Repeat, subject is disarmed and secured, over." Calm and cool, like, all biz.

Heavy boot on my neck now. I'll be goddamned.

There's a crackling of radios, somebody talking about "fuse box, breaker," and with a clunk the lights come on. With my ear to the ground I hear an ascending hum as the building wakes up. Maybe I imagine it cause these floors must be four feet thick.

Guys running in my direction, light on their feet for the amount of gear they must be carrying. Radios, numbered codes being called out, call letters and verbal shorthand I don't recognize.

That's troublesome. I'm a military creature. Got a good recall when it comes to codes and such. Should be on my radar.

"Let's get those hands, top of your head. Lock fingers, let's go."

I do it, feel plastic being threaded around my wrists and pulled tight.

"Let's get some ID on this mook, now, now."

Attempt to shift my head but the boot is still pinning my neck to the floor, say: "Suit jacket pocket, right side. My laminate." Comes out constricted.

Trying to get a look at somebody. I hope they don't fuck up my suit. Every time I score a new suit . . .

Note the footwear, a couple pairs of hi-tech plastic and nylon in black, looking for a brand, something to indicate—

"Sending scan, over."

Déjà vu. I'm having mad déjà vu.

"That's a roger. Let's move, move . . ."

My hands are pulled back and a hood comes down over my head. It's cinched at the neck.

Think Abu Ghraib, that photo, crucifixion pose, it comes to me, and I gotta say I am ever so slightly fucking terrified. There's not even a pretense of civility, which would come with most law enforcement agencies. Wouldn't it?

I know better than to say anything further unless addressed directly.

These guys are vibing contractors, private army stuff, beholden to nobody. Better equipped than our own military, I saw that myself over there. In the later days, there were more of these motherfuckers than there were straight military. Always swanning around. Better guns, better body armor, better food, better whores, better digs . . . Got me to thinking I was on the wrong team. Hell, that's why I—

Up and away. I'm lifted like a sack of rice, dudes have

their hustle on, jogging me forth, swing right, down the stairs, slam through the door and out in the sickly night air.

As we're bumping down the exterior stairs, I'm hearing, "Subject in custody, awaiting go-to points," the guy sounding winded, makes me think this operation is an improv, a last-minute clambake. Not that this observation matters.

I'm unceremoniously deposited on carpeting, reckoning the interior of a vehicle, two metallic bangs, must be in the rear, most likely a van, "Go, go, go," they're calling, and the van lurches forward, I tumble with gravity, hit the rear doors with my forehead. Hoping they're locked.

Feel fucking naked. I got boxers and a hospital gown. And a goddamn Gitmo Klan Kap.

Messing with my head. Driver going in circles, right on 39th Street, left on Sixth Avenue, right on maybe 42nd, and repeat. Trying to get a man disoriented . . . and worse, violating the edicts of the System (details when I get a chance), not that I expect these thug-o's to be aware of such an elegant paradigm.

Radio squawk. Driver or somebody saying something, and next time we hit Sixth Avenue we accelerate, northbound.

T rying to count blocks based on our approximate speed. Reference my mental map, dig the interlocking grid. It's all there, laid out in my head, in 3-D, in full color.

North on Sixth, sharp right on what I figure is Central Park South. Fucking hell. Zoom zoom, I'm counting, hard left, I'm guesstimating onto Madison or Park Avenue.

This is making me physically sick, this . . . gross affront to the System. What kind of animal . . .

Flat-out northbound, gaining speed. Wracking my brain over this fine how-do-you-do. Could this be FBI? Likely not. FBI don't have no sexy boots, they just throw shit together, especially these days. More fallout from the Branco/Iveta cock-up, the Balkan imposed upon me of late? The only loose end would be one Brian Petrovic, and somehow when that man gave me his word, despite his shadiness, I fully bought it as good. Plus, old Brian was on a military flight to Paris last time I checked, and I did confirm that.

Didn't I? Not remembering key shit. Slipping up.

The girl. Iveta, the very thought of her, it hurts my chest, so I kill that line, kill it good and hard and throw a padlock on it.

The woman in the middle. Pushing the buttons. Yeah, I get it, people. Lady played everybody. Doesn't change a damn thing. The human heart is a strange, lawless planet.

No. This is some spanking-new static.

We almost catch air as the road dips, my stomach drops

. . . A block later we're climbing a hill, yeah, we're at 96th Street or thereabouts.

Screech left around about 116th, westbound, and I'm starting to lose my bearings. Something like five or six blocks and it's ANOTHER hard right, a further affront to my System; I know we're in the wasteland that is Harlem, but gotta face it, this brother is lost.

Trying to feel around, hands and feet, for some kind of blunt object, something I can use as a weapon, no luck.

Abrupt halt, again I roll as physics dictates and smack into a carpeted wall.

Doors slam, several guys I figure, back doors thrown open. "Let's go, let's go," again they get me in a football hold and the men are moving briskly over pavement.

Bang through a door into a building, I have a sense of spaciousness but am losing faith in my powers of perception. We come to an abrupt stop.

"Sixteen." I hear a series of dings, the sound of doors sliding open.

An elevator. Jah protect and guide me.

This space does not vibe public housing, so that aside there's only one remaining structure this tall above 116th Street in Harlem: that monstrosity, the Adam Clayton Powell Jr. state office building.

Here's where I start struggling. The old familiar fear gives me a big bear hug.

"Look, listen," I say, "I can't do elevators. Seriously. There's gotta be stairs. Please, you all, I'm not—"

Something hits me hard in the chest, my last thought before I black out is that I've been fucking tasered.

The indignity of it all.

did not authorize, nor do I suggest, nor do I endorse . . ." Basso profoundo.

"With respect, sir, he was armed and resisting—"

"Son, you let me finish. Nor do my office or I endorse the use of unnecessary force, coercion, and inhumane treatment of any individual when my wish is only to have a conversation with them, in person. Are we clear?"

"Sir-yes-sir."

Awake, breathing hot against the fabric, thinking about those files . . .

"Get this mother-lovin hood off of him."

The hood is pulled away and I'm blinking at a tall black man in a blue suit, maybe mid-sixties but built like a linebacker, and of course I recognize him straight off.

Say, "Senator Howard."

Senator Clarence Howard regards me, mustache twitching. After about five seconds, he speaks.

"Leave us be." This to the man who dragged me in.

Soldier hesitates, makes a sound in his throat. Clearly, however, his thoughts on this are not welcome. Exits, closing the door behind him noiselessly.

Blink, blink. It's almost sunrise, and the skyline is pretty much dark. An opaque layer of poison blankets most of the island, but I can identify the lights of the Chrysler Building, and the stillborn 15 Penn Plaza.

Somebody still manning the lights on the Chrysler.

Something beautiful about that. Miniature helicopters buzz around the building like bugs around a flame. The helicopters are a constant.

It's an absolutely generic office in here, beige everything, mid-'90s décor, seemingly unused.

The senator stands for a moment, his back to me, sagging a touch but every bit as large as his rep, at least within the neighborhood. Old-school conk: no self-respecting black man of my generation would undergo such a procedure. Only the trannies. No. Natural is the way of the righteous. I speak of course for myself here.

Howard inflates, rotates his large frame, and presents me an expansive politician's smile. Big man's got his famous cane on him, rosewood with a copper horse head, its tongue extended.

"Son, apologies are in order. I'm not in the habit of pulling people out of bed in such a way."

He's got one of those voices. Velvet, and a couple decades of cigarettes. A voice that sells Jesus and legislation.

"Yeah . . . well, fuck it, apology accepted, Grandpa." Rub my wrists, the red marks there. "Seen you on C-SPAN back when. I dig your strong position on immigration, sir. And on those goddamn uppity unions." I tsk, wag my head in faux disbelief.

If he reads my snark, the good senator makes no indication. In fact, if anything, he brightens.

"Ha. C-SPAN! Now that's television that'd put near any man to sleep. Whole lot of people talking to themselves just to hear themselves talk. Son, let me get right down to the nitty-gritty."

"Please do, boss," I say, trying to radiate togetherness but reckoning: this cannot be good on any level.

"I have . . . excuse me." The senator produces a silky handkerchief and sneezes explosively.

Can't help it, I flinch, thinking: New strain of the superflu? Something I'm not inoculated against? My noggin just goes straight there and lingers.

Man, for some Purell™. And me in my jammies. Surgical mask hanging around my neck, useless, how slack am I. Deserve whatever I get.

"Pardon me once more." The senator dabs at his nostrils. There's a monogram, CDH, middle name Douglass.

Fuck me sideways. The DA's files. I know exactly why I'm here.

Senator saying, "The air in these buildings tends to just plain dry me out. Well, sir. As it happens I am looking for a mutual friend of ours. I've fallen out of touch with the man of late, and I must say I'm just a bit concerned. District Attorney Daniel Rosenblatt?"

Squint a bit, as if trying to make a connection. Nod. This heading where I figured it would head.

"Yeah," I say. "Me, I've been trying to track him down myself."

"Is that a fact?" says the senator, smile locked in place.

"That's right. As you probably know, I do occasional work for Mr. Rosenblatt. Haven't seen him for, what, six weeks, thereabouts. Talked to him, though, maybe last week."

Making up smack. Spot where they hit me with that taser hurting like a bastard.

The senator purses his lips and leans back against a table. Taps his cane on the floor. Shit, this guy doesn't need a cane. I could use a motherfucking cane, and not just as an affectation.

"Well, that is a shame. Goodness, I would have thought

you'd be the man to talk to here. As it happens, son, you were seen only just last night, leaving Mr. Rosenblatt's office. Took us awhile to make the connection and track you down again . . . but when we did, I figured, well, we should have a little chat."

Trying to fuck me up. Damn. The possibility of a piece of the DA's implant in my arm still giving off a signal occurs to me only now. Though I thought it got dug out. I don't falter, having anticipated something like this.

Say, "That's right, and I was surprised to find Daniel wasn't there. We had an appointment. What's more, I think the joint was looted. The door was broken, whole spot looked kind of torn up, vandalized."

I'm just freestyling. Wandered into a big fucking mess here. Keep it poker-faced.

"Ah yes," says the senator, all molasses, "and this was before half the floor was burned up, destroyed by fire? You missed that part, young man, if I hear you correctly. Because that's what got us thinking. The fire. And that's what brings you uptown tonight."

Goddamnit. Project confusion.

"How do you mean? A fire down at 100 Centre?"

"Indeed. And it's just the strangest thing, as this must have been around the time you were on the premises yourself. Me, I got the call about a quarter to nine. I will admit, working on a Sunday . . . the work of this Union is much like the Lord's work . . . it ain't nine-to-five, mister, it's a twenty-four-hour thing."

He *winks* at me. Fuck's sake.

"Off topic, Grandpa," I say, "but aren't congressional sessions suspended . . . like, indefinitely, sir? On account of complete—"

Howard sniffs, fusses with his tie, the flag pin. "Well, there are those of us who continue America's righteous work, young man. That's about all I'm prepared to say about that, thank you very much. Now, we were discussing this fire, down at our mutual friend Mr. Rosenblatt's office . . ."

"A fire, one that I would surely remember. Let me think on it," I say. "Eight-thirty, yeah, that was around the time I was there, for sure. A fire? Still, these old buildings falling apart, loose wiring and whatnot, we see it all the time now. That's tough stuff, though . . . goodness me. Hope nobody got hurt."

The senator is humming a little tune, not buying my spiel for a sweet second. He's far too smart. A dead man could see that. Letting me slide down the slope on my own. Sussing what I know.

Likewise, I gotta keep poking at him, determine what he's hip to.

Senator Howard says, "No, nobody hurt in the fire, praise be to God, being a Sunday and all. But it's a funny thing. And, well, it's hardly my business now, so just pardon me for prying, but I don't want to be making assumptions. I'm told you were seen to be carrying a stack of papers—oh, files, or some such thing—as you exited the building. Is that correct, sir?"

I nod.

"See now," he continues, "my men would have . . . spoken with you right there on the spot had we made all the connections, as I mentioned. But, again, to err is human, it took us a moment, and so we were obliged to . . . inconvenience you in this way."

Wanna tell the dude I could give two flaccid fucks

about a dead hooker. Ancient history. Hand to God, no problem, lemme go home.

Though I'd be a liar. Talk about fatal flaws, y'all: I am compelled to nurse the weak, and it's this tendency that keeps landing my knob in shit gumbo. Thinking this. But say, "Yeah, well, about those papers, I had brought that material in with me for our meeting. Paperwork we had discussed—"

"What kind of paperwork, son?" The senator's eyes tighten a fraction.

"A questionnaire, it was something I had circulated among the larger work sites, mostly to do with ethnic distribution of the employees."

"Who issued this questionnaire?" Mustache twitching. Flashes of the scorpion that hangs just beneath the public face of all politicians/preachers.

"As far as I know, the DA's office, the DA himself, he was—"

"So let me understand. If I call the governor, or the Department of Labor, what do you think they're going to tell me about this questionnaire?"

Massage the area where I got zapped. "I don't know, honestly. They still open for business, the Department of Labor?"

"That's beside the point, son."

"Uh-huh," I reply. "Well, as far as I could tell, it came from Rosenblatt's office, like I said. His letterhead. It wasn't unusual that he would conduct his own unofficial polling, just to have a general—"

"Unofficial polling." The senator gives me a generous look at his front teeth, uniformly capped, exclusive stuff. "Son, I am the chair of the Congressional Commission on Appropriations. Now, do you have any sense of what that

is, educated brother like yourself, watching your C-SPAN?
What we do on this commission?"

I scan my head, seeing where I fucked up. Problem
with any lengthy conversations these days is I forget what
I just said.

Figure I'll play along with the man's delusion that
Washington operates in the way it used to. Well, he should
know better than me, I suppose, for I might as well still
be asleep in that army hospital in Frankfurt. Or at the safe
house in Islamabad. Wherever.

Say, "Civics, yeah. Been a good while. Didn't school us
on civics in the corp."

"Indeed. Well, then. We deal with defense, homeland
security, commerce in general. Most relevant, son, we handle labor—military and civic construction. See where I'm
going with this, young man? Are you 'digging' me here?" he
says, making air quotes with his stubby fingers.

"No sir, I'm afraid I don't—"

"Well, let's consider what you just said. If in fact our
mutual friend the good district attorney is engaged in collecting such information on his own steam, why, sir, I'd
have to say let's hold on a moment. That's illegal."

"I have to say I was not aware of that, senator . . ."

Howard shakes his hand in the air.

"That's you talking, and I have to accept your word at
face value. Being as you are a working man, doing what you
can do in these very troubled and troubling times."

"Yeah, I appreciate that."

The senator closes his eyes, holds up his palm. "*Bear
one another's burdens, and so fulfill the law of Christ.* Isn't that just
the way, son?"

Aw, Lord. Of course the big man is church-crazy. Well,

that's Harlem for you in a nut. Say, "Beg pardon, senator, I don't follow."

"Galatians 6:2. It's the One True Word, young man." Senator points his eyes at me. Teeth on display, that alligator smile.

Man, these fucking get-happy-Jesus sociopaths are the slipperiest. Him and his fucking wife, Senator what's-her-name. Koch. Bad crazy white woman.

Senator saying, *"Bear one another's burdens . . .* You tell me this: you tell me if the good Mr. District Attorney Rosenblatt is the kind of man who enjoys conducting 'unofficial' polls, collecting, as it were, information—unofficially, mind you—for his own edification and education, information to be used to suit his very own purposes, and perhaps the furtherance and glorification of Mr. DA Rosenblatt's financial and professional position. Would you say he leans partial to this kind of practice, young man?"

My chest hurts. I need a pill. Need Purell™. But I dig an angle. "Well, if you're suggesting he's a cagey motherfucker, capable of, well, extortion and blackmail, I'd say positively hell yes."

The senator's eyes light up. "Son, understand, the good Lord did not put me down here on this earth to cast aspersions on my fellow man, be he of any color or creed. But it has to be said, now, if this Rosenblatt is running blackmail schemes, extortion, etc., it pains me, but I believe this is the kind of person who might . . . take such activities one step further. Create fictions, falsehoods which might prove favorable to his person. Or, more correctly, his purse. Do you read me?"

Goddamn if this guy doesn't use fifty words when five would do the job. Makes for easier obfuscation.

Don't respond. I raise my eyebrows a bit, waiting.

The senator looks toward the door for a second, clears his throat. Leans in, gets all intimate.

"Son, it's no business of mine what you get up to with yourself, and it is not my place to dictate how a man may or may not be making a living wage. Understand this. But make no mistake. I want to be absolutely clear about one thing: whatever you may have heard, perhaps about myself, perhaps about some other individual, I want you to first consider the source."

Leans back, nodding at himself in satisfaction.

"Consider the source," says the senator.

I make solemn like I'm digging him deep. In pain over here, goddamn taser.

"The source," continues the senator, closing his eyes. "Well, let's just say it like it is, the source is a Jew, of whom Christ himself did say: *You belong to your father, the devil, and you want to carry out your father's desire. He was a murderer from the beginning, not holding to the truth, for there is no truth in him. When he lies, he speaks his native language, for he is a liar and the father of lies.*"

He says this then falls silent, just smiling this inward kind of smile, creepy, rocking his head back and forth very slightly.

I'm thinking: this motherfucker is once, twice, three kinds of crazy minimum. That's the same biblical passage crackers of old used to justify stringing up our people in Mississippi and elsewhere. Everybody knows this. The Good Book is handy that way.

The trembling commences. Without my pills? About ninety minutes before my brain starts to hemorrhage. I'll start worrying in, say, ten.

"Senator." I take a deep breath.

Howard opens his eyes, pulls at his tie again.

I say, "Why would you have a goddamn paramilitary team haul my simple ass out of bed, run me up here at gunpoint?"

Rubs his chin. "Son, I do apologize."

"Yeah, you ran all that already, boss. Exactly what is your business with me?"

Mustache fluttering. "Well, young man, I simply wanted to commune, from my heart to yours. I wanted to express to you my feelings about truth. And those who distribute untruths. I wanted to tell you, son, should you see this Rosenblatt again, why not send him my way? Or . . ." Again he hunches over and moves in on me. "If you have taken my message to heart, you will yourself see the folly in placing stock in liars and thieves. *But as for the cowardly, the faithless, the detestable, as for murderers, the sexually immoral, sorcerers, idolaters, and all liars, their portion will be in the lake that burns with fire and sulfur.*"

He directs a thick finger at my chest.

"You can be that lake. Or burn in it. Son, take the side of righteousness. Repent, turn it around, seek a noble life. That's just straight scripture, Revelation 21:8."

Had enough of this preacher talk. I say, "No doubt. I still don't feature, senator, you feeling the motherfucking need to drag me up here, just to listen to you spitting jive Jesus shit."

It's a much more complex smile that inhabits his face now. Talking to the real man now. Much preferable.

"Why I brought you on up, out your bed? First of all, to demonstrate I can drag your sad ass anywhere I care to, any old time, day or night. Next, to let you know that whatever you may have done or choose to do, you are now front and center on my radar. I see you, brother, day and night. God sees you too."

He leans in yet further. I smell his mouth, coffee and old teeth.

"Why, I know all about you, son. You think you're clever like that, that you can just disappear, young man? Don't mistake me, I salute you for your service, all that. You're a warrior. But let's call a spade a spade. Things seem to have taken a downturn for you, son. I know about Walter Reed. I know about NIH, the programs you took part in, son. Shit, I probably authorized that grant, who can remember? The grant done paid for the study, to which you so generously gave of yourself. You were the star pupil, head of the class, son. What I heard. Hell, I know about this business with the Russian gangsters and what-all, socialist no-God cracker garbage."

The man enjoying this, darkness yawning wide behind his tongue.

"The Lord giveth, the Lord taketh away. How much do you love your precious library? Love is a powerful thing, I know that much. But I love the Lord Almighty, and a library ain't nothing but a pile of paper and rocks, built by the hands of men. Power of the Lord knocks it down in a heartbeat."

My lips go cold, and a spasm runs the length of my body.

"What are you getting at with all this, Senator?"

He waves me off, on a roll, saying: "I know about this white woman from the Balkans, you dig me now? War criminal, isn't she? Sure, I know where she's at this very moment. Imagine our friends at Interpol would be interested in that too. Son, I know what you and Rosenblatt were up to, oh goodness, know all about it, every detail. And I figure I know what became of the DA Jew."

The Senator draws a forefinger across his throat, slow. Then points it at me, cocks his thumb, pow.

"Doesn't take a genius. Fellow had it coming. Been watching. We. Know. Everything. So, young man, imagine stepping into the Jew's shoes, if you figure you know a thing or two about anything or anybody, including myself, I want you to remember the eternal words of our living God." He pauses, breathing heavily. Then, "Recall: *A false witness will not go unpunished, and he who breathes out lies, will perish.* And remember our little conversation here in this room. Proverbs 19:9. Godspeed, Mr. Decimal."

The senator rises and walks straight out the door.

Cued, black boots hustling in, the hood raised up and coming down on my head once more.

"Jesus fucking wept," I say to nobody.

"Come again, motherfucker?" Scratchy voice.

Lips parted, in my shroud, say, "John 11:35."

And the cocksukers tase me. Again.

Outside the projects, midwinter. I see my breath, feel the ice crust on a beard I no longer have.

Always the same dream.

Stand before the Gun Hill Houses. Behold the architectural brutality of American public housing. Behold the banality of economic segregation.

Observe the empty playground, and the singularly ghetto debris strewn here and there: frosted forty-ounce bottles of Olde English Malt Liquor, Doritos bags, chicken bones, a stray toddler-size Rocawear sneaker.

Note all of this. Disregard it.

Enter the building. All surfaces are subway-car metallic, impervious to graffiti.

Enter the elevator to a cloud of piss and beer. Push the correct button. None of this is unfamiliar.

Exit the elevator, follow the hallway to the correct door. Take out the key.

Key in lock.

Listen at the door.

Inside: a female, I imagine, holds a trembling hand over a child's mouth, and wills this child to be silent, for mercy's sake.

And mercy is what I'm all about. It's why I'm here.

Heft the weapon. And enter on my own time.

Always the same dream.

Come thrashing out of it, fully disoriented, soldiers misinterpret my little seizure as resistance to their caresses.

"Get his legs, his legs."

They renew their grip and I'm hefted onto cool stone. The hood is whisked away.

Eyes fluttering, focus, and I'm home, in the atrium of the library.

Little solace here, though, cause I'm crowded by five heavily armed men, black body armor and flak jackets, spooky in goggles, helmets, and foam rubber ski masks.

A particularly big guy leans over, me knowing it's foolish, but I'm saying, "Tase me again, friend, so fucking help me . . ."

He grips my trachea, pinches it closed. "Faggot, here's the sit-rep." It's the scratchy-voiced dude, clearly the alpha of this crew.

I can't breathe but that's the point. At least he's got gloves on. Small miracles. Involuntary tremors from the pill withdrawal, otherwise I don't bother resisting.

Through the mask the man says, "Should've picked you up right off the street last night downtown. Had a feeling. You had us running in circles for a bit there, but we found ya, motherfuck. Yeah. Always will." He clears his throat, continues, "Listen here. We've scoured this shit shack for any paperwork you might have regarding the senator. Happy to take this fucker apart slab by slab. Got reason to believe you've concealed certain documents, and that's government property, Decimal. Huh? But rather than wear my people out, we're going to do it like this and give you a chance to man the fuck up. Courtesy the senator is extending to you. Not me."

He readjusts his grip, I get a quick breath in, not much but enough to keep from blacking out if this keeps up.

"I'm doubling back here in eight hours with my unit. Any intel you might have regarding the senator goes in my hands. Understand you're locked down, we got you monitored. You so much as cough, we'll know about it. All exits are covered. Produce these materials and we got no problems. Consider this eight hours an act of grace, respect for a warrant officer. Broke-dick as you are."

There, the patch on his breast: *Cyna-corp*. The familiar circle-and-swoop logo. Contractors. As predicted. Gives me an Iveta-jolt, her file . . . something about her working with these guys . . .

Releases my throat. I'm coughing, think maybe I'll try vomiting on the man's overbuilt shitkickers, though there's nothing in my gut to puke up. Throatful of liver juice.

Guy rises. "That clear enough for you, sir?"

Try to speak, nothing but that burn, have another go, croak: "Solid copy, my man. Stay peace."

Dude draws a ridiculously huge diver's knife from his boot and cuts my plastic cuffs. Takes the opportunity to jab his knee into the spot they've hit me twice now.

Then he's back up, saying, "Yalla, yalla," and the crew piles out awkward through the revolving door.

The hustle bustle produces echoes, I lie here, listening to them dissipate. Dig the heavy empty space of my adopted home.

Well, well.

Gotta get to my pills. Left-hand suit jacket pocket. Please please let them be undisturbed.

Drag myself upright, and upstairs. It's not easy. Acute pain has been piled on top of the low-level hum of my body's permanent discomfort.

These Cyna-corp shitbirds go by many names and logos, and they have all but replaced the United States military . . . first overseas, and then domestically. Just more cost-effective. Oh, and then you don't have to concern yourselves with pesky details like international law, or the traditional rules of engagement.

Cyna-corp doesn't just do military. Cyna-corp does catering. Office supplies. Janitorial and laundry services. General infrastructure, and construction of all types.

Kick it from this angle: they get paid to knock it down, and paid to build it up again.

Funny little world.

Hey, shit, I told you blackmail wasn't my gig of choice. Witness the potential repercussions. This here how-do-you-do would be one reason why I'm just not into that bizzle.

Irony here is I never had any intention of trying to extort anybody. Did I? Fuck no. I'm just attempting to get through the goddamn day. A process that doesn't become any easier with time, now does it?

But this current beef. It's not about blackmail anymore.

Iveta threatened, though I don't take that too seriously. She can handle herself, to put it mildly. Pity the bitches that wanna come at that lady.

Hey, though. Threaten my library? Can't abide it. Won't

allow it. But that's not the worst thing the good senator seemed to imply.

Nope, the real worry: yours truly facing my most profound nightmare—being exposed to myself. My true name. Nothing I wouldn't do to wriggle free of that one.

Gimping down the hall, swing into the Reading Room; the place has been tossed, no question there.

Prior to further assessment I make straight for my suit jacket, hanging as I left it, thanks be to Buddha, and shaky-hand snatch the pill bottle out of the pocket. Dry-swallow one. Think again, dry-swallow another.

Scrubbing up with Purell™, I eye-sweep the room, yup, stuff scattered every which way, my agonizingly thought-out stacks of this and that toppled. I guesstimate a week of cleanup, without distractions, and it doesn't seem like I'm gonna see a week like that for a spell.

Gonna have to clean. Everything.

A look at the dumbwaiter tells me they tried to jimmy it, unsuccessfully. When the door is closed, it's closed. Plus, recall, I jammed it.

Occurs to me: there's got to be a good reason why the devout senator didn't just have me killed straight out the gate. Then his boys could take their sugar-sweet time ripping up this spot, and not have to concern themselves further with tumbleweeds like me. I'd just blow away, no muss and no fuss.

Yup, there's a reason I'm still alive and on the scene. And I suspect it's cause these clowns are chasing their tails and don't know what's popping, or how a player like myself might factor in the mix. I suspect they reckon I might, in my actions, feed them more tasty intel, that pesky missing puzzle piece.

Which means that despite the senator's tough talk, these boys might be nearly as deep in the darkness as I am about who's fucking who. Hoping I can throw 'em a bone.

So the man of God reckons the DA was running an extortion game on him regarding a small matter of a hooker and an infant, cut to pieces and stuffed into a tub of pickled cabbage. And now the good senator is concerned that I'm picking up where the DA fell off. That I intend to run the very same racket.

Well, at least I'm getting an idea of where I'm at.

Starting to feel more like myself. Trying to Zen it with respect to the mess.

To be sure, I do not doubt that I'm on camera. And I don't want to linger here.

Get my suit back on. Paul Smith, a rusty-brown wool number (I say this like it's not my only suit—it's my only suit, okay?), a joint that's either too hot or too cold this time of year, depending, but what can you do? The high price of fashion.

Naturally, my fucking guns have been confiscated Goddamnit.

But just a moment.

Dig in my cubbyhole, more good luck. They missed this one. Well pleased with the camouflage door, a new addition I made during a manic more-paranoid-than-my-baseline-paranoid episode.

I slide the Serbian CZ-99 into my hat and press it against my chest. Also a folded towel, within which are two 9mm magazines that will fit the 99. Note the dumbwaiter faceplate and controls in there, undisturbed.

Assuming cameras throughout the main room.

Grab a handful of gloves, an extra surgical mask. Spare

bottle of pills and two four-ounce Purell™ dispensers. My new laminate, and a couple small leather-bound badges. A penlight, and the night-vision goggles. Handful of jerky sticks. Wanna bring duct tape but I'm fresh out of pockets.

Head to the bathroom. Enter a stall, unfurl the towel, load the pistol, shove it down my waistband in back, drop the extra magazine in my pocket.

Take a moment. Roll my sleeve back, have a look at my forearm. Pretty well healed, of course there's plenty of scar tissue, but . . . what are the chances the implant didn't actually get removed? That bits remain? Do these things fragment and remain functional? Cause if that's the case and they're on my frequencies, this whole charade is moot. I'm a floating blip on a screen somewhere.

I simply gotta believe this ain't the case, otherwise . . .

Come out of the men's room dabbing at my face with the towel. Press on my hat.

Yeah, starting to feel better and better. Ready to bounce.

Praise Jesus. This fucking politician. The way I look at this, you can't bullshit a bullshitter. The senator knows more about me than I care to, quite likely every little distasteful thing the DA put me on to. Dangling this over my head like a guillotine. I can't have that. Worse still: ten-to-one the man knows my name.

This will not do. Got to get a leg up on the senator. Have to steal some leverage.

Start with what you know. That's the way of the System.

A dead, dirt-dredging DA. Dig the power vacuum therein.

A loony-bin legislator, likely the subject of extortion, looking to cover up a cover-up.

A sad-sack brother like myself wanders in ignorance straight out onto the field.

Senator, scared I'm gonna be his new tormentor. Scared, but not sure.

Nightmare team of military contractors, in the service of said senator, sent to settle my hash before I settle his.

Gotta move. Gotta move now.

Exit the Reading Room, dropping the towel in the doorway.

Midmorning sun struggles through the smoke and the atmospheric shit, and weakly illuminates the passageway.

Wing tips go clippity-clap, lopsided in accordance with my limp.

Betting these yahoos, however seriously I might take them on the j.o.b., couldn't get into the basement. Would be a surprise, as I've made some structural alterations that won't show up on an architect's plan of the joint.

Shuffle with stealth through the Bill Blass Public Catalog Room, with its collection of dead computers . . . hustle on down to the second floor and the Lionel Pincus and Princess Firyal Map Division. I enter and drag the outsized faux-brass doors behind me.

Looking for cameras now. It's a superficial search I make, but it's not likely they would have rigged this room. There's nothing in it.

Except for the wood panel covering a section of the westernmost wall, which sports an outsized eighteenth-century French map showing the West Indies and the Lesser Antilles.

Press my palm into the sepia splotch representing Trinidad. Birthplace of my bastard father, and his bastard father before him. Apply pressure, and the panel swivels on a central axis, opening up an eighteen-inch gap into darkness.

I take a moment and breathe the air of my adopted home, not knowing when and how I'll return. Alls I know is my little haven is under direct siege, and extreme protective measures are called for.

Click on the penlight and slide in, drawing the panel shut behind me, proper haunted-house stylie.

I clomp down metal spiral stairs of pretty recent construction, a fair descent.

Downstairs, underground. Backtrack toward the dumbwaiter shaft.

Damp. Endless recess of shelving, worn leather binding. No rats thus far, but man do they grow larger and bolder.

Old paper, smelling of feces and dirt. Beyond that, trace odors given off by the garbage fire pits that once made up Bryant Park. Maybe I'm imagining things.

Natch I don rubber gloves, check the fit on my mask. I see this labyrinth as if from above, its curvature well known to me.

If the Reading Room is the library's heart, the subterranean cathedral with its miles of shelving is the joint's brain, containing all things, all knowledge. I alone remain to bear witness.

When I come upon it, the DA's box is upturned at the ass-end of the dumbwaiter shaft, contents having partially slid out across the concrete floor. A single floodlight is still operative so I click off the penlight.

I quickly see what I'm looking for, make sure it's intact, and flip open the file.

Given the DA's sloppy habits, this is a comparatively

tight and well-organized set of papers, photographs, and subfiles. Laid out well, which I appreciate, and I start from the top.

A crappy set of fixed-point shots of a black man and Asian woman in various states of sexual congress. The pictures are infrared and of poor quality.

Timestamp has events taking place between two fifteen and two thirty-five p.m., and there are Korean Hangul characters indicating *Room C* on the lower corner of the stills. The photos date back twenty-one years.

Yeah, I both read and speak Korean dialects, courtesy of the U.S. taxpayer. See, I told ya. Fucked up, right?

For the most part the male has his back to the camera, but the accompanying documentation has this activity taking place in a brothel on East 53rd Street. Identifies the seventeen-year-old female as a Korean national named Song Ji-Won, a.k.a. Jackie, Sunny, or Kiki Oda, known also to profess to be Japanese. Born outside Seoul.

The male is ID'd as U.S. Senator Clarence Howard, age forty-one at the time of the report I'm reading. I know all this background jazz, but a primer:

First African American member of the Republican Party to have been elected senator in New York, largely on the strength of his relationship with a funky mix of mainstream politicians, going further back to more peripheral figures, Harlem king-making preachers, etc. Plus the support of the predominately white establishment in the boroughs and upstate. Et cetera.

Howard straddled several very different worlds, and cantered on down to D.C.

A socio-psychopath, deft compartmentalizer, and a born politician.

This story, the whorehouse, etc., is only interesting be-cause Howard came into full bloom on an old-school "fam-ily values"–style platform, viciously antigay, antiabortion, anti-Muslim, antiunion, pro-gun, yada yada.

Prior to 2/14, the big man was busy aligning himself with the post–Tea Party folks (after their much ballyhooed splinter and the RNC riots/multiple shootings) who had recently surged into power. He was a loud supporter of the actions against New Persia (sorry, the Islamic Republic of Shariaistan), one of the last gasps for our threadbare military overseas.

And perhaps most significantly, Howard was the prime mover in the antiunion contingent that emerged to combat the evolution of domestic workers' groups. Or "domestic terrorists," in the parlance of the senator's kind.

He and his ilk stood unapologetically responsible for events that followed, such as the Valentine's Occurrence of February 14. That's just my own vibration.

And, of course, the man's wife of thirty-five years is her-self a ferocious force, archconservative socialite/heiress and fundraising genius Senator Kathleen Howard née Koch.

Her command of basic English and her understand-ing of history and function of government were so deeply compromised that nobody took her seriously. Nobody took her seriously as the schools commissioner for the State of North Dakota. Nobody took her seriously as the mayor of Bismarck. And when she ran for state representative, well . . .

But Kathleen was nice with a slogan, had cash to burn, and her hair was never less than white-lady perfect. So it goes.

First husband-and-wife team with a hardcore agenda, just body-checking motherfuckers on the floor of the Senate.

The very picture of modern, media-friendly American political extremism. Modern, modern, modern, and biracial at that; the union of a golden Son of Harlem with blue-blood corn-fed Midwestern stock proved a powerful one. Something for everybody, like.

A loose photograph slips out of the file, depicting a girl I assume to be Song Ji-Won. It's a still from a security camera, high-resolution this time, cropped so I'm only really able to see her and no context.

Song is laughing, her hand blurred slightly in midgesture. Maybe eighteen to twenty-one years old, wearing a gray waist-length fur. Black or very dark red nail polish. She's a stunner, vibes extreme confidence. Looks smart, and like she's enjoying herself.

I slide this photo into my inner breast pocket.

NYPD file. Dated eighteen years back.

Crime scene photos, an industrial barrel bearing the stencil PROMISE LAND IMPORTS, a mass of cabbage and what appears to be a scalp, or the top of a human head, as well as a protruding stump. More photos along these lines, which I choose to leave alone.

The text is minimal, two bodies:

—Unidentified 19–21 year old Asian female remains, dismembered, minus hands/feet/teeth, face burned off/soldered really, perhaps by blowtorch. Partial silicon breast implants (serial numbers removed/unreadable).
—Unidentified child, approximately 2 years old, Asian mix, dismembered and incomplete in the same manner as other body.

Within ten hours of the discovery of the dead came

the arrest of one Kwon Man Seok, a.k.a. K-Man, a twenty-three-year-old midlevel Kkangpae lieutenant in the Korean mob, coowner of Promise Land Imports and the Executive Comfort Lounge, 18 West 33rd Street, a hostess bar, both businesses known funnels for human traffic, narcotics, and prostitution, according to the report.

The female was presumed to be the "property" of a competitor, no identification necessary. Unknowable turf disputes were cited, and I find no further mention of the child.

Case frickin closed + enjoy your weekend, boys.

But hey now. What have we here? K-Man strolls out the joint in May 2006, according to his parole report. Free and clear and nary another mention herein.

Damn, I know a hooker isn't worth much to our justice system, but a child? To walk that early, it's downright stanky.

His rap sheet. Small-time syndicate stuff. Suspicion of human trafficking, drug possession, reports of illegal organ trade. All dismissed or deferred.

Rosenblatt also included a page with a single CCTV photograph showing Senator Howard and a man identified as Korean mob boss Danny Ya, who would have been K-Man's senior officer, in front of the Tribeca restaurant Nobu. The date is two weeks before the discovery of the bodies.

A day prior, we have a printed transcript of Howard holding a conversation with two men at the Calvisius Caviar Lounge, Four Seasons Hotel, NYC—one Nic Deluccia, "formerly of the NYPD," I get a za-zing cause I know that name; and an unidentified "active ATF agent"—during which the senator makes such regrettable statements as,

"She is asking for too goddamn much now," and, "[*Garbled*] easiest to make the whole motherfucking thing [*fingersnap*] disappear."

Hold up. Nic Deluccia? I get an image, a small room, scarred-up wooden table, white dudes, a can of Tab . . . cops.

Nothing more for the moment. It may or may not come, so I move on.

Deluccia is credited with this zinger: "Just have to know the right people in that community, fucking bucketheads [*garbled*], but these things can be very simply resolved." To which the senator responds: "It's a question of perception, how this thing is made to appear."

And most distasteful of all, at least to me, is this exchange:

Sen. Howard: Kids?

Deluccia: No sir.

Male 2: My boy is thirteen . . .

Sen. Howard: Tough age.

[Laughter.]

Male 2: Tell me about it . . . and my eighteen-year-old, ah, daughter, starting up at Barnard this fall. Big transition.

Sen. Howard: That it is. Good school. Bit free-thinking, if you catch my meaning. I'd keep an eye on her.

[Laughter.]

Sen. Howard: But a fine school. Children, biggest blessing in life.

[Interruption, passing waiter.]

Sen. Howard: [Garbled] will forever haunt me, involving the . . . But I don't see how . . .

Deluccia: Can't concern yourself with that, sir. [Garbled] as collateral, unavoidable and of course very unfortunate, a very difficult thing.

Sen. Howard: God forgives. We have only to ask.
Male 2: As you say, sir.

No photographs accompany this section, but we have a dated CD in the plastic slip holding the transcript. I assume this to be audio of the conversation. If I want to listen to it, I'd have to find a goddamn *CD player*, which sounds so motherfucking exhausting that for the time being I'm happy to take the transcripts at face value.

Peep the disc sideways, hold the penlight to it. Could be holding data too for that matter, it's been awhile since I've seen one of these.

Nic Deluccia? Think. This skull of mine. Sealed-off sections, vaults, like Al Capone's: maybe containing a stale absence . . . maybe choked with radiant gems. All I can dredge is a televised news conference . . . Gotti-era mob sting?

I go deeper. A blue-uniformed Nic Deluccia at a podium, brass buttons, a bouquet of microphones . . . and Jesus, if I have the perspective right, I'm up there too. Among the uniforms. Deluccia or somebody saying, ". . . what we can accomplish when working in cooperation with local communities." Held aloft is a *New York Post*, headline reading, "Bronx Baby-Grabber Nabbed." Scattered applause. I must be a kid, cause everything seems outsized, too big. Flash cameras going off. Nic is turning toward me, headless, and another flash wipes the scene.

It's in there somewhere. I know this man. I'd have to run a more intensive scan. Let that simmer. I've learned I can't force it.

Also learned I can't trust it either. False memory a distinct possibility.

Bite my penlight. Back to the papers, the big picture.

Rosenblatt was a world-class bullshitter, and he must have known that some of this here is pretty thin, but gut level says it's real. With highly dubious and circumstantial aspects, but real enough.

I replace the file and rise, wincing at my fucking knee. Automatically shake the pill bottle in my pocket, pop it open, and drop one down my gullet.

Well, Clarence Howard, I do believe I've seen enough to make an initial assessment.

What nags is that all this material is so frickin old. Given what the public and private sectors have had to struggle through post–9/11 and particularly post–2/14, I find it hard to fathom why the whole narrative couldn't just be dismissed. Who gives a shit, really? We got fresher fish to fry, all of us.

But it's a profoundly ugly story. And the senator seems very anxious to kill it, even at this late date. I sense movement between the lines.

Listen here: I fear no man, save myself. Power has been redistributed with the upheaval brought about by 2/14. The playing field leveled. The agents of Babylon, they no longer hold the best cards. They may have more men, more bullets, but when it comes down to it, instinct and mojo trump cash money.

It's a knife fight out there, intimate, cheek-to-cheek. And I was raised on that tit.

Flow proactive.

Happy minding my own, but if the senator wants to raise a ruckus, I'm only too willing to oblige. Smack me, and I smack you back. That's real.

This dude concerned about exposure with this nasty hooker cut-up? We'll give him exposure. Realness: on the street, you hit first and you hit hard cause you never know what the other guy's got.

Fucking threaten me, man? Fucking threaten the New York Public Library? The books are *eternal*, nigger. The books, they're bigger than all of us.

Plus, I'm not into hurting the ladies. Don't countenance chopping up kids.

Next moves. Starting points. Scare up some Koreans, and see what shakes loose.

On the back of the folder is a Post-It, a couple phone numbers, which do me no good, as landlines are a thing of the past. Hell, as are cellular networks if you're not military, and even then . . .

But we also have a couple loose addresses:

Club Enduring Freedom, 8 West 32nd, suite 602
Bubble Teen Tea + BBQ, 38 West 32nd, ninth floor

I peel this off, and take the page detailing Promise Land and the Executive Comfort Lounge. Commit the moniker "K-Man" to memory, easy enough though my memory is spotty.

Did I mention this?

Shoulder everything relevant to the good senator. Down a couple aisles I deposit this pile amongst upward of seventy-five editions of Dante's *Inferno*, of various vintages, languages, and bindings.

From here, I move to the area I affectionately call "the 600," which is Melvil's class code for "Technology and Applied Science." Have to count aisles but I'm almost at the point where I can find it on feel alone.

Enclosed by wire shelving, the mess in this forty-square-foot cubicle disturbs my sensibilities, but these pockets are bound to form when one is engaged in ambitious projects like mine.

See, as I come across material that meets specific classification criteria, I've begun simply dumping it in the appropriate area like the 600 here. It makes for temporary unsightliness, but allows me to kill two birds without losing focus on the work I'm doing when I come across volumes that obviously belong somewhere else.

In the midst of this chaos, two steamer trunks. One contains a generous amount of heavy-duty explosives. To be frank, I don't know where this cache came from or what use I could ever possibly put it to.

No, ignoring the accumulations of books and drifts of loose papers, as this mess is already making me sweat, I crack open the other box, a big blackened Louis Vuitton, and have a gander inside. Dig: two extra bottles of pills, twelve-pack of Purell™, army blanket, yet more jerky.

Without knowing exactly why, I grab an old CD. Call it nostalgia. *Enter the Wu-Tang (36 Chambers)* . . . used to listen to this record before going out on an assignment, made a boy feel bulletproof.

More of a talisman than anything else. Like I'm gonna run into a CD player, dead tech as it is. I assume they once had them here but I arrived after the major looting had played itself out.

And now the items I'm actually looking for: an ankle holster containing an ultracompact Sig Sauer P290, this pulled off yet another deceased Serb; what the hell, I strap it on, and whilst doing so I peep some items that give me a new idea with respect to the current weather . . .

A pair of miniaturized Maindeka limpet mines.

These I snaked off a digger up at the Bryant Park site on the surface above my head, and I take them now, anticipating the same construction firm I borrowed these from will have (again) sealed the exit for which I'm bound.

They seal it; I blow it up using their own shit. Rinse and repeat.

What I don't appreciate is that this exit is not part of the original library's fabric—so I have absolutely no qualms about destroying a nonoriginal door.

My horde disorder and enhanced paranoia paying off large, people. I'm geared up.

Feeling a touch on the smug side, I pop a pill. Make for the tunnel, due northwest. Beyond the seemingly infinite shelving.

Thanks to the Army Corps of Engineers, the passage I'm headed into now is going to provide me with a way out that the Cyna-corp fucks will not be privy to. Hopefully.

Just after 2/14, public buildings were prepped for use as mass shelters. Alternate in-and-out routes were essential. Hence the newish underground traverse beneath the length of Bryant Park, likely forgotten by the few who were aware of it in the first place.

This will deposit me at West 41st Street and Sixth Avenue. At which point my plan is take a mellow stroll downtown.

And hope against hope I don't get myself dead en route.

Dirt walls packed tight, reinforced by heavy plastic and wood, the penlight trained on the ground so I might avoid organic things and areas of wet. Focus focus focus, cause I don't like tight spaces, plus too jacked to get neurotic—hey now, I've got my wing tips moving and I'm feeling myself in a big way. Color me jaunty. I'm mentally whistling a little tuneless something, and I come around a final soft curve prior to the exit.

Yonder, I clock the slotted metal gate that will allow me access to the Avenue of the Americas, watery daylight weak as '80s bodega coffee, illuminating no more than the last six feet of the hole I'm in.

And not for the first time in my raggedy life, I marvel at my breathtakingly stupid ability to overvalue my own acumen. For, unsurprisingly, a pair of bodies are parked at the head of the egress, just outside the gateway, sporting the future-ninja signature dress of Cyna-corp soldiers.

Always in twos. I sigh and click the penlight off.

The Maker would perhaps at this juncture have me hearken back to the last such situation, the similarities too glaring to sidestep, a desperate Dewey Decimal on the run with a gun, careening into a duo of soldiers standing point, blocking passage, at least from Dewey's altered perspective, between the darkness and the light.

Perhaps we have here a cosmic test of sorts. To see if a less messy solution is achievable. Or indeed desirable.

But fuck the theology. I bring my good knee down on

the clay to stay out of sight and give myself a moment, part of my brain veering immediately into concern for my pants—yeah, but this is vanity and vanity is weakness. Scope the two bruisers for possible nonfatal target points.

Hmm.

What makes these cats so freaking intimidating is primarily their vastly superior kit. Featherweight, powered exoskeletons (brought to you by General Electric), sexy custom A-15 machine pistols, drool-inducing smart headgear, 360-degree selectable view, built-in GPS, etc. And most relevant: voice-activated com systems, making it virtually impossible to disable the wearer quietly without a high-impact headshot. And even then the helmet sends an alarm to a central location.

So what's a simple fella of modest means like me to do? I wash down a pill with some bottled water. Look at the hands: steady as she goes.

In sharp contrast to the cyborgy cock-extensions in which these prim donnas swish around is the soggy cardboard crapola Uncle Sam issues its own in the field. Hell. I conjure up another (mind you: possibly implanted) memory of trying to keep sand out of my mouth, as my entire patrol and I struggle to bang corrugated scrap metal into a shape that might conceivably protect us from antitank fire.

Slapstick stuff. Physical comedy.

I pause at the notion of kicking this motherfucker off. There will be nasty and hasty blowback. To the extent that a man can, I know my own murky heart. I am foresworn to protect this building and its contents. But the ignoble truth breaks down like this: I'd rather risk watching everything implode than be confronted with my own name.

Dig me, I think I got this, with some help from the System. Think I can get over. And what's more, somebody's gotta get these fuckers away from my library, even if it means burning a few books.

Now here I squat, a mini-limpet mine burning a hole in each jacket pocket about the size of a late-twentieth-century nine-volt battery. I finger them, leave my gun in place.

Remember this well, people: unless you employ maximum violence with these psychos from the jump, they will kill your ass faster than you can spit.

So let's opt for the head-on approach. Rising with a grunt, I send up a prayer to Shiva that we can do this with a minimum of mayhem.

They're talking quietly, two beetles on their hind legs, perhaps chatting with each other (or perhaps not, given the headwear), one of them with his/her back to me, leaning against the sealed gate, the other idly rubbing a polymer forearm.

Slacking. I shake my head at this, for shame. Snap to it, earn that priccy gear.

Call to them now: "Hey, yo! Letting you know, I'm unarmed!" My voice thick. Thirsty.

Lowering my surgical mask, I limp their way, overdoing my legit handicap, gloved hands in the air.

The soldiers jerk around, one steps awkwardly and stumbles slightly, laser sights swing my way, the other saying, "Hands! Let's see 'em!"

Jiggle my hands like, duh, Al Jolson, jazz hands. "Already got 'em up, my brother, got nothing on me."

I'm about ten feet away, other guy calls out: "Stop where you are, pal."

I keep coming like I haven't heard.

"Just an appeal . . . Look, I'm stuck down in here, I understand that . . ."

Dudes have their fancy A-15 machine pistols trained on me. Red lights up in my grill, feel them on my forehead.

"Subject at my location, flight attempt, please advise, over," mumbles one into the headgear.

Holding up my right hand, slow down, I'm saying, "Hey, I'm in here with absolutely no fucking food supply whatsoever, okay, you people got me on lockdown, I dig that . . ." My left hand goes to my jacket pocket and I withdraw a limpet. "Just requesting some rations, whatever you all feel like you have on you . . ."

Reach the gate, "Back the fuck up!" calls one of them.

I get ahold of a thick metal slat on the gate, put my palms to it, press the limpet on there good, press hard now to engage the explosive, twenty seconds, count 'em down, saying, "Honestly, y'all, this isn't a hostile—"

"Back the fuck up!" repeats the beetle. So I do it.

"All right. Easy now. Just hoping to appeal to your . . ."

Backing up, fifteen seconds, guy muttering, "Subject moving northbound through tunnel A, permission to pursue and detain . . ."

Me saying, "I get it. I get it." Spin left (as per the System . . . more later), hobbling forth, twelve seconds.

"Down on your knees!" calls a beetle. "Down on your knees now, hold it right there!" Ten seconds.

I take off running. When I say this I mean I limp faster, the verb *run* is perhaps too strong. I speed-gimp from whence I came. Seven seconds.

Hear a beetle raising his voice, "Subject rabbiting, permission to engage, over."

The beetles hopping up and down, excited, pressed

up against the gate, shoving their fancy guns between the slats. Four seconds.

Stiffen my back and maintain the fifty-yard stagger. A dirt clod next to my right foot erupts, in this way I know they're shooting at me and shooting low. Must've gotten the thumbs-up over the com. Start to zig and zag, another bullet zings past my calf, giving off heat, I'm thinking less than two seconds, for serious hoping I've thrown up enough distance, grind my teeth and really try to give it some mustard, and whomp there it is, the force of the blast popping my eardrums like a sudden loss of altitude on a jumbo jet. Hurl myself flat against a wall, anticipating shrapnel.

None is forthcoming. Gingerly now, I hazard a glance behind me. A heavy cloud of reddish dust obscures my escape route.

Begin to stand and my fake knee goes wonky, weeble-wobbles, but I don't fall down, thinking daaaammn if I'm not on life number eight and a half.

Pull up my mask. Get the gloves off, reapply the sweet P™, new pair of gloves, another pill.

Seem a bit much? It's like I said: gotta use broad strokes with these people.

Cautious now. Oddly quiet save a muffled groaning and far-off helicopter.

I hobble forward, the air clearing, and am pleased to see the ordnance took off the gate completely . . . I note one beetle on his/her face, that's the one moaning. Momentarily dismayed to observe beetle number two has gotten a metal rod though his/her shoulder/armpit, unfortunately the most vulnerable area when one is togged out in such armor; this unlucky bug is lying sideways and if not dead already must be in considerable shock.

The skewered bug's matte black Smith & Wesson A-15 is sitting loosely in its extended right hand, too sexy to by-pass . . . I step though the hole carefully, eyes on the prone groaner, lest it be a ruse, and relieve the goner bug of its weapon. Heft the gun, a nice polymer, sleek and light. I loop the nylon strap around my shoulder. Prod at the survivor with my left foot.

"Don't say a fucking word into that radio. You hear me? Or I take you out quick fast."

Thing tenses up. It's drawn a pistol but it just dangles from its paw.

"If you hear me and wanna comply, set it down slow."

"Hit this position . . ." comes a weary female voice from inside the helmet. I gather she's called in an air strike or what-have-you, see what I'm fucking saying with these kids? Wanna hurt her but my Code won't let me. Let her bleed out slow.

Even less time than I had reckoned. I mount the steps double quick, squatting so I might peek around the corner . . .

Due north a couple Cyna-folk to the rescue, moving along the wall, I hit the soldier in front, pop pop pop, and he's down, guy behind him raises his weapon and I aim for his chest second and head first, boom boom, and he's deflating on his buddy.

Listen. I hate to play it like this. I really do. But trust me here, subtlety will only bring you sorrow.

Plaster and stone pop-rock in front of my face, pepper-ing me with little pebbles, ouch, and I reckon I'm being engaged by the black (natch) Joint Light Tactical Vehicle parked at the curb only slightly south of my position, duck back for a second, then boogie straight on out into the open, scurry across the sidewalk and behind the vehicle.

Me thinking left, left, left. The System. Even in a fire-fight, gotta work it proper.

Whereupon my attention is drawn skyward and I dig an MD-530F helicopter as it comes floating out over the top of the library like a big charcoal tuna, and boy am I dismayed to observe several Hellfire missiles mounted on its underbelly, as well as the expected M60 machine gun which is already spitting bullets. I hug the south side of the JLTV, hearing the ping-pong as fire is deflected off the other side of the vehicle, head south toward the driver, passenger door comes open and a Cyna is halfway out before I shoot him, trying to be sparing as I understand these mags to be thirty capacity at most, kicking the body out of the way as I swing into the vehicle, just flowing now, lean across the seat and push the gun into the driver's ear, as he/she is in the midst of turning back toward me, 9mm in hand.

"Shit. Take it easy." A male voice, he's lifting his hands, I pull the door shut, reach over, and force his headgear off, this is a sandy-complected white kid, all-American, thick linebacker's neck, blushing and blotchy, wincing as some of his hair comes away with the fancy hardhat. Despite the slight chill he's sweating. As he should be.

"Right, my nizzle. Gun on the floor, hands on the dash."

Kid does like he's told, keeping it cooler than I would have expected and thereby goosing my ill paranoid vibe.

Thinking about them Hellfires. Seen them atomize small towns.

"Kid, grab that fucking com and tell the chopper to back the fuck off."

"I'd have to . . . I'd have to put the helmet back on."

Think about this.

"Naw, fuck that, start her up and let's go—I mean let's go *now*."

He does as he's told, the chopper's blades loud even inside the cab here, presses the ignition button and pulls out onto the avenue, sideswiping an actual *rickshaw*, Jesus Christ, Asiatic eyes wide in some sort of headscarf as the driver disappears beneath the vehicle. We bounce ever so slightly and slide off headed the wrong way down Avenue of the Americas, southbound.

There's a half-assed blockade at 40th Street, a couple blue-and-whites, NYPD Chevy Volts (real cop cars, it's been awhile). And another JLTV, moving too slow down 40th to beat us to the intersection.

Couple beetles on foot, trying to work it all out . . . Here comes one of their own vehicles, dudes are all what the what, one of them raises some sort of carbine, but it's way too late, we're on top of them, careening off one of the police vehicles and spinning it sideways, we're past them, the two crabs laid flat, a cop getting out of the Chevy and ducking back in quick because:

The chopper comes in low and close, very close, and hangs on our bumper, its runner about six feet off the blacktop, risky business. It could cut loose with the gun (fuck, or missile) at any time, no problem.

The vibe is *ill*; the vibe is overkill, headed downhill quick. I drop into the wheel well.

"Oh Jesus. Aw shit," says my companion, saying it for me, he's really sweating now, gripping the steering mechanism. "I don't think they'd—"

Ah, but they do, they open up on us with the chain gun, "bulletproof" tinted plexiglass absolutely everywhere, All-America is hit countless times, I have to gag as his blood

Pollocks my face and suit (thankful the suit, as mentioned, is a dark brown, thankful for my mask, these small things), even as I'm reaching for the bottom of the steering wheel to steady us I'm thinking blood on wool, *blood* on *wool*, it's going to be a bitch to clean, and I lean across the sputtering soldier trying to speak through half a face, red bubble where his mouth was, throw open his door and give his soon-to-be-lifeless husk a solid shove, we're moving at a good clip and he folds up without protest, tumbles sideways, and is gone, helicopter lets loose another volley of bullets, perforating the front windshield but not shattering it, leaving a polycarbonate sieve, weird, me pushing down the gas pedal with my right hand, trying to steer with the pinky of my left, also trying to maintain a hold on my pistol, keeping my dome low, only as the noise of the chopper banking up and back hits me do I realize I've not been hearing anything since the first round of fire, fuck, we jump the curb, I'm up in the driver's seat and see only rust-colored masonry rushing up at me, jerk the wheel blindly to the left and the vehicle skids into a wall side-on, I note the words RESIDENCE and MARRIOTT and am then hurled through the driver's window, something smacks my mouth hard and lands in my lap.

All movement is sucked out of my world, and I am still.

It's a nice moment. Meditative even. My ever-flowing lip wound is open again, and I lick at it, metallic and salty. On automatic I fish out a new face mask and swap it leisurely with the old one, blood-misted and nasty.

Facing north up Sixth Avenue, a Cyna-corp helmet covering my crotch. Now the front window gives, just sort of sloughs apart in an understated way like melting ice, and small chunks plexicarb/glass mix quietly, spread out across the dashboard, the seat. I take a breath.

Not sure if I've hit my head. I watch the black helicopter idly, a block down, describe an elegant turn, on its way back . . . to me.

Snap to, Decimal.

I hustle out a pill, lay it on my tongue, and choke it back. This is far more ultraviolence than I anticipated. An x-factor is in effect here. Under normal circumstances these people are highly disciplined—hell yeah, they're killers—but they tend to fuck you up more by their tenacity than sheer wide-net mayhem.

Well, let's make some lemonade.

My CZ is still grasped loosely in my left paw. Look around, look around, a few things I could grab, up above the windshield is a racked shotgun, this I jerk free with my right hand, very very little time so I'd better make some good decisions, I'm extremely calm and can see the ridiculousness of my situation, all this unnecessary ruckus over little decrepit me and some prehistoric political sex-murder, slide my ass across the front seat under the assumption that I am not injured, and knock the passenger's door open with my shoulder, which is painful, falling out onto the street, lose my footing for a moment as my hands are full of guns, steady, spin a full circle in accordance with the System (left turn, left turn), now hoofing it south toward the rear of the vehicle, which I notice is smoking, thank God for the metal skeleton on these rides or I'd be chocolate flapjack, I'm not the fastest thing on one and a half legs but I am able to lunge sideways behind the JLTV as the gun on the chopper coughs at me again, taking out what remains of the rear windows, bullets pinging hither and thither off its armored shell.

Shit is getting real here. Way too real.

Don't I wish I had a minute to think this through, aw jeez, it occurs to me I can't stay here, once the heli gets in front of me I'll be wide open, no choice but to move, note the four-story corner building south of me, façade fire escape on the front facing Sixth Avenue, I figure hey, I'm up again, hunching over, hustling across the street, making for a doorway, you know, I have to hope and pray it's unlocked, a ragged orange awning advertising POLISH ME, chopper loud loud loud like it's already on top of me but I don't look back, hit the bar, and boom through the entry, praise Jesus, into darkness, the outline of a stairwell, and as I mount this I reckon I clock some heavy rain but those are only bullets painting the space I just occupied, halfway up the stairs now and bam, a wall of stink gets me face-on, physical and unmistakable, it's the reek of dead animal, press my mask to my face and take air through my mouth, no choice but to move into the cloud of body stench, death in front and death behind me, and sure enough, on the first landing is a balled-up form covered in black plastic, I make it as once-human, little nuggets bubbling under the tarp, probably feeding, shit, I leave this mess alone and keep on keeping on, looking forward to my next opportunity to disinfect.

Do believe I hear the chopper head past me along Sixth Avenue, probably in order to spin around again, second floor I kick down the flimsy plasterboard door and I am in what remains of the nail salon, yes, wall of windows facing Sixth Avenue, rows of sinks and footbaths full of fetid water, white and purple plastic scattered every which way, blots and trails of color and sparkle decorate the floor like a nail-polish de Kooning, I'm looking for something heavy, something substantial, I see nothing, it's all flimsy crap, think about some Purell™, nope, I'm out of time.

Shove my 99 into my waistband, rack the shotgun, and approach the windows low, helicopter headed north my way, back up the avenue, soon it'll be on me, and in a heart-beat blades and engine are all I hear as the big black thing swings exactly level to my second-floor foxhole, thinking it's balls-out but this is never going to work my man, stand up and unload both barrels through the blackened win-dow, approximately where I assume the front cabin would be, boom, and I duck back down.

Based on what I hear the chopper loses altitude fast, falters for just a moment, a short sharp raking of metal on brick, but the engine regains and the boys bank back up, guess I missed the pilot but I must've ruffled their feath-ers, again they arc skyward, hear it turning around, which is what I want.

Toss aside the shotgun, pull the pistol, and fumble around in my pocket for that second limpet mine, got it, kicking out the windows but waiting inside, hear the chopper come level with me again to the north, heading this way, wait for it, I hop awkwardly out onto the decay-ing fire escape, one guardrail giving a puff of reddish dust as I go to hold myself steady, fuck it, I swing my gun left and am firing on the Cyna-corp soldier leaning out the side door of the chopper, he's doing the same, the matchstick stairs vibrate as they're smacked with bullets, I don't hear any of it over the helicopter, dude goes slack and falls out the side, bouncing off the runner, not watching him hit the sidewalk thinking, shit, as tedious as this action-movie noise is, it's a rush no doubt, wakes you up, dig? Plus you can't make this jazz up, the chopper is trying to pull its mounted guns around as it comes flush with me and I haul off, lean way way out, holding the creaky railing, over-extend, and slap the smoke-glass dome of the cockpit— mind you, this is a moving helicopter so I'm spun around and knocked down—but the limpet mine is no longer in my palm, if it went where I intended I will know shortly, can't feel my hand, cover my head and the flying machine swoops beyond me, get up get up and get down the brit-tle spiderweb of a staircase, thanks be to the Maker for my malnourished state as I would surely have broken this flimsy thing at pre–2/14 weight, as I think this of course everything is going far too smoothly, so the stairs give, and I come down a-tumbling.

Luckily it isn't more than half a flight that I've fallen, and this broken by a waterlogged awning, catches me for a split second then snaps, I actually slide down the length of it and land on my feet like the motherfucking kitty cat who ate the cream. It's the slickest move I've busted in years and I'm damn proud to be me at this very moment in the progression of time. Wish a certain woman could have clocked this ninja move but her name, her name is momen-tarily lost to me.

My legs are shaking. Still just totally gobsmacked at the speed with which this pandemonium has unfolded. This crew is going to dog me for the duration of my natural life, which at this point might only be the next couple of minutes. Better make 'em count.

Wishing now I had hung on to the shotgun cause here comes the cops and the other JLTV, whole mess of armed dudes popping out the vehicle like clowns in a VW, some-body shouting into a broadcast system, made nonsense by the sound of the helicopter as it turns to head back our way.

Nothing to do but start running. Straight at the convoy. This way the heli won't fire on me. Or so I hope. Plenty of guns and helmet-clad heads are angled my direction from the vehicles up ahead. Figure I'm extending my mortal tenure by about ten seconds. And I don't remember how this all kicked off. Hope it was logical. Dig, the increasing pressure of a dozen or so trigger fingers.

Well, folks, I reckon it's been rizzle. I get mentally prepped to get shot a whole fucking lot. Think about: Iveta, that's her, the young Hakim Stanley, and my imaginary ex-wife. My mother. My books. And weirdly: the name Nic Deluccia. How the fuck do I know that man? Funny what crosses your mind.

Shit, I don't regret a damn thing. I did my best with the bullshit cards Jesus dealt out. Scatter my ashes across the silent Cross Bronx Expressway.

I get into the middle of the intersection, and that's when the chopper explodes.

Lopsided, leaning down Seventh Avenue past 37th Street, do now believe I'm clear of any kind of perimeter the Cyna-thugs would have thrown up initially.

Some might express shock that I lived through such a mad crazy scene. Some might express disappointment.

To the disappointed, I extend two middle fingers heavenward, à la the Trade Centers of old.

To those who might be surprised by my seemingly superhuman demonstration of power and subsequent impossible escape, I say simply this: Y'all bitches don't know me. At least not yet. But stick around.

I only *appear* wretched, wraithlike, hollowed-out. It's an illusion. The life force in me is strong, baby, and I don't break easy.

After the chopper blew up I managed to bounce through the smoke and confusion that ensued. It was really that simple.

But hey now, do I feel a twinge of guilt, a sliver of regret, knowing I caused the demise of more than several fellow travelers?

Once again: y'all bitches don't know me.

As Cyna-corp is regrouping, which will take them a bit for sure, I'll be high-stepping to parts elsewhere. But what do I know, I could be kidding myself big time, thinking I might be able to slide out of this pileup.

Nevertheless, made it thus far. Christ Almighty. Allah be praised. I take this moment to squeeze out some Purell™, and apply. Feeling peppier already.

In doing so, I only now realize that my right hand looks a bit off. Classic boxer's fracture, a jackknifed bone. I can jiggle my thumb, but my fingers don't respond to my commands.

No big wonder my skeez is wrecked: I high-fived a fast-moving military chopper. Perhaps not the slickest plan; but I got results, did I not? I'm unconcerned. Dr. Feelgood will prop me up. Point a gun just fine with my left hand.

Wonder how much time I really have: I'm under no illusion that those guys can't get to me, hunt my narrow ass down even if I leave the city right away. If they go after something, they do not miss in the long haul. Too many resources and too much time. And here I am, just down the block. Understand that I am now in cheek-deep, but I'm resigned to it. Not scared of commitment like other brothers.

And perhaps most importantly: I'm happy to say I am sticking to System protocol.

No time to explain earlier, my apologies.

See, prior to eleven a.m., the System prescribes left turns only, whether in a vehicle or on foot. This is all for a larger purpose that I can't articulate but understand to be necessary for the maintenance of internal and universal balance.

If you've got internal balance, you can radiate that balance externally, exercise control over your environment.

Don't expect everybody to dig the System. Though it's like I say, you work it, it works for you . . .

Moving again, I soon find myself back at Sixth Avenue. I peep north and clock the burning wreckage of the chopper, chumps wandering around, hamstrung, what to do? Clowns. I spin left left and left as the System dictates, with the intention of heading south and—

Wham bam stop dead at West 36th Street and Sixth Avenue. I'm having a freeze.

Scan the street for indicators of what the fuck. Plywood-covered storefronts, FedEx/Kinko's, McDonald's, blank, hollowed out. Mounds of garbage, which look like somebody tried to "organize."

Think: snipers.

Make for cover, expecting a pop and a shot to the back, scramble under a partially collapsed scaffolding, scoot into a recessed doorway to the dusty remains of one of those dodgy mobile phone shops. A sign reads, WE UNLOCK THEM, and I think: hajji mart.

I know I'm armed, touch the ankle holster, feel the pressure in the small of my back, produce the gun I find there. Crouch and have a long look at the windows, bank after bank, dirty/broken/blank, telling me zilch-o. I'm frozen, my head idles between first and second gear, nowhere.

Forgot what I was doing, see? I don't know why I now squat at this particular place, at this particular moment.

Fun with PTSD. My shrink back at Walter Reed would just love to see this, the snooty bitch. Making notes, shitty little smile, arching those thin eyebrows like I'm confirming all her private theories.

The point is, doesn't matter where you go. Where there's people, there's buildings; where there's buildings, there's windows; and where there's windows, snipers. Think: don't let 'em draw you out, rule uno.

Call it in. Feel for the radio that isn't there. Look left.

A couple blocks south at Cooper Square there are two

civilians, old folks, dragging one of those garment district rolling clothes hangers, covered with what looks like fur coats. Seems like hard work, slow going. I consider calling to them, tell them to get out of the open, but think again: smokescreen.

Beyond that a Humvee is parked side-on across the avenue. Three National Guardsmen are milling around, an open manhole spewing steam. Oblivious. To the threat of snipers.

Stand. My leg protests. I spin around, look uptown. Lone moving vehicle in sight this direction: ugly bronze Prius, headed against the nonexistent flow of traffic, toward some kind of bonfire, industrial wreckage, hard to see what is going on up there. The driver is all over the road, going slow, clearly impaired. Not like it matters. He peels off at 37th Street.

No action. Please, give me some sort of clue.

Fuck. This happens. Need to be patient with myself. Always feels like: this time it's going to be forever. I'll get stuck in this antistate. And I always recover. So I don't stress it, but it's a challenge.

Don't panic, man. I replace my gun.

Start patting myself down, that usually does the trick. Notice again my broken hand, which indicates nothing. My usual kit, the Purell™, extra gloves. Jerky. In my breast pocket, a photo of a lovely Asian teenager. And a fucking compact disc? Wu-Tang . . . what is this, the twentieth century? No jingles yet. I put both back.

Some sort of condiment splatter on my suit? Nope. Blood. How could this have happened?

From my front pants pocket, I withdraw a folded piece of paper, addresses, within mere blocks of here, Chinese stuff . . .

No, Korean. Song. K-Man. Senator Howard. Oh yeah, here it comes, all at once like a hot blast of air to the noggin.

Back in it. Dizzy and embarrassed. I strip off my gloves, hit the hand and a half with Purell™, new set of gloves for both. Toss back a pill, which lodges in my sandy throat for a panicky second, then dives.

Pull up my mask. Heart slamming but gradually, gradually slowing. Counting backward from twenty. I get to zero and continue south.

Have to check the dosage on my meds. Freezes coming more and more frequently.

In passing I lift my hat at a Guardsman, a fleshy albino. He's watching the burning helicopter up yonder, but directs his gaze my way. Pink eyes. Looks right through me like I'm already gone.

Unlike the low-lying sprawl they have going in Los Angeles, New York's Koreatown was always a compact, vertical affair.

Never really expanded past its horizontal block-and-a-half radius, but the area seemed to be in a perpetual state of skyward growth. New floors would metastasize on top of new floors. Mysterious extensions and unreadable neon sprouted like lichen. Thirty-second Street was garish and impossible to miss, but ultimately unknowable.

A tangle of offices, nail salons, electronics stores, BBQ joints, bars, karaoke spots, travel agencies, bridal shops, plus the plentiful manifestations of the jizz-biz: wack shacks, tug parlors, whore stores, sexy shoppes spanning the spectrum of class and cost.

Nobody actually lived on this street and a half. But day and night, business was frenzied and dense.

That was back when.

This is now.

Koreans have always been smart, and the moves they made post-Valentine's bear this out. Ever the pragmatists, they threw their lot in with the Chinese. Despite all historical hullabaloo that would make such a union seem inconceivable.

The scene got a lot more desperate in a hurry for the Koreans when the North did what it had been saying it was gonna do for decades and set about lobbing dirty bombs into central Seoul. Extremely ugly stuff. Everybody acted all surprised, but if you look at it, this was a long time coming.

The action on 32nd Street has hardly slowed since the Occurrence; after the bombing of Seoul the Koreans got a lot tougher, and a lot more thick on the ground as they flooded the city looking for a job; these folks now make up a fair percentage of the workforce on the island. Korean, Chinese, and Korean/Chinese contracting firms lay claim to some primo gigs. Landmark stuff.

But today the street is stripped down, less frenzied and gaudy, less eye-candy. Basically only three types of businesses remain: construction, food importation/service, and the hostess bars that keep it all lubricated.

Yeah, the bustle holds steady.

Even this early in the morning, work gangs haul themselves onto electric buses. Trucks unload wooden crates of seafood and building materials. Men and women fresh off the boat blink in the filtered sunlight, as they're corralled by gun- and nightstick-toting Chinese soldiers, tan uniforms laying down a constant flow of verbal abuse, this in Mandarin.

Chinese famously treat their own people like slaves, you gotta wonder how they treat the "lesser" races. Bar none, the Chinese are the most scary (and best organized) motherfuckers on the island. I steer well clear of them at all times. They do not play well with others.

Here on 32nd Street, gray folks in gray uniforms weave in and out, heads lowered, sucking up the garbage as fast as it's created. Under the dead gaze of Chink gunmen.

It's a clean street.

Clean, but the Stench, which is everywhere, sits over the area like cloud cover. It tastes/smells . . . different in these parts. More rotten seafood in there somewhere.

The men, the fresh meat coming in, are directed toward the buses, the women steered toward various buildings.

Appealing to me: Organization. Structure.

Then again, the same could be said of Dachau. Or the sugarcane plantation my great-granddaddy worked.

Woulda made a shitty slave. Too uppity. I'd be quick to cut massah's throat too, that's no joke.

All this I observe from the intersection of 32nd and Broadway, crouched in the stairwell of the old Herald Square subway station. Bear in mind, I've made a left turn off Broadway to get where I am, so the System and I are in full step.

Already know I'm not welcome. Even in happier days, any non-Korean was viewed as the Other, and there was only so far one could go before hitting a cultural wall. The unspoken message was: *You have your neighborhood, and we have ours. We'd like to keep it that way.*

I intend on waiting out the busloads of new bodies, but they just keep on coming. It's a dirge. Like watching a film loop. Nothing new happens.

Check this: I have Bubble Teen Tea down at 38 West 32nd. This address is just opposite me at an angle, an angry-looking steel-and-stone office building, though strikingly featureless for this block.

Well. Here I am. So this is where I start.

Plus, might as well be inside when Cyna-corp rolls up, as they inevitably will. Oh yes.

Without moving too quickly I tilt my hat forward, readjust my mask, step into the street. I have a Michael Jackson moment. One of many differences being I got two gloves on, and they're blue rubber.

Nobody's clocking me so I stroll on over, just past the entrance, reverse, and take the prescribed left into the building's foyer, through double glass doors.

I'm presented with another set of doors, locked this time, and a daunting array of buzzers, ancient-looking unit numbers, and layer upon layer of yellowed tape. Label-maker squiggles describe names and business in a mashup of Korean, English, and Chinese characters.

Let's see, ninth floor . . . Not surprisingly, I see no Bubble Teen. Scan the ninth floor, zoom in on suite 907, Club Enjoy. I get inspired.

Deep breath. It's a nasty filthy business, this wall. Pick at the buzzer's marker, gagging, easily peel back the *Club Enjoy* label. Behind that are Korean characters that simply indicate *BAR*, which I peel away as well, in tiny strips. Revealing *BUBB TEEN TEA*, and that's good enough for this guy.

Apply pressure to the buzzer with my working hand. It's a straw-grasp. No idea really what or who I'm looking for. I only know I do not appreciate being threatened, not by anyone.

No response from suite 907. I bust a New York classic, hold my breath (weevils, fungal clouds) and lean both forearms across multiple random buzzers. Sure enough, a speaker crackles, and the door clicks. I push on through with my elbows.

Stairs, walk on in despite the Korean sign advising me to *DO NOT USE STAIRS*. Let's give those gluts some attention. Drag myself upward. Thinking about a name: Nic Deluccia. Now this is gonna bug me all day.

Farther on there's a point in that stairwell where it becomes absolutely pitch dark, and I observe myself begin to bug out.

Ridiculously enough I conjure Hakim Stanley, handsome and rangy, bullet hole under his strong chin. Behind me, on the stairs. Reaching for my ankles. I feel him panting ragged. He's close, really close.

Shoes slapping concrete, echoes ping-pong between the walls. Sounding like more than one pair of feet.

I fucking work through it, *command* my focus forward.

My lungs report serious taxation, count seven, eight, one more flight, and nine, yeah, okay, I get frantic, panicky, feel for a doorknob, no dice, kick at what I believe to be the door and it flies open, dousing me in weak light.

Stepping out into the hall, shaky legs, I rifle around in my pocket and draw a pill. Pop that thing. Spritz me some Purell™.

Gotta be a grown-up man here. Phantoms, spooks, shapes in the dark, that's schoolyard hokum.

Hakim Stanley: a young, beautiful black brother I never knew. Kind of guy this world needed back when, and needs today. A soldier I cold-blood murdered.

Could have been avoided. It's this fact that makes him loiter, occupying corners of my head, leaning into the picture at unpredictable times.

Shake it off, Decimal. Proceed down the hall.

Hovering at 50 percent disuse minimum. Evidence of recent activity. Suite 902: *Samuel Moon, DDS*, a brass placard. Note voices within. I'm thinking, how could a freaking dentist stay in business? I move on, mapping my rotting choppers with my tongue. My mouth starts watering, which reminds me to pause, grab my pill bottle, and take another one of those blue babies.

Opposite side of the hall, 903 and 905 seem unoccupied. Club Enjoy announces itself in a tastefully small, if pink, plastic sign, with a pair of dancing musical notes.

Consider my blood-misted suit, my gnarled hand. Figure it's dark enough. I locate my bogus Health Department badge. I got a badge for every occasion.

There's a doorbell, with an itsy-bitsy *Thank you, members only, OK* sign in English and Korean. I tweak the bell. Within, I hear a synthesized tune. Give me a second . . . yeah, it's "We Wish You a Merry Christmas."

Déjà vu. Don't know from what. That's why they call it déjà vu.

I sense a presence behind the peephole. Inside: "Place close." Female. "Come back lunchtime, members only."

I hold up the badge. "Health Department."

I hear locks being turned, the woman saying in Korean: "You've gotta be fucking kidding."

Door swings open, reveals a small, skeletal woman, wearing some sort of smock, black page-boy haircut looking wrong on someone in her sixties, at least. So hard to tell really. Vibes cleaning lady. She waggles a massive cluster of keys at me. So goddamn thin I'm shocked she can stand upright. Is that the vibe I radiate too?

"Nobody come here. Close. This for members, private club."

I show her the badge again. "Ma'am, I'm with the City Health Department. The premises are scheduled for an inspection. Is the tenant available?" Sounding bored.

"Close," she says, starting to shut the door. I get a foot in.

"Ma'am. Listen. Where's the owner? We have this visit scheduled, there's penalties for rescheduling inspections."

I'm aware she's likely digging a mere fraction of what I'm saying. Wonder if I should jump over to Korean, figure that'd freak her out.

Doesn't matter really; one of the bonuses of living in a dying city is nobody knows for sure what the fuck is going on, one example being: is there a functioning Health Department? Of course not.

But are you *sure*, health code violators? See what I'm saying?

"Ah, you go! Place close . . ."

"That's right, and this is when we do the inspections, so as to not disrupt your business. Might I speak with the tenant of this unit?"

"Nobody here, you come back."

"The owner. Of this place. Your boss." I make loopy hand gestures trying to illustrate my intentions.

"Boss, this place?" She stops trying to close the door on my foot. Steps back.

"Yes, the boss, I need to speak with the owner. I need to contact the owner."

Behind her I clock hardwood floors, rice lamps, fake flowers. Looks fancy.

Cursing me out, the lady leans back across some sort of receptionist's podium and plucks a card off it. There's a stack of them. "Owner, here." Handing me the card. "Now you go, place close!"

She's shutting the door and this time I withdraw my foot. As the locks are set back in place, I'm reading the glossy card:

CLUB ENJOY
38 West 32nd Street
Suite 907
PRESENT THIS CARD FOR ENTRANCE
Rose Hee, managing director

This in both English and Korean.

Ring the bell again. Footsteps, swearing.

"Place. Close." The lady groans once more, beyond exasperation.

Press the card up against the peephole. "Rose Hee," I say, then in Korean: "Tell me where to find her. I have jerky, good jerky. Beef . . . and spicy beef and cheese."

A pause.

Then the locks start turning again.

At the third address I've been given by the cleaning lady, I spot Rose straight off. Cho Dang Gol Restaurant, West 35th Street. These people must come correct in the food department, otherwise the local mob wouldn't see the point in floating the joint. No other way for a place to stay open, not without backers. Single Chinese soldier to the right of the door, making stone-faced like the joint is Buckingham Palace. I'm not worried about him, but he rocks a big old-school AK-47.

Rose perches on a high chair at the bar, legs crossed, leaning over a bowl of something hot. Blowing on the spoon. Has to be her.

She's a bizarre sight. Like in a really good, pearl-in-a-pigpen kinda way. Long dark hair up in a complex bun, held together with chopsticks. A white jean jacket pulled over a formal silk dress, gold with some detail I can't make out. Matte black heels, strappy bits tied up her shin. She bounces her leg, absently. Blows on the spoon again, brings it carefully all the way up to her lips.

The spot is pretty much dead as it is, but trust when I say shit goes *silent* when I saunter in, past the wax sentry at the doorway, whose attention is focused west anyway.

Two dudes with identical over-gelled haircuts, ties tossed over their shoulders, the guys straight freeze, jaws loose, eyes on me. A bit of meat falls out from between one gent's sticks.

Black folks do not come here. White folks do not come here.

An employee is moving rapidly to intercept, perhaps to tell me exactly this; out of the corner of my eye all I see is teeth and a pair of glasses.

I raise my index finger at him and with my busted hand indicate Rose. He fades out, fast. Somehow I knew he would.

Pull on a new pair of gloves, grab a menu, and head over to the bar. Take a seat right next to the lady, catching her air, it's not perfume exactly, it's pricey body wash or shampoo.

Nix that: she smells like the stuff folks try and fail to make expensive products smell like. The essence of the thing, the thing itself.

Rose doesn't even remotely acknowledge me. Her dress has little butterflies set in the gold.

Flip open the menu. Authentic. Scan it . . . I don't know from Korean food, not the real thing. Stains on the laminated plastic. I get nasty chills. Close it.

My opening, in the main Korean dialect spoken in Seoul, I say: "Hard to imagine getting fresh cuttlefish. Locally, I mean. What do you reckon, miss?"

Rose sets her spoon down. She's working on some kind of simple porridge. Dabs her lips carefully. Half turns to me. Gives me a long look up and down. Lingers on the hand. Without expression, her makeup understated.

Turns back to her food.

"Fuck off, cop," she says, in English. With a pinch of the city in that accent.

Can't help but smile. I dig her already. Hell, I do vibe all kinds of cop.

"Rose Hee, I presume."

"You presume correct. Did you miss the part where I

told you to fuck off?" She takes another spoonful of the porridge, pops it in her mouth.

"Let me guess," I say. "Flushing? Elmhurst?"

Rose doesn't respond.

"I'm not a cop," I say.

"Oh yeah? Well, still, like I said, fuck off."

I take the photograph out of my breast pocket. Place it on the counter. Slide it over next to her bowl.

"Song Ji-Won," I say.

Her hand floats up to her mouth. At first I think she might be choking, my brain scrambles to dislodge my fossilized CPR skills, but she separates her fingers and says, "Put that away."

Big knot of muscle in a do-rag and cook's apparel comes out of the kitchen, holding a dish towel, black eyes on me. "Yo. Is there a problem?"

Rose brings her hand down, covering the photo. Says, "No, Kim, it's cool. It's cool." Smiles at him.

He looks from me to her and back again to me. Tattoo on the meat of his hand between thumb and forefinger, a stylized fish. Good-looking kid. I smile too.

"Think I surprised her," I say. "It's been years."

Rose nods, going with it. "Queens College. You can chill, Kim, really."

He shrugs. Gives me a look, and disappears back into the kitchen.

Rose slides the photo back to me, palm down. I take it, she's dabbing at her mouth with her napkin. Says, "Jesus. Not here. You better not be a cop. Or a rapist freak. Walk with me."

She swivels, grabs her purse off the counter, and is up, heading for the door.

I follow.

The maître d' or whoever he is bows at Rose as she exits. Simply stares at me. Likewise the soldier's gaze swivels and tracks us out the door.

Outside, Rose is headed toward Fifth Avenue, goddamnit, a right turn and it still hasn't gone eleven a.m., so I cheat a little, turn in place, three distinct left turns, saying to myself: left left left.

Dude still gawking through the window. Soldier trying to look unreadable. Like, what's that funny black man doing?

African fucking dance, bitches.

Proceed east, Rose's heels clicking up ahead.

Me, trifling with the System. Not good form. I catch up to her.

"I want to see some ID," she says, without breaking stride. "Don't talk to me, let's just keep walking, but show me some ID."

Fish out my laminate, my proper City laminate. Hand it over.

Rose frowns at the thing. "Decimal, Dewey? Is that like a . . . old-timey library joke?"

"My folks had a cornball sense of humor. What can I say?"

"And Class-A? Are you kidding me? You have to be some kind of cop. I don't need this."

She speeds up, starts crossing the street. I keep pace with her, saying, "I'm not a goddamn cop. Hand to God, ma'am. I'm a, uh, independent agent . . ."

Rose snorts. Granted, "independent agent," that came off shady, delusional.

"Agent of what? See, I don't want any drama, what

makes you think it's okay to just waltz over here and wave that photo around? What's your damage?"

"I have information on a club, Bubble—"

"Just, no talking, let's get off this street."

We take the left onto Fifth Avenue, heading south. I'm trying to mentally steer her. Rose ducks into a recessed entryway, arms folded, defensive posture, saying, "All right, I'll give you two minutes to explain what the fuck you want."

"Listen, will you just relax?" I need to turn this around a bit and get a better position here. "I am not a cop, I have nothing to do with official law enforcement, so you gotta stop with that. I apologize if I disturbed you with the photograph, I had no way of knowing you'd respond to it, so let's just start over fresh here. All right?"

Rose is looking down Fifth. Back toward Koreatown proper. She nods.

"Thank you," I say. I take out the card from Enjoy. "This your place? Your name is all over the card, so I'm assuming yeah."

Rose shifts her gaze to the card, then back to the avenue. "Shouldn't be talking to you at all." She readjusts her arms, hugging herself.

"And why is that, Missus Hee?"

She stares at me for a second, then returns her attention downtown. "*Miss*. That's just how it is around here. This is not your neighborhood, you have no idea what goes on."

Fair enough.

"Okay, that's fine, you don't have to say shit. Let me lay things out, kick it to you from my angle."

I fetch the photo of Song, her frozen laughter. Rose flinches.

"I'm looking into the circumstances surrounding the death of Song Ji-Won. My reasons for doing so are private, and I'm working on my own. As in, yo, by myself. Now, from your response to this picture, I take it you knew this woman, am I wrong about that?"

Rose shifts her weight to her left leg, doesn't respond. Holding herself, tight.

I press forward: "Okay, so, mixed up in the info I got on Song, I have some locations, addresses, and one of them is your place of employment, which was formerly know as quote Bubble Teen Tea unquote. Yeah? So it's not crazy that I'm standing here, wondering what that has to do with Song."

Rose is looking more and more uncomfortable, and has nothing to say. Focused downtown.

"I have names too, I'm going to throw them out there and get your vibe. Again, you don't need to say shit. K-Mart." I'm trying to recall the files . . . damn, should have written these names down. Maybe I did, somewhere . . . "K-Man. Kwon somebody."

That's a bull's-eye, Rose's eyes dart left, blinking. Not looking at me.

"Some company names, some clubs. Promise Land. Some kind of import company. Executive Comfort, another whazzat, *hostess club*, like your spot . . ."

Rose speaks, still looking south: "Enjoy is a legitimate business. You said hostess club like you'd say whorehouse. You clearly don't understand shit. None of my girls are into anything on the side. They get caught doing dates, tricking, drugs, whatever, they're fired. Full stop. And trust me, they need that fucking job, so—"

"Okay, Rose, I feel you, I get it."

Turns to me. "Do you? Where are you from?"

"South Bronx. However, I've traveled—"

"Right, so you don't know how people do things down here. All that goes on at Enjoy is a whole bunch of sad men binge-drinking, doing karaoke, and talking a lot of bullshit that my girls have to sit there and listen to. That's fucking hard work, believe me."

"Hey, I'm not a complete, uh . . . I've read a lot about the cultural function of—"

"Yeah? Oh, you have? So who the fuck are you, a sociologist who does a little cold-case murder investigation on the side? What's up with the suit?"

I dig plucky, but Jesus, man, her attitude is a touch too much, say: "Hey, Rose. I didn't come down here to disrespect you, or to research fucking Korean male bonding or whatever you wanna call it. I don't care what you do, I don't care what anybody does, I'm only concerned with anything relevant to Song Ji-Won, her murder, and the murder of her son. That's it."

Rose covers her eyes. I continue.

"So. Why do I find the address of your . . . fancy-ass karaoke spot amongst all this information on Song. Everything about your behavior tells me you know exactly what I'm talking about."

Rose's position doesn't change. Pressing her palms into her eyes.

"Be real, Rose. Still think I'm a cop? You think the cops give a fuck about a dead Korean hooker, some small-fry gangster stuff from eighteen years back? Especially given the current state of things? Please. Think they gave a fuck back then? Be real. Plus, from their perspective, that book is closed. Forgotten. Ten-to-one there's nobody left who ever even heard of this shit."

Rose takes her hands away. Lids and lashes smudged and wet. Silence for a while, I ride this out.

Dig industrial noise from three directions. Closest site being the Empire State Building, which looms huge. To the west, probably Penn Station. The day revving up.

I can now make right turns.

I want to disinfect my hands. I want to take a pill.

Rose sighs. "I gotta go to work. I'm gonna look all puffy."

Want to observe that she's gonna look great, puffy or not. I withhold that thought.

Then she does this: she touches my tie. Reflex, I blink and step back, smashed flipper aloft.

"Easy. Jesus. Look," she says, "maybe we could talk later. Talk about why a guy like you gives a damn about a dead Korean girl. Reintroduce ourselves."

It doesn't vibe flirty, honest to Jah. I should be way dubious. This screams stitchup. But life is short, apparently.

"What happened to the hand?" she asks.

"Caught it in the cookie jar."

She looks at me sideways. After a while: "And your mouth?"

"Tried to kiss a Korean chick and she kwon-do'ed my shit."

That buys me a laugh. Again she reaches out, rubs at a blood spot on my lapel. Then, "Come and find me?"

I say, "Yeah. I'll find you."

Rose nods, brisk, glances both ways. Jams her petite hands in her jacket pockets. Takes off south, toward the rigid tumult of West 32nd.

I try and fail to not watch her ass.

As she crosses over West 34th, I see the red Lexus hybrid idling on the east side of Fifth Avenue. Retro twenty-inch chrome rims. Smoked-over windows. Pimp extras. Automotive bling, stands out against the drab military vehicles like a straight brother at a Barbra Streisand gig.

Good morning, Scarface. How long has the car been lurking? Wonder if I should be concerned. Too fly for Cyna-corp.

Rose clears the street and is moving down the block. My view of her is broken up periodically by the slow flow of workers in and out of the Empire. There's another gaggle of soldiers out front too, Chinamen, looking two-dimensional and robotic in their loose poop-brown getup.

The Lexus creeps away from the curb, does a surprise peel out, gunshot loud, burns it westward on 34th.

Rose starts, looks around. Looks back at me. I think. Can't see her face clearly. She turns and I lose her completely in a sudden surge of figures in yellow spacesuits, disembarking an impossibly decrepit Fung Wah bus.

An angry black Hummer swings out from behind the bus. Cyna-corp, no doubt, what with me sleeping . . . I spin and head back uptown, cussing myself out for not staying sharp. Telling you, those boys will hunt me down, just sand in the hourglass, yo.

Try to look, I don't know, less black or something. More gray. Blend into the concrete.

The vehicle speeds up and rips past me. Whew.

And I'm thinking: maybe I would be better served watching my own back than getting sidetracked by a pretty ass.

Two-stepping it north up Fifth, realizing I feel good. Back on my grind. Important to have projects, goals, even if they're not immediately clear.

Group of Central American thugs slouching on a corner. One of them gives yours truly an eye-frisk, then returns to his can of Goya beans. Probably trying to figure out what's next after the Chinese gave those beaners the racial high-hat.

Thugs, scavengers, and gypsies every which way. Disgruntled worker bees looking to smash and grab, and who can blame 'em?

A big crash in the sky draws my attention northward, top of the Empire State Building. Something hypnotic about the comings and goings around the tower on that iconic building . . .

From street level, hard to know what they're doing up there.

I pause.

Yeah, what the fuck are they doing up there? As far as I recall, there wasn't any major structural damage to the Empire. Just the shooting on the observation deck, a replay of the shootings at the same spot way back in 1997. Details are spotty. A lot of people got dead, but that event was overshadowed and sidelined by the larger whole of 2/14.

Reckon blowing up the Brooklyn Bridge upstaged most everything, as dramatic and sexy as a terrorist act can get, even if it didn't quite take the structure down. Highly visual, the exacting distribution of the explosives, boom boom boom. Shit, if you're a career insurgent, where do you go from there? How do you top it? I didn't witness it myself but it must have been some spectacular theater.

Strikes me, concerning the Empire State. As I watch a crane heft a massive girder: they're actually constructing something new up there. On the observation deck, however many floors up. Visible only from above. Maybe from upper floors of the Chrysler or 15 Penn.

Clock the helicopters buzzing around the spire like hummingbirds. Always with the helicopters, be they NYPD—Apaches and Super Cobras—or matte black and unmarked, vibing Roswell, "enhanced" interrogation, secret CIA prisons. The familiarity of such stuff should chill me out, I did enough time in such twilight zones. But it doesn't.

Choppers make me nervous. Ghetto-birds. Always have. Especially now.

Catch myself standing out in the wide open, wrenching my neck backward, spacing out. Sloppy. Time to step. Pop a pill, pull up my surgical mask.

Continue north, trying to put some space between myself and freaky-deak Koreatown.

It occurs oh so obviously that I can't return to the library, as the Cyna-corp crew would surely be up and in my ass in a poker-hot minute. Pause for a moment, unsure as to where I should be headed.

Mere blocks away but it gets quiet in a hurry as I move beyond the construction sites. Dead spooky.

And splat, something gray hits the sidewalk in front of me. Jump back, jack. It's a dead pigeon. Wham. Make that a pair. I look up, slide back against a building.

A third. Smack.

Christ. Even the vermin can't hang on in this void shell of a burg. What the fuck am I thinking, out in the open like this? Looking for a nook to duck into . . . Get shuffling again. Foot traffic is almost entirely absent. I slide closer to the walls, slip in and out of alcoves. Should get off the street.

Take a moment to sneak another pill. Psyching myself out, it's easy to wander into that headspace. Again I think of snipers, but I have some grounding context now and don't let myself slide down that slope.

Need to cook up a plan. Make some power moves.

Drag about my suit. Try finding a dry cleaner in this fucking beat-down ghost town. You'd think with all these Chinese . . . but that's straight racist, and this brother shuts that line of thinking down.

One time I got so desperate to get my threads shiny I busted into a boarded-up dry cleaner on Grand Street, way east, disturbing a huge community of raccoons. Raccoons, in a dry cleaner's on fucking Grand Street! Like a dozen of them. Believe it or not.

At the corner of 37th and Fifth I'm trying to determine what's best, cutting down a side street or staying on the avenue.

It's at this moment that I detect color and movement to my rear, and I'm turning, clock four electric motocross bikes nearly on top of me, Jesus they're dead frickin quiet, now sliding to a stop, two jumping the curb and flanking me, the other pair coming to a halt in a showoff-y but elegant V shape, essentially pinning me to the window of a former Citibank.

Reach around and put my hand on my gun. Hold it

there as I savvy that I'm confronted with four young punks, teenagers or early twenties, Koreans, all in civilian kit save the one dude I recognize: tough-stuff from the restaurant, hand tattoo, the knuckle-dragger who popped out of the kitchen to defend Rose's honor. He wears hospital scrubs and a hairnet.

So. Mean-looking children with colorful bikes, all of them puffed up aggro like gibbons. I let go of my gun, say: "You kids outta be wearing helmets, y'all know that much."

I mean it. Not a helmet among them. It's shocking.

"Kim, be chill, I think this monkey is strapped," says one kid in Korean, hair a stark white-colored pompadour per the current fashion. The street slang sounds stilted in that particular language, old-fashioned.

The hero in scrubs ignores this, says, "Hey, guy. You know who I am?"

Push down my mask. In Korean I say, "Lemme guess. You're either a busboy, or a male nurse in a hairnet."

Dude flushes up, his boys give a collective *ooooo* . . . down comes the kickstand and the guy is swinging off his bike, whipping off the hairnet as he rushes me. I figure, fuck it, and pull the gun.

Up in my face, my pistol shoved into his stomach, this kid not giving a fuck. In English: "Uh-uh. I'm the man who cuts off your fucking head and fucks your skull, money. Digs up your moms and nuts on her bones."

Ah, gangsta speak. This kid fancies himself retro-street American. Points for balls, I do have an automatic weapon jammed into his stomach. I gotta let him down easy.

Note one of his buddies has produced a Glock and has it trained on me, sideways and above his head like this is a video game, like anybody ever really shot someone from said position and didn't wind up hurting themselves. It's no way to hold a gun, who made that nonsense up? And it announces them as ass-clowns, as if the haircuts didn't say it all first.

Still. A gun is a gun is a gun.

Kim breathing on me. He smells like food, cooking oil. Prods me with a finger. Note again that this is a good-looking dude, beautiful eyes, jet-black hair cut close. Says, "You come up in my neighborhood, start sniffing around our women? Are you fuckin simple? You bring heat and point that shit at me? You must want to die. You're gonna tell me who the fuck you are and you do it fast, best believe I am showing great restraint not ganking you right here and now."

I'm nodding along. When I think he's done, I respond, "All right now. Let's all take a cleansing breath and recast that energy. Reel it in. Ready? Cleansing breath . . ."

Close my eyes and suck in a deep one. It stings the back of my throat, dry and granular.

Open my peepers. Kim is giving me a flickering look, trying to maintain his hard bearing, but my weirdness threw him. His buddies swap glances, wavering. Kim rallies. "Yo, are you fucking *laughing*—"

"Namaste. No, listen, for real, Kim, I blame myself, had I done some homework, had I only known that you were the big boss-dog round these parts, I would have come correct with due respect. Bearing gifts, whatever. Chalk it up to my cultural insensitivity."

"Man, I'm not trying to claim—"

"Cause now I know you're the top man, I see your posse is strong, and I reckon I can talk to you. And hey, I got no need to seek out civic leaders like K-Man or Danny Ya . . ."

Kim displays serious discomfort, glancing back at his boys.

"Listen, man, yo, I wasn't trying to—"

"Hey, it saves me some time. Saves me the hump. I talk to you and I know I'm speaking to the boss man. Look no further."

"Not trying to say I'm the boss."

I pull a surprised face. My gun hasn't moved from his midsection. "I must be reading you wrong, Kim. Is this or is this not *your* neighborhood, *your* women? Cause if that's not what you were trying to communicate, well, shit if I wasn't feeling you all wrong."

Kim grits his teeth and takes me by the lapel. Hanging tough. "Motherfucker, listen to me now. Did I say I was running things? No. Just consider me, like, a concerned citizen trying to keep my hood clean and shit."

That makes me smile.

"Ain't no such thing as a clean hood, Kim. Never was. Now come with it, player, I respect your stones, barking at me with my nine in your gut. Due respect. This is your world, and I'm just a little-bitty squirrel. Now if you have your boy put his Glock back in his pants, I'll do likewise and we can talk like fully grown men. How's that sit with you?"

Wanna give the impression that we've got a stalemate here. In truth, I could sort out all these kids in a spiffy jiffy, but an appeal to vanity is never a bad move.

Kim's breathing out of his nose. He holds my gaze for another ten seconds, then tells his flunky to stand down. The kid does it, huffy. Kim moves back a couple strides.

Good faith, I stick my pistol in my waistband.

"Jah bless. That's much more civilized, I appreciate it, Kim."

Poof. Like magic, a black jeep comes around the corner. I lose focus, cause shit: Cyna-corp beetle-suits standing on the side runner and up in the back, a big-ass .30-caliber machine gun swiveling this way and that, hell, I drop fast. Hoping the haircuts will blind them to much else. Willing them to ride on by.

"Man, what the fuck are you doing?" Kim is looking askance at yours truly. He swivels to clock the patrol.

"Head rush," I say. "Head rush, just a moment."

The jeep slides past. I come out of my crouch, shaky. They'll get to me eventually, but the longer I can stave that off . . . On a positive tip, I'm now pretty sure if I've got any more implant fragments in me, they're not broadcasting my location.

Back to these teenyboppers. "Head rush. You were saying." Wink at Kim.

Kim cracks his neck and sighs. "Don't get you at all, yo. Man, what you want with Rose, huh?"

"Like the lady told you, we went to Queens College back in—"

"Bullshit, man. You're like fucking fifteen years older than Rose, minimum."

"Continuing ed, Kim. What, you never heard of that? New beginnings."

"Bullshit. The sense I got, man, you straight-up cruised her, right there in my house. Then you come flex on me and my boys."

"It's not like that, Kim."

"She's my cousin."

"That's good to know. See, now I know."

"So I take an interest when armed bitches I've never laid eyes on in my life start dropping by, flexing, you know what I'm saying?"

"Indeed I do, Kim, and you're right to feel that way, though I would argue it's y'all doing the flexing on me."

Kim takes a breath to continue his rap, glances back at his buddies like he's showing this strange nigger what's up, right, and I spin him around by the arm, smooth, getting out the gun, jerking his elbow up and noting a little snap, easing the boy to his knees, me with my Serb niner up against the back of his skull, super-klassic execution-style. Except I wouldn't be able to pull the trigger anyway, not with this prop hand I'm wearing. But these boys needn't know that detail.

His posse is shouting this and that. Kim spits, tough stuff, but embarrassingly his voice marks him as poopy-pants scared.

"Jesus, word to God . . . fucked up my . . . fucked up my arm, that's not cool."

I keep my peepers on his dome, and address his buddies in Korean. "Boys, can you hear Mama calling? Hurry on home now, Kimberly's got detention."

Nobody moves. Silence save what sounds like a massive pile of metal getting knocked over blocks away.

I sigh. "Or. If you're still here after I count to three, that's an expulsion—for Kimberly. Like permanently. I could give a shit either way. So. One . . ."

Well, my hand is crying uncle but my thumb works, so I pull back the hammer with a deeply satisfying click, always a scary fucking sound if you're on the wrong end of things. Kim doesn't like it at all.

"Like he says! Do like he says, I'm all right, okay?" says

the young Korean. And over his shoulder, "Just chill, word to God, son, I'm sorry if . . ."

The bucks linger, hesitant.

"Stay right, children," I say. "Scram."

"Go, motherfuckers!" Kim screams. They jump to, rev their engines, and split, their softness palpable despite the haircuts and hard looks. Cut hard around the corner, frightened and colorful birds, off and gone and it's me and Kim and the CZ-99.

Chinese dude in a yellow bodysuit comes around the corner, savvies us, not scared, bored even, just walking down the street, spins on his heels and scoots right back where he came from. Well played.

"Hey comrade!" Kim calls after him in crappy Mandarin. "Hey! Beijing! Hey, getting robbed back here and all types of shit!"

Poor fellow. I pat him on the head. Tap him gently with the barrel and put the gun away.

"Get up, Kim."

The kid is trembling. I feel a wave of tenderness, fuck knows why.

"Who's in charge around here, huh? K-Man?"

Kim lifts his shoulder, won't meet my eyes.

"Maybe . . . maybe not. I don't gotta conversate with you, nigga," he mumbles.

I don't like that, but hey. I poke him again.

"C'mon, get up, nobody's gonna hurt you. Just don't approach folks you don't know with that negative attitude, there's all kinds out here and plenty badder than you. Humility, brother. I respect athleticism, but don't matter how much tae kwon do kung-fu-Manchu you know, nobody faster than a bullet. But I'm not that guy, dig, so stand up and be thankful for another day in paradise."

Kim points his face at me. "Best be glad you had that gun, man."

I nod, solemn. "Always am, Kim."

"Fucking pull out your heart with my bare fucking hands, man."

Clown. But I maintain a serious tone. "Don't doubt it."

"Fuck a bitch up."

"Well, Kim," I say to this man-boy, "the moment you see an opening, I suggest you take your best shot. I'm right here, brother. Meantime," put a hand on his arm and point him back toward the distant hubbub, back toward Koreatown, "take me to K-Man Seok."

Middle-aged Korean saying, "I didn't do it."

Cigarette-stained fingers touch the dog-eared photograph I've placed in front of him, the fur coat, the frozen gesture.

He repeats this gently, as if to himself: "I didn't do it."

Kwon-Man Seok is probably about my age, if not younger, but the dude looks a full decade-and-change my elder. Salty, greyhound-thin, prison- and street-hardened, sharing the same fish tattoo as Kim in the meat of his right forefinger and thumb, faded blurry-blue ink, gang signifiers. Leathery all over, plenty of scars. K-Man.

The both of us rocking SARS masks.

I'm a people person and a sucker, and hey, I dig the guy's energy, even in this dingy sixth-floor office on 34th Street. The man radiates class somehow, and a certain calm. Old-school dignity, old-school code.

About which the young Kim would know nothing, as he hangs back now, gum-smacking with some fellow thugs. A couple Koreans, one or two Chinese as well. Keeps throwing a worried glance over at us, did he fuck up bringing me here? Not like he had options.

We're seated toward a yellowish chicken-wire window overlooking the street, tea cooling in front of me. Haven't touched it, I'll admit.

I might have a good vibe, but I'm not stupid, y'all.

My vibe is positive, sure, I got that PMA.* But this joint is dirty, dirty, dirty.

On the table a Korean paper, ashtray, gold stub of a pencil, a deeply weathered book of sudoku puzzles, newsprint sienna, gone over once or twice, erased, and gone over again.

I've been relieved of my 99. Still got the little guy around my ankle, but there seems no pending static, and this situation feels pretty chill so I don't anticipate any need arising.

Defeated, that's the flavor of the air up in this place. Has-been. Past tense.

I am perched on my chair, with as little of my ass making contact with the seat as humanly possible. Chiggers, lice. Wanna Purell™ up but don't wanna offend.

I don't see it happen but Kwon produces a pack of cigarettes, Chinese, and I accept. At this moment I really have no recollection as to whether or not I'm a smoker; I have a hunch I am. Pull down my mask. Lean in to accept a light from him.

Inhale, exhale, yet more lung pollution. K-Man's in a fugue of sorts, thumbing the photo.

"Didn't do what? Didn't take the picture? Didn't know the girl?" I say.

"Disrespectful. You, you come in here . . ." Flashes mad for an instant, then he straightens out his face. Big sigh. The dude deflates even further, and dude was deflated already. Just a tarp of skin, draped over a rack of bone.

"Doesn't matter," says the man, monotone. "Doesn't matter anymore."

---

*PMA: Positive Mental Attitude. Ref.: rock group the Bad Brains, song "Attitude," released 1978. MUS 782.42 Library of Congress.

"Uh-huh. Now, sir . . ." I begin, unrolling my spiel, but Kwon cuts this off.

"Who you work for?" he says, quiet yet, but with teeth. "Police? ATF?"

"No sir. Self-employed. I work for me, nobody else. I'm not here to fuck with you in any way, sir."

Kwon gives a pained grin. "Mr. . . ."

"Decimal."

He mouths the word, dismisses it. "Been expecting one you guys, long time. Huh? Must work senator's office, Secret Service, or—"

"Absolutely not. In fact, I was not aware of this whole . . . situation until agents representing a certain congressman accosted me only this morning. Think we're both talking about the same guy. Yeah, you could say I have a beef of my own to settle with those motherfu . . . people."

Kwon smokes between thumb and pinkie, watches me. I continue.

"I'm here strictly in an information-gathering capacity."

Kwon speaks now, says, "Old shit. Old story. Who cares? Korean whore, one more, one less . . . same, same." He makes a weighing-the-scales gesture with this hands.

My thoughts exactly, but I wasn't gonna be the first one to say it straight up.

"Yeah, well. Plus the baby," I remind him.

Kwon bats this away. Indicates my paws. "Why you wear these . . . on the hands?"

I look at the surgical gloves. Speak frankly and switch to Korean. "I am, well, concerned about bacteria, germs, general hygiene, vis-à-vis protecting myself from exposure and possible illness or disorder arising from such."

The man laughs; I know what he's thinking, what with

everything we're breathing up in this tar pit, everything we're touching . . .

Switching back to his native tongue, Kwon says, "Strange man. Speak Korean. You hurt your hand."

I regard my flipper, hold it up. "I slapped a moving helicopter."

Kwon scans me, deadpan. I blank him back.

Dude says, "Why do you know our language?"

Again I find myself feeling sure of the answer, as sure as I've ever been without actually knowing, so I'm candid. What the hell, tell the man: "After my military service the United States government subjected me to a battery of unsanctioned and invasive experiments and tests. One of these tests involved enhanced language aptitude. I have had many of the world's languages downloaded into my brain. That's about as far as I can understand it, I'm constantly surprising myself."

He grimaces and switches again to Korean. "You actually believe this?"

I dip my chin, yes. Do I? I do. "Yes I do."

Kwon knits his brow. Looks back at the photo. "And you are not police, military, government, working perhaps for another contractor . . . working for Chinese . . ."

Nod my head. "Hand to God. I'm my own man."

K-Man thinks about this. Squints, peering at the blood on my lapel. "I understand most but not all of what you say. You use strange words."

I shrug.

The man casts his gaze around the dingy room. Sighs a couple times. "Well, I am an old fool who has nothing to say that affects my people."

"Appreciate the trust energy."

Kwon frowns at the odd terminology, but nods curtly. Dude seems prepared to talk to me so I jump on it.

"Sir, I'm here, obviously, because you went upstate for the—"

"Murder of Song Ji-Won, yes, I did."

"Well, sir, it's my instinct . . . I should say that your, ah, confession is the only bit of evidence on record, so I'm, you know, inclined to believe you are—"

"Not responsible for the murder of Song Ji-Won and her infant son," he cuts in. "No, it hardly matters now so I can freely say I did not, could not have committed this . . . most brutal, heinous action against two innocents."

We sit with that, the natural follow-up question heavy in the atmosphere. Start to say it: "Okay. So if not you . . ."

K-Man makes an impatient sound. "Look at us."

I don't get it. "Sir?"

"I mean, we used to be captains here. These American streets. Edicts of Seoul were observed equally here. A direct connection, a business arrangement here was a business arrangement there. We had order and hierarchy and respect. Now it's Beijing says this, Beijing says that. And with the war . . ."

Wags his head. Sad.

"All this Chinese ass-fucking, and what do they understand? They understand people as numbers, as pack animals. It's a gigantic mess, extremely volatile, you know. The Chinese don't understand our people, the people they subjugate; for that matter, they don't understand their own people . . . and when you don't understand your slaves, well. Your American history bears this out." He looks uncomfortable, then bobs his head, quick. Continues, "But these fucking Chinese . . ."

I glance over at the clutch of young folks.

"Don't worry, they would never waste the energy learning our language. No, it's our lot to learn theirs. Ugly language. And look at that. The younger generation knows nothing of history. Look at that, they eat together, commune together, sleep together, live together. Disgusting."

Cluck my tongue, yessir: it's a filthy shame. But in truth, this is where I diverge from racially pure old-school cats, cause we know the kittens are gonna play together, break bread, make multicolor babies, and hey, I reckon that's a major positive. It's really the only process keeping our species headed down the evolutionary path. Without mixing it up, we go the way of the dodo or the high-top fade.

Plus, as any breeder of dogs will tell you, like my old neighbor who dealt purebred rottweilers: eventually they start popping out retarded.

But hey.

K-Man is in a mood but the guy gets to the point nonetheless. "Sure. Doesn't matter now, so I tell you this. How do you say, I *took one for the team* on Song. This was my honor. But don't think it didn't break my spirit, sir. Song was . . . well, many things . . . but we always understood each other. We knew each other's hearts. And I always made sure . . ."

He looks down at the sudoku, the pencil. Looks back up, his eyes are just a little glassy. The barest suggestion of something soft, and that's as far as it goes cause the K-Man is rawhide like that.

"I always made sure Miss Ji-Won got along okay. All the girls, of course, but Song in particular. We spoke a lot, spoke a lot about home, you know. Korea."

I nod.

"Did my job. Danny Ya ran most everything, he was big from way back in his family history, Inagawa-kai, a very old and respectable family, yakuza from the beginning."

Danny Ya, the big boss . . .

"Might I be able to speak with Mr. Ya . . ." I begin, and Kwon is shaking his head.

"Pancreatic cancer in 2008, he went very quickly. Huh. Too quickly. No plans. His sons were junkie brats so that left me in the driver's seat. By default. But, you know, I'm so tired . . . so other arrangements were made. At least one of his kids, pretty sharp. Though I kept business going, in the short term." He waves his hand. "Witness my former kingdom, sir," he adds, wry.

I get the picture. "So it was Danny Ya—"

"Who asked that I step forward for the . . . what happened, with Song."

"That's a lot to fucking ask. Even in your circles. As I understand it."

Kwon eyeballs me like I just walked in the room. "This is a life thing we have here. I just told you it was my profoundest honor. Unlike—" Pauses, as if getting his anger under control, continues: "We don't try to move in on each other's territories, sir, or poach other's property, we're not like the Italians or the Russians, killing each other, lying to each other. This is a life thing, and a true family. The Sicilian thing, they're vain, spoiled children. No, you would not understand."

Don't like this. "I understand the concept of loyalty, Mr. Kwon. Ran with my own local gangs. And I was a military man."

Kwon bobs his noggin, acknowledging my snippy tone. "Not meaning to offend. Yes, of course you know loyalty to state, maybe to fellow soldiers, to comrades. Well, we take this one step past loyalty, this to us is family. You don't cherry-pick your family. You do whatever it takes to protect them. Can you understand that?"

"Yeah," I respond. Insulting he would assume I wouldn't understand such basic shit. Want to get him back on topic. "That's positive energy you're putting out there, Mr. Kwon, but hey, with all respect to your family and your sacrifices and whatnot . . . and, you know, considerable time having passed now . . . I'm here looking for the guy who did Song. And if that's not you, I'd like to ask if you might point me in the right direction."

Kwon fiddles with the photo, the girl, hand to mouth, frozen laugh . . .

"That's a horrible, disrespectful expression." I think he's talking about the photograph, but: "*Did* Song. Using the verb *to do* as a substitute for . . ."

I wince. "Apologies for my poor Korean, sir, and for my manners, Mr. Kwon. I've been wandering in the desert so long. Forget where to put the salad fork."

Kwon blanks me.

"Meaning to say, I apologize for my coarse language."

Kwon returns to the photo. Rubs at it.

Laughter from the direction of the exit, the gaggle of kids, Man throws them a sharp look and the laughter stops.

"No," he says to me, eyes on the boys. "My honor is my honor, and I don't have a lot left to lay claim to, sir. I will say this, however, and then speak no more on the matter."

Hands me back the photo. I gag inwardly, thinking about those parasites that thrive on human dermis, but I take it gingerly between gloved fingers.

"My family behaved as a smoke screen. That's all. The

people you're looking for, they're not *my* people. I suggest you look for answers to this . . . tragedy in more exclusive neighborhoods. Or maybe even in government circles."

He's growing progressively more emotional as he speaks. Feel myself recoiling, and without looking around, I mentally review my exit options.

"I don't control things here anymore. Not me." He starts pulling himself out of his chair. "Now I've said enough. You're a stranger here. It's best if you leave quietly, and kindly don't molest us any further. We have enough on our hands with these motherfucking Chinese."

Seems like the smart play, just walking. What's all this about not running things, though? If this guy is not the boss, why am I sitting here gum-flapping?

I rise as well, but can't resist one last grasp at the man. "Mr. Kwon. If you are no longer in charge, I respectfully request an audience with whoever . . . Song seems to have meant something to you. Would you not want to see . . ."

K-Man has clearly had enough of my nonsense, makes a gesture at the boys. Something revs up deep in his throat and before I know what's what, the man hawks a dark hunk of spit near my right Florsheim, causing me to stumble backward a bit. Jesus.

". . . those responsible . . . brought to some sort of . . ." I fumble the photo of Song, and it falls to the floor.

All of this is brought to a halt as everybody in the room clocks gunshots outside. High caliber, very large guns. The first is lost in industrial noise but the second is unmistakable.

Hustle to the grimy window. The boys crowd me.

Mexican standoff.

Situated just east of Broadway on 32nd Street, we are treated to a comprehensive bird's-eye view of two black

JLTVs, tricked-out with a Saab antitank weapon and a .50-caliber machine gun, respectively, these vehicles flanked by upward of a dozen black-clad soldiers on foot—yup, Cyna-corp has not so subtly made the scene.

This grouping is faced down by a heavily armored Hummer with some sort of mounted RPG, looks like a 40mm, and at least twenty Chinese militia buffering on foot, with more approaching rapidly from the east . . . It's not clear who fired what where, but by the sound of it I'd say it was the RPG, which having been directed skyward is now coming to rest, trained on the Cyna-corp brigade.

As well I note Chinese/Korean snipers taking positions on rooftops opposite, and long nasty-looking barrels pointing out of opaque windows. Un-uniformed folks, citizens and laborers, are scattering, making for doorways. I hear choppers, but don't see them.

Huh.

Kwon, taking his time, leans over to pick up the photo, straightens, squints out the window for a bit. Then has a long gander at me. Hands me the picture and heads back to his table.

I find Kim and a couple of the other boys staring at me. Kim's eyebrows are raised. I return the look, like, what the fuck would I know about this?

Turning to Kwon, who is in the process of reaching for his worn book of sudoku.

I clear my throat. "Well, I'd best be off then," I say. "Mind if I get that gun back?"

Once the barking match between leaders of the two military units reveals a lack of a common language and therefore a total inability to communicate, things out on 32nd Street go quiet-ish for a spell, while both sides, presumably, contemplate their next move.

I faintly hear the Cyna-corp captain calling for a translator, reckoning I can link that voice back to the intimate rasp in my ear early this morning at the library. Or maybe I'm tripping.

Some homeboy hands me my pistola, everybody's peepers on the street action, and I use this lull to haul ass out of K-Man's hidey-hole . . . through a dingy hallway and once-yet-fucking-again into a darkened stairwell, lit every second floor by a smallish window.

Taking the stairs in pairs, fumbling for a pill, nearly losing the whole bottle, fuck me, out of breath I dry-swallow and choke it back, not sure if I want to charge out there and make a suicide dash, go out tragic, which would mean getting shot in the spine and hopefully taking a few of these fucks with me . . . or if my intention is to genuinely engineer some kind of escape that will allow me to pop and lock another day.

Right now I'm just running. I forget why. The Boogie Oogie Man. No. I'm old, an old man, and so much has happened in the meantime. Enough to make me irredeemable.

I've been stumbling down dank-ass stairwells most of my life. Seems to be a theme, a coda, a tired refrain in a long, sad godamn song.

Now on the landing of the seventh floor, pause to sneak a peek out onto the street, through brownish glass I confirm the stalemate continues with each respective side in a huddle, I know this hiatus in the action can't last long, not with so many people with their fingers on so many triggers.

Ditch my gloves and get my Purell™ on . . . thinking, major chutzpah is involved with stepping en force into Chinese-controlled areas, surely the Cyna-corp folks, be they out-of-towners or not, should be aware of this. I cradle my beat-up flipper, which pains me like the dickens. Oh for a Percocet . . .

Not trying to say it's all about this guy, but if the shoe was on the other foot I'd be pissed off and looking to fuck me up too. Otherwise why here, why now? No thinking person would jostle the Chinese hive without good reason. So paranoid, or my working assumption is that Cyna-corp has traced yours truly to these quarters.

The Chinese aren't interested in nuances and should be expected to lose patience with this situation at any time, and just start shooting people. They're famous for it. In fairness the same could be said for Cyna-corp, but in contrast to the Chinese they tend to be knee-jerk and all emotional about it, I recall temper tantrums over in the sandbox that would leave scores of civilians dead, the boys in a frenzy, abusing their weapons, young, dumb, and full of cum. One infamous incident in particular, publicized for a moment and quickly hushed up, the American participants swiftly pulled out of the country. You may or may not recall.

A traditional headscarf decorated with brain matter and skull. A prepubescent girl raped and mutilated over a period of a week and a half, dead after a week, amongst the corpses of her family, who, it's estimated, had lived long enough to see their daughter and sister violated multiple times by a dizzying number of Western men. It doesn't matter at all now, does it? The slate is wiped cleaner than clean.

Reaching the ground floor in time for some feedback and the crackle of a bullhorn.

"CITIZENS," comes the oddly synthesized voice in Mandarin, they've got one of those translation-robot thingys . . . I crouch in the atrium, tucked back in semi-darkness but separated from the action by only a glass door.

"CITIZENS," repeats the robot. Not exactly state of the art, sounds like Stephen Hawking. Remember that space guy, black-hole dude, the guy in the wheelchair? He was a funny motherfucker. Dirty mind.

"WE HAVE COME HERE IN A PEACEFUL SPIRIT, WE RESPECT YOUR CLAIM TO THIS AREA, AND IN-TEND NO HARM NOR ENCROACHMENT ON YOUR JURISDICTION."

Somebody outside calls, "Just fucking shoot 'em!" and I stiffen up but nothing happens.

"WE SEEK YOUR ASSISTANCE. A CRIMINAL IS AT LARGE WHOM WE WOULD LIKE TO QUESTION. THIS INDIVIDUAL PERHAPS WITH ASSISTANCE DID WITHOUT PROVOCATION ATTACK SEVERAL OF OUR VEHICLES AND PERSONNEL, RESULTING IN MUCH DAMAGE TO CYNA-CORP PROPERTY AND THE DEATHS OF SEVERAL OF OUR PEOPLE. AT THE VERY LEAST—"

Crackle pop pause. The machine seems to be process-ing the next bit.

So yeah. I'm not high on my own supply; see what I'm

saying? These people HATE to be shown up. They're like the gangs of old in this respect.

The Chinese fire up their own PA system, through which a woman speaks in English. It's fuller and much more hi-fi. This is why America fell on its ass, we used to have the best sound systems, the best everything. But look, we got fat and China blew right past us, all casual like see ya on the flip.

"TRESPASSERS. PLEASE REMOVE YOUR VEHICLES AND REPLACE ANY WEAPONS IMMEDIATELY, OTHER-WISE THIS WILL BE CONSIDERED AN ACT OF AGGRES-SION AND WE WILL RESPOND ACCORDINGLY, AS PER THE BOWLING GREEN ACCORD."

The Cyna-corp voice computer catches up, comes with, "INDIVIDUAL GUILTY OF MAYHEM AND MULTIPLE HOMICIDE. HE HAS BEEN TRACKED TO THIS—"

"TRESPASSERS," says the Chinese gal again, battling sound systems, "PLEASE REMOVE YOUR VEHICLE—"

And then it's just a big loud smear as they talk over each other: ". . . DARK-SKINNED MALE, FIVE FEET TEN INCHES, APPROXIMATELY 135 POUNDS, WEARING A BLACK OR BROWN SUIT . . ."

". . . ACT OF AGGRESSION AND WE WILL RESPOND ACCORDINGLY . . ."

". . . TWENTY THOUSAND YUAN OR THE EQUIVA-LENT IN FOOD SUPPLIES FOR INFORMATION . . ."

". . . THAT THIS IS THE FINAL WARNING. TRES-PASSERS. PLEASE REMOVE . . ."

Everything speeds up, folks start hollering, dig the Chinese Hummie start to inch forward, the Americans like-wise push eastward ho, take a deeper peek and the soldiers on foot are up in each other's faces. It's about to jump off.

Of all the situations I've helplessly witnessed deteriorate into chaos and/or mass slaughter, finally one over which I have a touch of control. Or so I imagine.

Can't allow this to go down, y'all. Slip sliding right into an absolute bloodbath, and I won't sit idly by, I'm not that fucking precious about myself.

I'm going out there.

Up on my feet and I'm pushing at the door with my shoulder, more or less braced to die, who cares, right? Me calling out like I'm the freakin mayor, "Hold your fire! Hold your—"

Grabbed from behind with much force before I can get out the door, neck jerked back, I'm in a headlock, trying to breathe, inaudibly mouthing, "No, no," hit the concrete atrium sideways with somebody hanging on me, gunfire erupts and almost immediately the glass door is decimated, my attacker scooting us back and away from the exit, me stupidly thinking no, no . . . no what, Dewey? Writhing around in broken glass and rusty water, try to reach around and get a grip on my pistol but I find I've already been relieved of it, confirmation arrives as it's shoved in my ear.

Kim has to shout, I'm not particularly surprised to find myself in his embrace, kid has righteously been itching to smack me stupid since back at the Korean snack shack.

"Don't fucking fight me, man," I hear him say. "I've been told to keep you breathing, but trust this, if it were up to me, yo, I'd just let you walk right out the door and get what's coming to you, you devil fuck."

Cacophony of bullets outside, sounds like microwave popcorn as Kim jerks me to my feet.

Yet more blood figurative and literal drenches my suit and soul. Just add it to list of evil shit for which I will pay dearly in Hell.

nderground it's all connected, I mean ant-colony tunnels connect basement to basement here beneath 32nd Street, burrows probably as old as the island itself, occasionally opening up into larger caves where I peep open fires, livestock, tents, entire families pausing to look glassily at Kim and me as we shuffle past, me discombobulated, trying to regain my already compromised footing, must've smacked my head on something. The deep gloom of these tunnels is disrupted by the battery-powered lanterns spaced at approximately fifteen-foot intervals.

Always suspected something like this subterranean hive, always detected its pulse, its movement. I want to vibe further on this new vista but my heart is sick. Register the gunplay, even down here. Knowing it's on me, my spiritual rap sheet, it's all in my lap.

Dizzy, scrabbling for my pills. My vision keeps going wiggly. Time is liquid, I want to set this misunderstanding right, but my internal pragmatist knows it was already too late the moment Cyna-corp rolled onto the scene.

Kim is sufficiently comfortable to at least allow me to hobble along without jabbing my kidneys with the pistol. He's fallen a step or two behind, and it occurs to me the boy has been talking all the fucking while, him saying, ". . . bring your ill shit up in here. You think we need this static? Like we don't have enough bullshit . . ."

Retune this noise out. If he was geared to whack my sad ass he would've done it by now, and why the fuck not?

He's an eager beaver, is Kim, a street soldier just executing instructions.

So the Koreans are willing to shield me, for what purpose I can only guess at.

Earth gives way to a concrete incline, terminating in a wall sporting a flimsy-looking ladder which at one point was painted yellow, extending heavenward into midnight black.

"Climb it, bitch," suggests Kim.

Turn to him but can't really make out his features. Not sure if it's the lighting or my own frayed synapses. I dig that I've been slumped against the wall, stargazing. Missing tiny scraps of time, my connection to the continuum is intermittent, glitchy.

"Where the fuck we going, Kim?"

"Nigga, you don't get to ask questions. See the boss. The boss gonna sort you out, no doubt, now fucking climb it."

Okay. The boss. I withdraw a fresh pair of gloves. Withdraw my pill bottle, twist, and fish one out.

"You're one straight freak, man."

This I ignore as I swallow the little pentagon-shaped pill, but it's true enough.

Trust my depth perception is still functioning, I grab a cold rung, and hump my corpse upward.

I t's a serious haul, a long ascent into a species of dark that I've only seen before in nightmares. Doing it more or less one-handed, which is trickier than it sounds.

As I'm enfolded in blackness, the spirits who populate my sleep make themselves known.

Whoosh. Here's Hakim Stanley, the handsome, brave brother with a hole in the top of his head. A hole I put there. Stanley's simply observing me, expression unreadable. U.S. Army attire with a wide collar of blood. He salutes in slow-motion. I know not to speak to him lest I make these visions manifest.

Whoosh. Here's District Attorney Rosenblatt in a worn shit-colored bathrobe. Absent is a sizable chunk of his skull. Another head-shot brought to you by Dewey Decimal. He appears drunk, leering, eyes just slightly to my left, which makes the effect all the more fucked up.

Decimal. Your file. The stuff they did—

Shove that away. Won't be played by phantasms.

Whoosh. Here's some abstract art, no, a jumble of body parts. This is a new one. I'm forced to watch as they assemble themselves into a young woman, outfitted in a grayish fur coat. I am looking at Song Ji-Won. She's admiring her nails, singing to herself in Korean. It's not a number I'm familiar with, I don't think I've ever heard anything like it, and she sings soft, sweetly, in the manner of one who thinks she is alone:

Did I dream you dreamed about me?
Were you here when I was full sail?

It seems extremely goddamn important that I hear more, I can get with this tune, but my dome smacks what I immediately believe to be the ceiling.

"Open the fucking thing. There's a handle." This from Kim, sounding winded behind and below me in the blackness.

At this juncture I could do a couple things. Reckon I could stomp on Kim's hands, kick him in the face, knock him back into Hades, be done with the punk. Then cash in life number nine getting the Fu Manchu out of Koreatown.

Or. I could see where this whole mess is going to land, and what my protectors have in mind for me. Meet the boss.

"Motherfucker, what's the fucking holdup? Open the shit!"

Kim has got to learn to ask nice. Nonetheless, I choose option B.

Loop an arm over a rung to hold myself in place. With my good flipper I sweep the area above me Helen Keller–style, find a cylindrical grip, twist it. As if spring-loaded, the door in the sky flips open, and a mildew-laden basement draft douses my upturned face with microorganisms.

Emerging from the basement into yet another multistoried building, Kim keeps me hustling up the stairs . . . the gunplay outside seems to be tapering but is still very much in effect. Again I resist the urge to make a break for the ground-level exit, jog headlong into a hail of bullets, remind myself that at this point such a move would be for naught but self-murder. Even at a canter, I get my pills out and make sure one slides down my gullet, nearly spilling them before I can get the cap back on.

I think I might vomit, but my vision is better. All of this on me. Have to remind myself that a soldier is not a civilian, a soldier forfeits his human value. Doesn't make me feel better but there has to be that distinction.

A sign in Korean, *DO NOT USE THESE STAIRS* . . . Hang on.

Third floor, and in almost all respects this building, this stairwell, is indistinguishable from the last one, and the one before. I am assuming I am still on 32nd Street. Things are looking more familiar than they should, I must be losing it a touch. Kim is silent, wheezing slightly, smoker's lungs, surprising for such a young kid.

We pass though another stretch of darkness, stepping gingerly now, and it hits me as I'm pushed though a door marked 9, déjà vu again, hang on: we are on the ninth floor of 38 West 32nd Street, just as I was only hours ago.

"Kim, man." I try to turn but Kim gives me a shove.

"Shut up, yo. Come on."

The big machine gun outside goes bada bada bada.

Window open or broken at the end of the corridor. Couple guys crouched under the frame, trying to get a look. Dude in a lab coat. Fucking doctors, blood tests, needles . . . oh yeah, the dentist. He's a dentist. The dental practice. Chill, Decimal. Crazy noise from the street boomerangs up and down the hallway here on the ninth floor.

Practically shouting over the din.

"Kim, listen to me now. I gotta do something about this, youngin, you gotta let me get down there . . ."

Kim is taking a pull off an asthma inhaler, which makes me like him more for some reason, and does a decent job of fronting hardcore AND keeping the gun on me, no easy trick. When he can speak, "Bitch, don't fuckin tempt me. Just keep stepping. 907, you know where we're going."

I guessed as much but am at a total loss as to why. Try again.

"Kim, I'm telling you, man, if I don't try to help fucking sort out that madness down there, I'll never be able to forgive—"

Gun is inserted into my eye socket, which does have the effect of silencing me.

"Keep. Stepping," says the young man.

The very fucking moment the door to Club Enjoy swings wide, I'm sucked in and group-tackled, for what seems like the umpteenth time today, by a knot of burly bodies shouting in a collision of Korean and English, "Get his hands! His fuckin hands!"

If you must get my hands, please do so gently, I amend. Wishful thinking. Worse perhaps than the gangbang physical assault is the tsunami of body odor coming off this crew. Coughing, once again I suffer the indignity of finding myself pressed to the ground. My hat is gone. This time the wood floor tastes like Pine-Sol, which takes me back some. I go slack, try to just relax into it.

Note a gaggle of maybe six slinkily clad teenage girls, made up like Japanese courtesans, clinging to each other in the corner, shrieking theatrically.

"I got his gun!" I hear Kim shout over the babbling flunkies and squeaking ladies. "Yo! Listen up. Nigga is helpless like a baby, y'all can get up off his ass, gonna give the old motherfucker a heart attack. Get him up, up on his fuckin feet."

Somebody's got ahold on my nappy head but they're having trouble getting a solid grip as I wear it short. They settle for the back of my neck. I open my eyes and take it all in, my first thought being the flowers which I had initially thought to be fake are real. Live flowers? Impossible.

Rose Hee, perched on a barstool, legs crossed. That gold dress. Smoking what looks like a Capri. She's applied geisha-style white base since I last saw her, and black lip-stick in a painted pout. Another live flower.

I'm crowded by maybe four or five dudes, overbuilt, clones all, who have gone Zen-temple quiet. The gals in geisha garb huddle, whispering amongst themselves. Be-hind me is Kim.

"Whaddya say, boss? Call it," says Kim. Deferential. Me thinking: who's the fucking boss? Why does this gotta be so confusing?

Rose takes a long drag, bouncing her leg. Black lipstick residue on the filter. Blows a couple smoke rings. Tapping her long nails on the bar. Shots through the door and down the street, distant and increasingly sporadic. She speaks: "Clear out, gentlemen. I want to talk to him. Alone."

And only now, slow dumb-ass that I am, do I get it.

S o you're the boss. Miss Runnin' Thangs."

We're alone in a wood-paneled cabin. Rose ignores me, says instead: "Never dated a black guy."

She plops two long-stemmed champagne glasses on the low table between us.

Rolling with this. I grin and try to relax into it despite the anxiety in my gut regarding the doings outside. I gotta get a plan together quick, but I play casual: "Well, I'm only 75 percent black. Grandma was from Manila. Still makes me black as far as the rest of the world is concerned. And you know what they say. Once you go black—"

"Shut the fuck up, mister. You're slick but you talk miles of shit, you know that? Gets boring. Just hush."

Pop goes the cork on a bottle of Cristal (Cristal!!), a sight and a sound I have not beheld since . . . well, since Shaq was still hooping. In a heartbeat I am almost positive that I've been reborn within a Hype Williams–directed hip-hop video from the early 1990s.

Add to this an overhead projector casting a sharp digital film of various exotic fish, the suggestion of a hazy coral reef, candy-colored bubbles, in 360 degrees, creating the pleasant but disconcerting impression that we've landed in a sexy cartoon aquarium.

I can't sit. Agitated. Trying to focus, I slide my gloved hand across the tan leather of the wraparound couch, here in this smallish room . . . Yes: real leather, worn but intact.

Inwardly I shiver, leather being so . . . absorbent. Porous. I check my fingertips.

Rose holds the bottle away from her, making a frowny face, and when no froth appears she bobs her head in satisfaction, leans over to pour me a couple drops.

I should refuse it. Mixes poorly with my medication. But I don't. Thinking: want to give the impression that I'm loosening up, slowing down. Getting slippy-sloppy.

She attends to her own glass. Saying, "I want to remind you. There's any number of armed men outside who would love to see you dead. For bringing those foreign soldiers here. I'm not pleased about it myself."

Sets down the bottle, straightens up, hands on hips.

"Just in case you were looking to get fresh. Fair warning. Okay?"

Pick up my glass with my broken paw, hold it at eye level. "I'll behave. Cheers now."

Rose gives me a hard once-over. "What the fuck kind of person are you?" Flat, more statement than question.

"Compulsive do-gooder," I say. "I right the wrongs as I see 'em. Otherwise, I'm a scarecrow, I'm nothing. I haunt and get haunted and I ride the highway to Hell. Cheers, Rose."

Regards my mask, which hangs slack around my neck. My gloves. My fucked-up hand. One pretty shoulder lifts, and she picks up her own glass.

"Poetic. Salut. Chin-chin," she says. Offers a smile.

We touch champagne stems. Must say, it's been a long time since I found myself in such a civilized situation. But dig, for all the conviviality my stomach tells me it's a good fucking thing the muscle never did think to frisk this guy, leaving my ankle holster in place.

Take a small mouthful and allow it to flow back into the glass. Still get that sweet, woody aroma that reminds me of nothing so much as an eve of high-rolling and gangsta-leaning back in the ghetto. Waking up broke.

Head drifts over to the melee outside. It's my problem to solve, and I'm all jagged edges. Say, "I get the vibe. Take it then, your daddy was Danny Ya. Y'all are like . . . K-town Cosa Nostra and all that. Mobbed-up, right? That's your steez."

The lady doesn't respond to this directly. "Will you sit?" she says.

"Rather stand. I'm a bit . . ." I'm a bit what? I'm a bit responsible for the bloodshed outside.

"Do what you want," says Rose. "I just had a conversation with the chief of Cyna-corp . . ."

Snap to. Hold up.

"Sorry, what's that?"

Rose throws me a look. "Come on. Cyna-corp? Nic Deluccia, that's the boss over there . . ."

Nic Deluccia. So there it is. I get a very fucked-up feeling.

". . . upshot is that we give you over to his team. Or else," Rose is saying.

I gesture vaguely in the direction of the door. "Seems like they've already come down on your people pretty hard."

She laughs, flops her hand, bracelets rattling.

"Oh no, that's really just a bit of street theater. More for the public benefit. Buncha shooting in the air. Rubber bullets and all. This is more common than you'd think. Keeps us Koreans in line, knowing Beijing has our back. It's all bullshit."

Stockhom syndrome–type psych-ops. Right, I'm thinking. Makes sense.

"You know, the thing with Cyna-corp, we're always arm wrestling over construction contracts, there's always some issue to be resolved, but it's never too serious cause in the end we work together, and we all serve the same master. No, I've known Nic since I was a girl, and our conversation was actually quite matter-of-fact and polite. As usual, Nic's a gentleman."

Don't know what to believe, but sweet Jesus, if that's the truth, this is a load off a brother's mind. For the moment. But Cyna-corp . . .

"Those Cyna-corp people are straight-up psychos," I say. Lamely. "They don't care who they hurt. I've dealt with them a lot, and trust me, Rose, they're some bad cats who've done tons of bad shit."

Rose regards me. "Yeah? Well, I've worked with Cyna-corp plenty in the past. Generally had a good experience with them. Plus, they're extremely important allies to my people. Business associates. Us Koreans . . . well, I should say me, I have my own private relationship with Cyna-corp. We need them for a little counterweight, so the Chinese don't consume us completely. They need us cause we can at least communicate with the Chinese. And we have people, plenty of able people. And that's all I'm really concerned about here. My people, and keeping them working, keeping them fed. You get it?"

I get it, but I'm duty-bound to drill some sense into this woman.

"Hey Rose. Due respect. You do not know what these guys are capable of. I've seen these crazies get up to some sick madness that would make you—" Thinking specifically of more than one gang rape in which . . .

Rose cuts me off: "Don't you fucking dare lecture me

about crazy, mister." She's pissed but her voice modulates controlled and even. "You're the one against the wall here, not me, but you're putting my people and my organization in a tough position, and who the fuck are you anyway?"

I don't say jack. The woman clears her throat, regaining her composure.

"Listen here. I have to make a decision about this thing, like right now. Help me out here cause I'm trying to do the correct thing, but you know I'm having trouble," says Rose, sitting and adjusting her skirt, "understanding exactly why you've just . . . sailed in here, asking well-informed questions about a dead girl who could have meant nothing to you. And furthermore, we wonder why a fucking private army like Cyna-corp would be calling for your head on a platter. Cause Nic did not provide me with any information. Only the demand."

Now I speak calmly and quietly: "Rose. I'm a private investigator. Been telling you from the jump. Cyna-corp is under the mistaken impression that I have information I mean to use against one of their clients. Absolutely not the case. Unless I can verify that the intel I have is accurate. This is where Song comes into play, so I think you might know what I'm talking about."

Rose watches the far wall, struggling with her face. Clearly she's hearing me. Clearly she knows what I'm talking about. I push forward.

"I'm truly sorry that your people got in the middle here, but I am simply doing some follow-up, and this leads me straight down to your hood. No way around it. That's my word, that's the truth. Now, of course I never knew Song. But in my own fucked-up way, I wanna see some justice done up in here."

My little monologue is met with silence. I wait it out. After a full minute, she speaks.

"Well, buddy, I'll put it to you like this," Rose says, setting her glass aside. "It's my responsibility to make sure things run smoothly around here. As for justice, I don't have a whole lot of faith left." She clears her throat, shifts gears. "Look. My one purpose, I mean, all I'm good for, is to keep business flowing in this neighborhood. I'm talking about our construction contracts. My father . . . anyway. This is all we got. And at this point, you pose a threat to the business side of things here. You get me? I have a board to answer to, believe it or not. Shareholders. Rocking the boat, this is a tricky thing."

Swirl my glass, the amber liquid. Pace the tiny area I have available to pace.

Rose is gauging my energy, my language. Am I for real? Sure I am.

Eventually homegirl says, "It doesn't add up, mister. Unless you're completely crazy and just want to stir shit up. Now sit!"

Still fucking antsy but I sit. Cross my legs casual-like, which sends a jolt of pain up my right side and causes me to blink. Between my leg and my busted-up hand there's jockeying going down as to what can pain me the most.

Rose shifts ass cheeks, tensed on the couch like a hummingbird, her aura buzzing and raw.

"So, this is your big chance to charm me, Mister X, you get This. One. Chance." A fingernail taps her glass thrice, accenting each word.

Her tone is light and easy but I know better. Here in this video fish tank I swim with the barracuda. Straight, calm talk is in order. Clear my throat and take that one chance.

"I got no interest whatsoever in your comings and goings and whatnot. I know how it is out here. Don't give two fucks about construction contracts and all, entirely your scene."

I carefully place my glass on the table as well, lean forward, an earnest gesture. My hand that much closer to my gun. Leg shaking. Talking faster now.

"All I wanna know is the skinny on Song's murder. That's it. You wanna share, you wanna help me out, for the sake of a girl who I know featured in your life somehow, darling—don't deny it now."

Pause to read the air. She's trying to vibe steely but I sense subcutaneous emotional activity.

Say, "Those tears earlier? Doesn't take a detective to savvy those tears, they come from a deep, real place." I lightly tap my chest.

Rose is watching me. Eyes a touch unfocused, part of her elsewhere, lips parted, she says, "More bullshit from an expert bullshitter." Quiet-like.

Spread my fingers and press them to my chest like I'm pledging allegiance.

"I'm just as this cold world has made me, Rose. Yeah, I can bullshit, but when I get locked onto something I don't let go, especially where I smell some injustice. That's real, Rose, what more can I say? Got a compulsion."

Rose taps out a Capri, eying me.

"Uh-uh," she says, nodding at my gloves. "Looks like you got more than one compulsion. Okay, I get it. Senator Howard put you up to this. You're working for him. Somehow you fucked up and now he let out the dogs on you."

"No, flip that around. Howard put the dogs on me first. I had no prior encounters with this motherfucker. Naturally, I got interested in the man when I discovered what he's accused of."

She's studying her Capri. "I take it you're referring to . . . Song Ji-Won."

"Yeah," I say, hoping this is headed in the right direction. She lights the cigarette, leans in a bit herself.

"Let's talk more about you, shall we, Mister X?"

"Call me Dewey."

"I'm not calling you that. It's not your real name. I'm calling you Mister X."

Lift a shoulder, say: "Whatever floats your junk." Bounce my leg. Counting the bounces even as I speak. Can't help it. Forty-two, forty-three . . .

"Now Mister X," she continues, "you're up to your ears in four dimensions of shit. You got the senator, you got Cyna-corp, you got the Chinese AND the Koreans disappointed in you. You're looking for the exit, and you got nowhere to go but down." She grins at me, blinks those eyes. "Am I warm, Mister X?"

I don't say anything. She knows she's right. Gives me a sad face.

"Poor baby. Well. What can you do?"

More than aware it's a rhetorical question. I exhale, momentarily stumped. Exhaustion rushes in to meet me. Certainly must show cause she offers up the sad face again. Then knocks the ash off her cigarette and carries on.

"You're running out of gas. Less and less options. So I tell you what we can do here, Mister X. We can cut a deal."

I'm listening and I tell her so. My leg and hand are competing for most-painful-body-part status. I want to sleep. Wonder if I've been drugged, don't care.

"Here it is," says Rose. "We want Senator Clarence Howard. *Alive*, please, you fucking psycho."

"Were I in your skirt I'd feel much the same," I say, letting the psycho dig slide. "Why not get him yourself then? He's a big bastard, difficult to hide a dude like that."

Shakes her head. "Can't do it. Tried reaching out, he won't come out and play with us. Song and everything. He thinks we'll whack him. But his office hands out the contracts. We need their continued support, more of it. We need our own contracts, not just subcontracted Chinese shit. So if we look bad, negative ramifications on the business. Everything goes to the Ukrainians or your American Cyna-corp types. He favors them as it is. They're his boys, as you pointed out yourself."

She tips her head and blinks at me, girlish.

"The senator . . . well, he just needs a little convincing as to our merits. So we need you to pull him in, I take it from there. See our position?"

"I sympathize. But here's the thing: if you're asking me to do this, I can't know what you're gonna do with him. So I gotta know he's guilty of this murder. Directly or indirectly."

"Oh he's guilty, Mister X. But that's not why we want to talk to him, as I just explained," says Rose evenly. "I see an opportunity here to open up a channel previously unavailable to us. But don't worry yourself, he's a guilty man. This is just history."

"You saying you don't crave some payback? Please."

Rose shakes her head, expression like she doesn't give a hot shit what I believe.

I put out my palms, show her my gloves.

"Yo," I say. "Let's back up. I gotta independently confirm this man, this very powerful man, is responsible for the murder of a young woman and her child. It's a thing I have, a deal-breaker for me. Confirmation. And hey, you may not give a shit about Song—"

Rose snaps: "I cannot afford to give a shit. I have a business to run. A whole lot of people are watching me close, so I wouldn't fuck me around, Mister X."

A pause. Hit a nerve.

"Listen, I'm just trying to . . ." I stall out, then say, "Are you trying to tell me you want the senator's business, and are willing to let Song slide, just like that? I don't buy that noise for a heartbeat."

Rose doesn't respond, studying her glass.

"My read? You're gonna do your Black Widow–Ice Queen gig, and you're gonna look real good doing it. But it's not you. Ain't your heart talking."

"You don't know a goddamn thing about me," Rose responds thickly, raising her eyes to rendezvous with mine.

"Maybe not, darling, but gotta say I think it's truly fucked up that I'm the only dude around here who gives a shit about Song Ji-Won." I'm trying to think fast through a cloudy head. "I don't believe that's the case, I can't believe it. I see you struggling. Okay. I haven't figured you out yet. But I will. Okay? I'm gonna work you out, lady."

More silence from Rose. Then: "You are one strange man, Mister X."

Shrug. Shaking my leg. "I'm a shade quirky," I concede.

Rose chews on her lip. "You're a shade shady. Can you not fucking shake your leg? Let me fucking think."

I will my leg to stop. In my brain I'm still jiggling it. Rose puts her hand to her forehead, her nails carefully sculpted. See her hand shaking a bit. This is tougher than she's letting on. I clam up.

She rises, clear-eyed. "What would that require, Mister X? Confirming the senator's guilt, I mean."

"So y'all have no evidence here on your end, a little something you could share with me . . . ?"

She just looks at me. Take it as a no.

"Leverage. I'd need a heavy angle. I got nothing. I'm only one little dude, one little, slightly handicapped dude. I can't go straight at this guy. As you well know, those are his people out there playing at tearing up your block." I pause. Thinking. Say, "And more still. Gotta get past them, if I were to agree to your proposal."

The girl looks at my knee, which is bouncing around again. I can't help it.

"That's something we might be able to assist on, Mister X." Rose tilts her head, birdlike. "As for leverage, here's a tidbit—do with it what you will: Howard's wife arrives on the island this evening. We know when and where. Maybe that's somewhere to begin."

Upend my glass into my mouth. Chew on some ice, and this bit of new information.

"It is. Somewhere to begin," I say.

"Good—"

Cut her off: "But please, now—how could you be privy to such info, Miss Hee? These people are beyond paranoid."

Rose does her canary imitation again, a sideways tilt.

"We have resources. And this woman, she loves to goose her handlers. It'll be the thing that gets her killed." She runs her hands along her skirt again. "So. We'll get you to that white bitch. We'll get you that far. If we have an agreement, Mister X."

Chew on it further. Homeless. On the lam. This whole thing not making sense, but what the hell: nothing better on tap. What the fuck. Say, "Swapsies. In exchange, Rose Hee. Regardless of how it goes down with the senator, you all help me get my library back a.s.a.p. We do that first, or no dice."

Rose blinks, confused. "Library," she repeats.

"I live and work in the Main Branch Library up on—"

"I know where it is. Hence the nickname. What do you do up there, Mister X?"

I don't know how to answer that. Say, "Point is I need to get back in there, I'm gonna need what files I have on Senator Howard in order to get his attention at all, wife or no wife. Everything I got on him is in there. Can you get me back there, Rose? Key to your request, can't be done otherwise. I got those Cyna-folks in my way so it won't be easy, they got the building locked down tight. Throwing a lot of resources at it. I wouldn't be able to get five blocks from the place . . ." I trail off, realizing I've started to sound needy.

Rose is turning this over. I'm looking at her in profile. Both of us breathing. Watching the wall, the exotic underwater holograms.

The woman says, "You've got some balls, setting some pretty steep terms and all, hon. Look at you."

"I'd much rather look at you," I counter. It's true. "Far more pleasant."

Is she blushing? She averts her gaze, a small smile, vibing teenager. Flips her hair and gives me a stern look, gets serious again. So do I.

"Take it or leave it, sweet stuff," I say. "My terms. Otherwise, I'm happy to go my own way and play it as it lays, even if the odds are bad. If you can dig that."

Rose goes back to staring at the wall. She then starts to nod, almost imperceptibly at first, then decisively.

"Okay, Mister X. We're going to have to do this so we sidestep the Chinese as well. Only way to do what you're describing is to give you up."

"Not gonna fucking happen, honey bun."

"That's not what I'm talking about. I'm talking about handing over a body. Won't be you, darling. It'll buy us some time."

Oh, I don't like this.

"Body? What body?"

Rose wears a coy grin. I get it. My stomach churns.

"Oh, fuck no—"

"This is something we're good for," she says soothingly, "providing bodies. One of our primary exports. Now, we will do this your way, but you'll have to cooperate, sweetie."

I'm looking at bad bad and way worse than bad bad. Fish out my pill bottle and toss one back.

"Koreatown has a biohazard response team. Everybody else being so shorthanded," says Rose, thinking aloud. Looks at me. "Basically, we send our people into holes to die, as we're considered expendable like that. Anybody in town sees something suspect, they just call us and we get down there and remove it. At whatever cost. Anyways, that's going to be the ticket."

"I'm not following you," I say, cause I'm not.

Rose waves her nails in the air. "You don't need to. Do we have a deal, or what?"

Need time to process but I hear the survivor in me saying, "Deal."

She stands, slides open a closet.

"Deal," says Rose Hee, dropping a bathrobe in my lap and making air quotes. "Now, Mister X. Let's have that suit, and get you over to the dentist."

At approximately three thirty p.m. our biohazard response unit rolls up on the Forty-deuce Main Branch entrance. Kim is on my left, us sitting rigid in our gear like pastel-colored astronauts, he exhales audibly, I imagine at the sight of the concentration of soldiers, perhaps twenty-five heads total, who knows how many more at the other exits.

I'm seeing straight U.S. military in addition to the black-clad Cyna-corps, it's a two-vehicle-deep presence, NYPD as well, emergency bars cycling blue and red, the general energy frenetic, confused. All of which amounts to that snafu vibration.

Sigh. All this wasted energy. And for what? My damaged paw aches in anticipation of ill weather.

Fine, we're coming off a bit shabby in our converted airport shuttle, but I've seen worse when looking legit really counted. At least the mustard-colored electric van bears the biohazard tribal tattoo. A single cop moving out into the street to flag us down, fat, red-faced, jaw flapping.

A whole lot of complicated shit went down back in K-town in a very short amount of time, and I don't ever particularly want to read the fine print.

A pencil sketch:

I had a wax cast made of my teeth. Which I might add are like the Roman Forum in that they remain stunning, but a mere suggestion of their former majesty.

As I lay there in the dentist's chair waiting for the mold

to dry, I was informed about a biological "incident" at the Main Branch Library. I was further informed that no such incident had in fact occurred, but that I would be amongst the unit responding to this hoax.

Returned to an underlit room at Club Enjoy to "rest," Rose no longer in evidence, where I was unenthusiastically offered an "enjoy massage" by a bony teenager with mournful eyes. I declined as gently as possible. She left, and I was alone.

At this point I experienced another freeze, during which I was convinced the area I inhabited was under siege. Not finding any physical clues as to my current situation in the unfamiliar bathrobe, nor in the foreign room, I effectively barricaded the door by disassembling one of the wall couches.

When forced open I attempted, nearly successfully, to throttle a large Korean man with the terry-cloth belt from the bathrobe. I was subdued and reminded of my location and current condition. Whereupon I did my best to apologize, which was lost in the rush to get me into a Chinese version of a yellow Tychem-encapsulated chemical head-to-toe bodysuit, of the type I had worn in the military, the kind of suit I coveted and privately longed to be buried in.

At Walter Reed I as much as insisted I be outfitted in such kit at all times, which probably jacked up my ranking on the kook chart in a big way.

Additionally, the Koreans issued me a pair of "athletic" shoes, which I very reluctantly accepted. Picky about my kicks.

Prior to this, the surly Kim had returned my weapon wordlessly, and I was informed by an older man that Kim would not be leaving my side for the foreseeable future.

The prospect of this seemed not to thrill young Kim to the degree it might, had he known me better. Hell, I can be a motherfucking blast. But you all know that already.

I was informed an agent would meet us at the library and facilitate things.

Before the helmet was lowered on me, I made sure to take another pill. Who knew how long it would be before I next had a chance to do so?

As I was hustled out the front entrance, duly impressed at the level of organization and the speed at which this had all come together, I blinked in the diffuse sunlight, amongst a group of a eight identically clad jokers. I did not see Rose again.

My eye was then drawn to a small clutch of soldiers around what appeared to be a charred, still smoldering body. Mostly Chinese, and two Cyna-corp dudes, both vibing authority, one peering at the body sideways, hands on his hips, the other with his back to me, mumbling into a walkie-talkie.

The weirdly untouched wing tips on the corpse looked very much like my own Florsheims.

Wonder where they got a black guy.

Tried to get a better look, but before this was possible I was boarding the shuttle bus, idling noisily, and off we went, the driver in a hurry, not bothering to secure the door.

The fat cop intercepts our crew, arriving in midsentence, hoarse-shouted Brooklynese: ". . . said cut that fuckin engine! Now, what I wanna know is what took you so goddamn long, but never frickin mind already! Who here speaks English and who does not speak fuckin English, show of hands! Aw, fuckin forget it! Look now, we got us an alleged, said SUSPECTED, biological hazard. If you ask me, a much-ado-about-nothing kinda deal, but what the fuck do I know! I want you boys in and out as quick as possible with this thing cause we got other situations percolatin elsewhere, so let's fuckin get on with it! And don't forget who got jurisdiction here, you people talk to uniformed NYPD and ONLY uniformed NYPD, this is a City operation, not some private-sector shit, now let's move out!"

We do so, me thinking, damn, this guy is old-school, the kind of provincial street uniform we used to goof on and outrun up in Morris Heights, Keystone Kops–style. I'm stunned his kind still roams this earth.

Somebody swings wide the rear doors and we're pulling out shoulder-mounted thermobaric weapons, SMAW-NE. Oh boys, kindly handle with fucking care. Used to call these babies "bunker busters" in the sandbox, and I don't have to do any math to know it would be a very unfortunate thing to have such a weapon go off in the confines of the New York Public Library.

But I reckon this is how they clear a room, if they're

scared enough. That's certainly how we did it back when: came up on an enclosed space thought to contain hostiles, you just hit it with one of these bitches first. Only then you took a look-see. And what you saw was generally nothing but ash.

Which is probably just as well. Cause more than likely it wasn't insurgents you just incinerated. Kids. Schools. Makeshift triage stations . . .

Mentally salute my lions as we jog up the stairs, the Cyna-corp people hanging back and letting the locals sort this one out, giving the scene a wide berth, uncharacteristic of them . . . Fat cop is still bellowing, apparently there's some sort of territorial issue with respect to which outfit "owns" this particular situation. Feels mad intrusive to have all these costumed jackasses up in what has become my house, and I need to remind myself that this is a public space, others have the right to soak up its energy as well. Within reason. Once I get a leg up I'm gonna kick 'em all to the curb, and enjoy doing it.

"Decimal." A lone female cop in a gas mask has materialized near me, not looking in my direction. "Confirm by tapping your helmet with your right hand, okay?"

She has a West Coast lilt that dips up at the end like she's always asking a question. Am I that easy to spot? Guess I should calibrate my limp. I tap my helmet as requested, though I have to think left, right, shit.

Quip, in blackccent: "Sheet, I don't know nothing 'bout nobody, occifer."

"Gonna ask you to not speak, okay? Here's what's gonna happen, okay? Koreatown sent me, okay? I escort you people into the building, and from there you're to proceed upstairs unaccompanied. Apparently you're on point. Okay? If that's clear, tap your helmet once more."

Tap tap.

She raises her radio, there's a static fart, then: "We're moving, copy."

Through the doors, into the empty atrium, eight yellow-suited individuals and one officer of the NYPD. Cathedral arches make beautiful shapes overhead.

Once inside the cop ushers me to the stairwell. My crew inspects their weapons with focus. It gets quiet in a hurry, this marble is thick. A man I believe to be Kim nods slightly in my direction.

"Okay," says the cop in a low voice. "Here's the Cliffs-Notes, okay? I've been the liaison between Cyna-corp and Koreatown for the last six months so I have special access, okay? We disabled the cameras on the upper floors and au-dio throughout the building. They're working to get them back online, okay? So whatever it is you need to do, which is none of my business, you better do it fast. If you attempt to finger me I'll deny we had this conversation. Okay?"

"No worries, sugar. I'm all about discretion. And by what name do I call thee, fair lady?"

"Officer Fucking Friendly, okay, smartass? Now, this has to happen fast. So listen up, okay?"

I listen up.

"Okay. The incident report indicates a single speci-men, okay? I should know, cause I placed it myself, okay? But you know how that goes—if you see one, there's sure to be a whole mess of them nearby, this will be their as-sumption. Okay from here?" Neither her tone, nor the shiny black plastic mask, nor the reflection of my own headgear in her goggles, reveal anything I can grasp on to.

Specimen? I twitch my head. Mount the stairs. My goddamn stairs. Round the corner, ascending the second flight I lay the SMAW down. Specimen? Well hey, whatever I might stumble on, I don't want to bring that amplitude of death jazz into my place of peace, it portends crazy ill.

Rather, I fumble with my straps and zippers, tough going with my half-broke paw, and at long last withdraw my CZ, which strikes me as much more to scale here. Rack a bullet into the chamber and carry on.

Yeah, my stairs, my halls, my floors, my silence, broken only by my respiration, Darth Vader–loud in this spacesuit. But this very structure, my *space*, violated by any number of interlopers, all of them respectless, all of them unwelcome.

Come around the corner and go into a crouch. Sight this way and that, plenty of midday light, visibility clear all the way down the hall. Don't know what I'm looking for, could be an extremely small object, but all appears undisturbed. My improvised wall lights are out, remind me to check the generator. Get an eye-drop of sweat, which I blink away.

Nothing.

I check doorways, thinking about nooks and crannies but none come to mind, try to get a gander under the long display cabinet against the wall of the corridor . . .

Movement. Hadn't seen it before, but hitherto motionless something that had been poised in the windowsill drops to the floor.

Get an adrenaline kick, hard, as I bring the gun in line with the thing. Down the barrel I peep: a cat.

A house cat. Like a generic cat. A mottled-gray domestic shorthair. Just as quickly as the fight-or-flight rush came, it's replaced by fragile relief.

Do I shoot it? Of course not, though this creature could

give a feline fuck either way. It's taking its own time sa-shaying in my direction, then describing a slow circle, tail aloft, and I find myself pointing an automatic weapon at a kitty cat's asshole.

A freaking cat. I jam my gun in a belt loop on this clown suit, unlock my helmet, and haul it off as I stand. Jackass that I am. Take this opportunity to swallow a pill.

So the Koreans dropped a cat in here, that's what brought about this ruckus. Pretty crafty.

Let me clarify some things that might not be obvious, and pardon the jargon. I've read up on this here subject.

In brief, taking us back to 1985, domesticated cats in China were ID'd as the incidental host animal for a nasty hemorrhagic fever epidemic. Transmission was carried out via fleas. All very simple. It was perhaps the first ob-servation of the house cat as a carrier for medium-scale outbreak. Not far behind were typhus, Rocky Mountain spotted fever, and H1N2, all of which were found to be transmitted, among other routes, via feline fleas.

Which brings us to the superflu pandemic of 2013, oth-erwise known as H3N3, responsible for perhaps four mil-lion deaths worldwide.

Prior to H3N3, the cat was known to be a secondary host, which is to say that the organism hosts the virus for a brief stretch of time, but is not the source from which the mature virus emerges.

This all changed with the H3N3 pandemic, in which domestic cats from Damascus to Des Moines were found to be primary hosts. That fact changed the game.

Governments in all corners of the globe enacted aggres-sive feline euthanasia programs, in which most militaries wound up playing a large part.

Not exactly proud of this, but I have no emotional response when I recall participating in the mass gassing of house cats outside of Thessaloniki. We used a crop plane, and amused ourselves picking off the dazed survivors as they tried to claw their way out of the hole we'd dumped them in.

That event either actually happened or is a figment of some perverted technician's brain, inserted at the National Institutes of Health. Doesn't matter.

And the fact remains that I am immune to this particular feline-borne strain. I was inoculated against my will at NIH during my captivity there as part of a test run of the never-distributed vaccine.

In the now, the cat disappears into the Rose Main Reading Room. There's something . . . I inhale. I sniff the air. I really suck it in, heat going to my head.

Cellulose. Carbon. Burning. Paper.

Drop my headgear and I am running, though I can no longer feel my extremities, my peripheral vision is neutralized, and I'm plunging down a cloudy and narrow tube, begging any god to exhibit mercy, if any goodness and kindness remains in the intelligences that monitor this vile dimension, please let it not be so.

Between the columns of the entryway, I do not have the will to look directly at the darkened expanse that is the left half of the great room. I peer to the gilded ceiling, heavenward to the frescos, renditions of clouds moving in on a blue, blue sky . . .

Reduced to powder . . . many hundreds, many thousands of books.

It's so vastly worse than I could have conceived, I experience a kind of minifreeze. A wedge of time, don't know how long, slides away, and I come to on my knees, my hands quivering in drifts of silt and small irregular pieces of leather, the debris still radiating heat that finds its way through my protective suit.

This action, this meticulous desecration, is a recent one.

A second wave of anguish hits my stomach as I absorb the realization that this, very specifically, is the sum totality of my own work. Untold effort. But fuck me, fuck that. Irreplaceable things, irrecoverable. Singular items obliterated. The dizzying permanence of this.

Titles and covers flip through my brain at random, I am thinking of the second category in 000, this is the subsubheading "Knowledge," contained therein is the one and only first edition of the English translation of Immanuel Kant's *Critique of Pure Reason*, dated 1782, bound in a very early example of "straight grain" Morocco goatskin by the great Roger Payne in London.

On my elbows, as if praying to Mecca, I am nearly choking on my own snot, repeating a single syllable as if in repetition I might reverse this tragedy, "No," could I have been so arrogant as to simply walk away from these helpless jewels, my one true purpose, my only charge, leaving it all unguarded, open to all manner of harm, am I that much the motherfucking fool to have thought I could endanger this place so recklessly and not see any consequences whatsoever?

This. Is. On. Me.

I have disrespected the System, toyed with it. Treated it like a stepchild, a hood rat. Betrayed the spirits here. I have brought darkness and suffering to all that I have loved, and destruction to the only thing that has ever loved me in return.

What does such a creature deserve?

Cat rubbing against my leg. Resist a strong urge to stomp on it. Looks at me woefully. Something in its mouth . . . jerky. My jerky. My cubbyhole.

I'm across the room in a flash. Nobody fucks with my cubbyhole.

It's wide open, emptied out. Motherfucker. No, not completely empty . . . a handwritten note, single sheet of paper, weighted by a six-ounce container of Purell™. Next to the cubby, a stack of DVDs and a couple hard drives, clearly meant to be found.

Grab the written note, biting my tongue, fucking furious. Cyna-corp letterhead.

Read it, tremor in both hands making it hard to focus.

Son,

It's been an age. Won't say I haven't missed you, because I have. You've always been a resourceful little punk. I figure you'll find your way back here, so I figure this is the best way to get in touch, if slightly old-fashioned. But then I'm an old man now.

Son, we want you to come in from the cold. It's the only thing to do. So you didn't complete the operation. Let's let that lie, and honor our long relationship. To me, you're still that skinny street kid from the projects who brought down a serial child-killer. To me, you're still the finest deputy any manager could ask for.

To have watched you grow over the years, to see you fulfill your potential, this is of great value to me. It's time to heal this rift. Come back to your home team, and let us leave the past where it belongs: in the past.

Son, this includes any business with the senator. We

have him in a secure location and he is under our protection.
What's past is past, and I need you to let it go. Whatever you
may have in mind regarding the senator, understand I run his
security, so if you're fucking with him you're fucking with me.
I would just hate to see that happen, so if there's anything of
that nature going on, let's just nip it in the bud.

Simply hand over any weapons you may have, along with
this missive, to any Cyna-corp employee, and let's begin again.

Your friend always,
Nic Deluccia

p.s. You owe me approx. 1.3 million U.S. dollars, the cost of a
MD-530 chopper. Things being what they are, shall we simply
say this and any other outstanding debt is hereby forgiven? ND

I read this. I reread the whole thing. I stare at this paper until I can no longer see it. I reach for the bottle of
Purell™. Let the note fall from my grip, and lather up. It
hurts so good, especially with my shattered hoof. I want
it to hurt.

"Yo, asshole!" It's Kim.

I jerk back to the present. How long? Must've fugued
out. Standing here rubbing my hands clean down to the
bone, wringing them out for who knows how long.

Kim has his hood off and rocks a dumb look of accomplishment on his chiseled mug. Holds up a clear plastic
box with the cat in it, and gives a thumbs-up.

"Got the fucker. He's not dead, I don't think. But yo,
if you got what you need, best we bounce before bitches
start looking at this whole thing too close."

Okay. Okay. Gotta pull it all together. Tell myself: this

is going pretty well, despite having just suffered perhaps the second biggest loss of my ridiculous tenure on this big blue marble.

Got my hand to my forehead, swaying.

"What's the dilly, chief?" says Kim. "Hit your head?"

Rally.

"I'm good. I'm good, Kim, thank you."

I collect the hard drives, DVDs. Shove them in my spacesuit.

Retrieve my gun from the pile of ash where I dropped it. Embers still glow here and there like fireflies.

Kim hands me another hard drive. Has today's date on it.

"What is this shit?" I ask the kid.

Kim rolls his eyes. "Fuck if I know, man, white guy just said get it to you, I was all *get out of my grill*, he was all *just get it to him*. So this is me doing what I'm told, yo."

I take the hard drive. In addition to the date, I read NYPL RRR. Surveillance video? Stick it in my suit as well. Pull my helmet back on. Say, "Lookit here. Gimme that cat."

"Yo, though. Hold up. It was me who caught this motherfucker. You try catching a cat, shit's hard."

I'm getting impatient with this child but I need him, so I make an effort at controlling myself.

"Kim, you're a fuckin American hero, I'm not trying to take credit for your brilliant work, homie, I gotta go downstairs to pull some important shit. Need the cat for cover. Promise I'll tell everybody you saved the fucking day. Now, I gotta go alone so just do your best to hold it down for me up here. Can you do that much, my brother?"

Kim doesn't look thrilled, but he carefully hands over

the plastic box with the unconscious cat, him saying, "Bitches trying to tell me what's up . . ."

"That's right," I reply, taking the bulky thing from him awkwardly. "Put your helmet back on. Heard me? And anybody comes upstairs who isn't part of our team, you shoot 'em. Chalk it up to friendly fire. Dig?"

The kid has more to say but I speed-limp out the door, holding the box, headed for the Map Room, hoping those fucking cameras are still on the blink.

Nic and company. Burn my house down, murder my babies, I come burn down yours. With you in it.

The dank, familiar subbasement again.

I am stuck, staring at the mystery trunk, the one full of explosives. I'm looking at it for familiar markings. I see nothing I recognize and yet what I do see looks familiar. These markings . . . starting to think . . . starting to think impossible shizz.

Funny, as long as I've occupied this place, I have known where this trunk was, and what it contained. Never meditated on it, never paid it much mind. The whys and the wherefores.

It's an interesting state I'm in. Sort of a mental semifreddo. I listen to the two halves of my brain duke it out. One section, on the right, says the following: we are starting to understand why the name Nic Deluccia has been so familiar. It's all in that letter, really. He knows me, has known me all my life.

There is another section of my brain, distinctly on the left, that calls bullshit on all of this. Player, please, it scoffs. Anybody could have written that letter, just to throw Dewey Decimal for a loop. Anybody could have put this crate here. Full of military-grade explosives. Sure, why wouldn't they? Because . . . because . . .

With a huge effort, as if this steamer trunk were magnetized, I turn and limp away. And with even greater determination I shut out the warring brain factions.

Whatever the truth of the matter, I am currently on the

j.o.b., and Decimal slacketh not. Either way, the correct move now is to dig up Deluccia. For which I will need every neuron firing properly, lest I be struck down.

Blame the head hiccup but it takes me a little longer than I would have liked to reappear upstairs, my whole crew plus Officer Fucking Friendly rotate their plastic faces toward me, and I come gimping out of the Map Room.

Officer Fucking Friendly is on me, grabs my arm and steers me to the stairs. I fumble the cat-in-the-box, holding it as I am with one hand and a wrist. Within the box, the animal is starting to stir, and the fat Clarence Howard file I grabbed downstairs giving me mad grief, jammed under my shirt. I'm hog sweaty and the manila is sticking to my flesh. I'm dying to spritz. Hose me down with Purell™. The very smell of my upper lip makes me want to puke, which would truly suck balls in this here spacesuit.

"The cameras are live again, okay?" she says between her teeth. "Don't know about audio, but just keep it shut."

Team Yellow jogs with us. I'm holding the cat-box out in front of me the way we used to handle unexploded ordnance back in the shit. Who says I never use my training?

"Coming out! I want a clear path to the vehicle, and at least a twenty-meter perimeter, okay? Move everybody back out there!" says Officer Friendly into her radio. Then to me: "There's a car waiting, okay? Stick the specimen in back and then let's roll out as fast as possible, okay?"

Bam, we're out the front door. The fat cop is still shouting, there's a general din. Fat cop screaming, "Coming through!" Everybody backing up, away from the "biohazard." Plenty of folks talking into radios, me thinking shit shit shit.

Clouds have moved in since we were inside. I yearn for a pill but I got an armful and countless peepers on me . . .

Four of our crew peel off, leaving two yellow suits, the cop, and myself, bearing the cat-box. The four departed members of Team Yellow are replaced by two Cyna-corpers.

What the . . . all this action vibing bad bad.

Another female voice. It's one of the two remaining yellow suits, the smallest of the two. "This is fucked. We've been made. Hey. In case we get separated." It can only be . . .

"Rose??"

"Shut up. This operation is a snafu."

"Rose, why would you come out here like this? It's just straight-up stupid."

"Didn't trust you. Wanted to make sure you weren't going to just dodge out," she spits, keeping it low. "Clearly a fucking mistake. Remember what we talked about, about the wife. Eight p.m., West 30th heliport. MPs making pickup. Diplomatic limos, UN garage, it's unguarded. License plate starts with *KKK* . . ."

I'm trying to process all that and she falls back behind me. We're being run down the stairs and toward what looks like a small refrigerated truck idling at the curb, the side proclaiming, *Peter Luger's*—

Hold up. This is out of fucking bounds. I'm not getting in there. Try to throw on the brakes but I'm being pushed from behind, I can't tell by whom . . .

"What the fuck is this?" I manage.

Officer Friendly is breathing heavily. Sounds like a smoker. "NYPD probably don't have a free vehicle, okay?"

A pair of soldiers get in front of us and jerk open the rear cargo doors, and before I know it the cop, two yellow suits, one of whom I know to my great dismay to be Rose Hee, and myself are inside, me saying, "Wait a fucking second." The doors are slammed shut and the vehicle peels out . . . We're in some sort of cold locker, nearly pitch dark, freezing back here, smells like carrion.

The driver has the divider open between the cargo hold and his area. And he's not alone, another human-fly CC soldier is facing us, and I recognize too late the barrel of a pistol peeking over the seat.

Fuck me. There's nowhere to go, we're in an enclosed six-by-twelve space. If this dude starts shooting, we're screwed. I consider trying to wrestle out my own gun, but I'd be a goner before I even found the fucking thing.

Officer Friendly goes down hard, bouncing off a box that reads, *Peter Luger Old-Fashioned Sauce*, falls flat on her face mask. Apparently dude has started shooting, which is unhappy news. I didn't hear the report but an exit wound is visible even in this half light. Happy trails, Officer Fucking Friendly. You weren't paying attention, darlin: didn't have the highest of hopes for you.

"Which one of you is known as Dewey Decimal? Indicate, fast!" says the shooter, his voice muted by his helmet.

To my eternal dismay I see a yellow-suited hand go up, and it's not mine. It's the shortest of the three of us. Goddamnit.

The shooter flips his weapon in her direction, and I take this opportunity to hurl the plastic-boxed cat his way, with no small effort. The cat within flipping out and yowling.

I just glance the man with the weapon, but it does the

trick and his gun is knocked loose . . . the shooter, cursing, tries to bring another weapon around.

Yellow suit I know not to be Rose kicks the back door once, twice, and it comes open. Poor excuse for daylight pours in.

We cut right hard and I lose my footing, and as I'm recovering Rose shouts to me: "Go! Go!"

I am about to make a noble speech to the effect that I would never leave her in such a jimmie-jam when my legs are swept out from under me, Yellow Suit #2 executing some sort of martial arts move, I think absently that it's racist to assume it's a tae kwon do number just because these are Koreans here, all this as I pitch backward out the rear doors of a fast-moving vehicle.

My next thought is that, seeing as I'm coming down on my head, this is what will probably kill me, this fall, and that seems pretty motherfucking anticlimactic considering. But no such luck: several inches of hard plastic somehow manage to keep my skull in one piece as it strikes the pavement, I bounce ridiculously a couple times, going limp like a rag doll, something I learned somewhere at some point which may or may not be effective, find myself sliding to an abrupt stop against a decrepit billboard.

Dazed, I look up at a massive photo of a female crotch in a see-through leotard, the word *APPAREL* in huge Helvetica font.

Get up, says the soldier who lives in my cranium. Not thinking it through, I attempt to push with my fucked-up flapper. The pain has me seeing blue pills and green clovers, and I'm still on the ground.

Brakes squeal and protest, they're making a U-turn, I gather pretty quick that we're at the corner of Third Avenue and 42nd Street. The van is a block away, driver must have not immediately realized what was going down.

Manage to drag myself to my feet using my elbows, my knee nearly snaps straight away, and I can't help it, I yelp like a dog and shove off at random . . . Beyond the billboard I see a broken storefront window, an upended Duane Reade drugstore, I make for the hole in the glass and am inside before the van is even completely turned around.

In the dark I crash headlong into some sort of shelving and hear the percussion of a ton of pill bottles hitting the floor. This and the pitter-patter of fleeing rats.

Must be the obscure/useless vitamin section. These spots got picked clean, and I mean bone-dry. Even I make the occasional run-through for some extra hand sanitizer (though I refer even to the generic brand as Purell™, which is what it is). And some vitamin C, cause ever hear of scurvy?

Now I'm down and am pretty sure I cannot get up again. I think I broke my hip. Why the fuck not, y'all? Everything else is rattling around inside this brother, all splinters and fragments.

The van careens around the corner, onto Third Avenue. I lie there in the dark and listen to the noise of the vehicle fade. They're gone, sounded like north.

Goddamnit, what did Rose think she was accomplishing? I had taken her for a clever young lady. This is now officially a disaster. If harm comes to that lovely gal, once again, it's on me.

Gotta get on the good foot before the rats return to check me out. That thought forces me up to my hands and knees. This alone takes an eon. Thankful for the spacesuit.

Only thing to do is get some painkillers and carry on as planned. Bummed the plan calls for me to shuck the outfit soon enough. When I'm out of this jam I'm gonna get one of my very own to curl up in, tell folks to work their own bullshit out. Take a holiday.

With a sharp inhale and a grunt I'm on my feet again, unsteady . . . A trio of helicopters, flying low, come up out of nowhere . . . I consider scuttling for better shelter but they're heading west and aren't interested in insects like me.

Yeah, carry on. With Rose in play now, the other side has double the weight on yours truly. I'm holding a losing hand here, in more ways than one. Thing to do is to stay peace, get an edge, if not a leg up and over these mother-fuckers, at least pull within stalemate range.

My internal clock reads about six in the evening, and when I'm on my game I'm usually within fifteen minutes of the correct time.

In a few moments I am speed-staggering north up Third Avenue, the one and only Chrysler Building soaring overhead as solid as ever . . . I could almost make like this was my city pre–2/14 were it not for the total absence of life, and the fundamental wrongness of the near absolute silence, with the occasional industrial rumble.

Third Avenue stretches before me, utterly blank, minus the rare abandoned vehicle, and that holds true as far as I can see.

Logos like FedEx and Starbucks and Cosi like hiero-glyphics. I pass a pile of dead dogs, various breeds. I pass a shopping cart from Staples filled with printer cartridges. A Le Pain Quotidien, one of their country-style "communal" tables half in and half out of the busted window.

I'll take a right at 49th Street, groove all the way east,

and I'm pretty sure that's where I'll find the United Nations parking garage. From there it's just a couple of elementary moves, and I'll have the good senator's wife trussed up like a pig waiting to get her belly cut.

See how the boys like that turn of events.

I t's an ugly ocher-tinged dusk as Kathleen Koch, in requisite patriot-navy Chanel pantsuit and heels, disem-
barks the chopper, that media-honed smirk affixed to
her square-jawed, masculine face, hand on head in a attempt to keep her sculpted coif impeccable as she ducks
under the slowing helicopter blades and makes a beeline
for the limo. Her vicious mouth, her weird jaw. I don't find
her attractive in the slightest, but apparently I'm in the
minority.

Me, in the driver's seat, in an outsized MP outfit.

No problemo. Thus far this here op is automagic simplicity. Thus far nobody's gotten seriously mauled. The
owner of the pants I'm wearing is no doubt still sleeping
off the chloroform, laid out on a bench on Dag Hammar-
skjöld Plaza, in my yellow biosuit.

From the UN it was a simple matter of gunning it all
the way across town to the specified heliport off of West
Street. My files, guns, and other supplies lie under a blanket in the passenger's seat wheel well.

Let's do this fucking thing. I'm chewing on an Aleve.

Now I clock Secret Service hustling ahead of the lady
and jerking the rear door open, one eager beaver panting,
"All right from here, Senat—?"

"Jeez, I'm fine, Tom, God bless ya . . ." that too familiar Midwestern nasality dismissing the man. Koch slithers
into the backseat, apparently already on a cellular phone
or radio cause she carries on, "Hang on a moment, hon.

Thank ya, Tom! See ya in a couple days for that . . . that thingamjigger."

Tom is saying something as she slams the door.

"Jeez, freakin *Mormons!*" This into the phone. "No, my freakin new staff. Freakin buncha freakin flamin Mormons!" Kathleen cackles.

Me thinking, shit, a *cell phone.* Didn't occur. On the plus side, no acknowledgment of yours truly. And why should there be?

Service guys backing up to get a look at my mug through the dash. Sure, they do look like a gaggle of Mormons, though this would be my first encounter with that particular subculture. Buncha duplicate white boys with nothing-colored hair anyhow, for which I praise Allah.

Cause to them, despite my varied ethnic background, a black dude is a black dude is a black dude. Especially as night approaches.

Salute 'em. Guy squinting through the window screen at my ID, all he sees is black male, whitey backing off, making the hand gesture *move it.* I hit the gas obligingly, not too fast now out the gates, and north onto the West Side Highway, marveling: those devils honestly do think we all look alike.

Not saying that's always a bad thing, y'all.

". . . oh gosh, just 120 percent," Kathy's saying. "Gay as a five-dollar bill. Part of the, ha, ha . . ." the woman just cracking up. "Part of the ol' vettin over at, whozzit. Quantico. Sir, can ya demonstrate that yer a big ol' freakin Mormon flamer?"

Koch is really knocking herself dead, takes no notice as I bust a screechy right onto West 33rd Street. Hit the power locks.

". . . ohhh yah. All of those Jews too, whaddya call 'em . . . ones with the pigtails and outfits? Riiiight. Mormons and those Jews wear that secret lingerie. No, I'm telling ya, Pat!"

This goes on. I am thinking this may prove to be easier than I had anticipated, Kathy might not actually be the sharpest knife. I'd always taken her for crazy, but like her husband I reckoned it was of the crazy-like-a-fox variety . . . Perhaps not.

". . . the one time I met that freakin robot Mitt, I promise ya, he had on lip gloss. And! Listen, Pat. I could see . . . ha, ha . . . I could see his bra strap. Would I kid ya?"

I hang a hard right onto Ninth Avenue, headed due south, annoyed that this woman is so profoundly wrapped up in her own sociopathology that she doesn't even have the common courtesy to take fucking notice when being abducted. It's rude.

Rise above, Decimal. That's her MO: she's a shit stirrer, riles up folks so that they get their panties in a twist whilst she leans back and observes.

". . . telling ya, all their menfolk are queer. Jews, Mormons, and Arabs. *Oh* yeah."

Kathleen is a fact machine. A factologist. A fact factory. A boundless fount of knowledge.

Only problem for Kathy is it's all bullshit.

Bitch ran for president. It was a squeaker, y'all. She had this miserable "Just call me Kathy!" ad campaign that made me wanna gouge out my peepers with a spork. Lady's scene got thrown cause it emerged that ol' Kath was subject to debilitating migraines . . .

This I can empathize with. I get headaches something

fucking awful. Like biblical headaches. Lays me up for days.

Yes. In fact, I plan to give her one tonight. A *migraine*, that is, player please. Woman is foul.

We blow the light at 23rd Street. Some neighborhoods, the lights continue to cycle around uselessly. Still feels satisfying to sail through a red light. Small pleasures. And I dig the feel of this fossil-fuel vehicle, perhaps the first I've driven in years. You can actually hear the damn thing, that's what it is, there's instant gratification when you step on that shit.

Well, I had something a little different in my mind's eye, but between the cell phone wrinkle and her complete obliviousness I initiate my second Plan A: confirm the car stereo's bass and volume are on max, make positive the fade is set all the way to the rear of the vehicle. Insert that audio CD I picked up out of the steamer trunk before all this madness got underway.

Gently press play. Even this gives me a hot shot of hurt up my arm.

Wu-Tang Clan's "Shame on a Nigga," with its clamorous kung-fu film combat intro, whallops me in the back of the head. And I'm not next to the speakers. Kathleen is, and she goes mouth to carpet, mitts to ears, one lacquered-nail hand still clutching the phone. Which is my first concern.

The track is deafening and I'm mildly impressed that the glass on this car, bulletproof as it undoubtedly is, doesn't atomize.

Speed up. We bounce over West 14th Street and I swerve to avoid a work crew, an open manhole spewing thick smoke.

Turn on the interior lights and in the rearview I observe an ashen Kathleen Koch coming to her knees, making her way forward. Begins sliding the "executive privacy" window that separates us. Her cell is in hand, to my relief, her mouth working. Can't hear a word. Keep an eyeball on the phone. On the stereo ODB roars forth. R.I.P. Big Baby Jesus.

> To the young youth, you wanna get gun? Shoot!
> Blaow! How ya like me now? Don't fuck the style, ruthless
> wild . . .

When she gets close enough and commences wailing, I reach back with my good hand and snatch her cell, a pink BlackBerry, gives me a retro zing, she's doing her level best to lunge across the seats, flailing left arm knocks off my MP helmet, but I'm depressing the button that controls that hard plastic divider, Kathleen quickly and wisely withdraws her hands, not before tearing off half my shirt collar.

> Shame on a nigga who tries to run game on a nigga . . .

I ease the car to a stop near Horatio Street and Hudson. Swivel in my seat. Smile wide at Kathleen, our faces mere inches apart.

All this expensive material sitting between Wu-Tang, the controversial far-right-wing politician, and myself creates an oddly noiseless experience. I feel the bass, observe her spittle and bared teeth, eyes boiling.

So much to despise in this woman and the interests she represents. Time was, she could've been the most powerful female on the planet.

Time was, plenty of folks in my current position wouldn't've hesitated a microsecond to simply off the terrifying bitch, by any means available.

I swear to Xenu my wrecked trigger finger twitches.

But people. Really. Dewey Decimal doesn't play that. I did tell you, now, my word is I don't harm the females. Unless extreme circumstances warrant such action, and even then . . .

So, this: I jerk the car forward a good ten feet. Turn and watch the fallen Kathleen "Call me Kathy!" Koch gamely endeavor to get herself upright again. Slowly start to accelerate . . . gain a block, then another, moving at a good clip now, glance in the rearview to check that the woman is unsteadily maintaining a hunched standing position. Slam on the brakes.

Wham-o as she hits the glass. We skid to rest at Bethune Street, just in front of the old nursing home.

Take a moment to really be in the moment. Something we so rarely do, ain't it?

In the periphery of my headlights, I note leaves red and gold on the untended trees. An abandoned, doorless DOT car. Pigeons crowding something or other, several seagulls in there too, nipping at the smaller birds. Clock a pair of orthopedic shoes just visible amidst the avian throng, still attached to . . . My gut shucks and jives. Let's leave that mess alone.

I sigh. So much unnecessary silliness in this motherfucking life. Look over my shoulder . . . a blot of lipstick, a touch of blood, and a little spit slowly sliding down the opposite side of the glass. Peep deeper, and there lies Kathy, flat on her back. She's lost a purple pump. Watch her chest. She's breathing.

And just like that I'm back in the honorable business of wife-snatching.

Butter. I kill the stereo. Do that Purell™. Reach for the duct tape with my good gripper.

—————————

I'm kneeling on a beige leather couch, facing a blank wall. Extremely thin, light-colored wood. I'm aware that there is a peephole about three feet above my head, and I stand so I might look through it.

I am observing a stunning young woman, seated on a similar couch. She wears a tight black or dark-colored (the footage is in black-and-white) reflective dress, looks like silk. She wears her hair in a single long braid thrown over her left shoulder, which hangs down below her left breast. On the table are two martini glasses, two smaller bowls, a pack of cigarettes, an ashtray, and a black cordless microphone.

She sits quite still, in silence, though very faint laughter and music is audible, probably coming from surrounding rooms. She seems occupied with her nails. At one point she looks at her watch, sighs, glances around the room. She returns to her nails.

My foot slips, banging against the wall. And with supernatural speed, the woman, whom I know to be Song Ji-Wong, looks up at me, flips upside down, and lands like a spider on the ceiling.

Come to with a big jolt, in the driver's seat of a Chinese BYD e6, sporting a brand-spanking-new suit. I look at the tag dangling from my cuff . . . black little pouch with a couple extra buttons. Paul Smith. Okay, right. A peek outside . . . groan, as the general filth and the presence of a mangy flock of chickens tells me straight off I'm ass-deep in Chinatown.

Chinatown is not what it once was. Which is to say: there's a hell of a lot more of it today. You could safely say that today's Chinatown stretches north to approximately East 6th Street, east as far as one can go, south to the Seaport, and west to Greenwich Street . . . but these borders are constantly shifting.

Shit. I spin and check for Kathleen . . . There she is, across the passenger's seat, sealed in a black plastic cocoon, securely wrapped in duct tape. For a moment I'm thinking I killed her, which would have been a bad move, but I can see her breathing, see that I cut a slit in the plastic near her mouth . . . I suppose this is a relief. Another moment of panic as I pat myself down for pills . . . blessed are the poor. The reassuring contours of pill bottle, Purell™, etc. . . . wince at my sorry digits.

Last night? Details hazy. Trying to piece this scenario back together . . .

Well hell, on our merry way down here to 154 Hester Street near Elizabeth, found myself with an acute desire to shuck those miserable poly MP duds and get back into something proper. I cut across Houston to Greene Street and (not for the first time) tossed the Paul Smith store for some flossy new gear. Kathleen was out cold and pretty well immobilized, so I took my time, wandering around the stockroom till I found something temperature-appropriate (one of the pluses of the timing of 2/14, with fall being upon us now, slightly heavier duds that'd been bypassed over the summer become suddenly useful). Nearly everything hung tragically off my emaciated frame, but I ultimately landed on a dope wool flannel gray-check double-breasted suit, with which I married an off-white shirt and a gray-and-black-striped tie. Completed the outfit with a pair of oxford brogues, a touch big but manageable, and with great relief dug up a black trilby-style hat with a blue band that fits my skull to perfection.

This Paul Smith dude, he brought it strong when it came to threads. Before, I couldn't have come near this level of elegance, but now, what with all things being equal and money being no object, literally, I'm free to enhance my carriage with an extra dash of panache.

As an afterthought I grabbed a black wool-and-mohair overcoat with a velvet-top collar; it's not that cold yet but it'll get there . . . or will it? I suppose we shall see, as each year brings new surprises on the atmospheric front. None of them happy surprises. Ill breezes blowing hardcore. Old-testament stuff.

Two extra dress shirts, some multicolored underwear that I don't love, and four pairs of stripy socks. A pair of calfskin gloves. That's me set for the next several months.

Also grabbed a green-handled box cutter out of the storeroom. I dig box cutters, they take me back.

Time to ditch the limo and acquire a new whip. Easy enough; I hot-wired a BYD e6 just nearby. Transfered the unconscious Kathleen. Tossed my new wardrobe in the front seat with the rest of my shiz, took a break to disinfect, swap gloves, and I biz-ounced.

That's as much as I recall, I don't rule out a freeze but the facts are it's about six twelve a.m., according to the dashboard clock, and I have come to the one place I could possibly pop up and be welcome with a hostage in tow.

It's the old Overseas Chinese Mission building, which has been occupied and heavily renovated by my man Dos Mac, with whom I enjoy a fragile connection.

Before the Valentine's Occurrence, Dos was the chief computer tech guy for the NYC government, having been hired on straight out of the Navy. Dos had written the code that controlled the weapon systems on all U.S. submarines, later adopted by most military forces worldwide, the British, the Russians, NATO, etc. This code was based on something he sketched up during freshman year lunch breaks at Brooklyn Tech, so it is claimed, on a napkin from Junior's (of cheesecake fame). And yes, Dos is a homeboy, raised hard in Brownsville, a brainy kid with very few options by dint of his economic status and skin color. In this sense alone I am proud to call him my friend and spiritual brother.

Dude owes me, in a large way. But I won't need to remind him that.

And Dos, who refuses to reveal his real name to me, just as I can't return the courtesy, is a . . . complicated man. Again, not unlike your narrator. He is to be approached with great caution, eyes and ears wide open.

Make positive Kathleen is secure . . . tinted windows

all around on this e6 . . . should be okay. The neighborhood stirring, old woman paying me no heed, squatting
as if waiting for a bus, gray workers sporadic in coveralls
wafting up and down the block, scarcely there.

Nearly every storefront has been scooped out like
a pumpkin and flipped to serve other purposes, this is a
hood where the original function of a given shop couldn't
always be readily determined pre–2/14 (though I reckon
Munchies Paradise across the street had something to do
with, like, snacks. But hell, you never know).

Aware that I've misused and abused the System of late,
I intend on following it to the letter in compensation and
hope all things balance out in the end. First we slap on the
Purell™ and scrub the bad dreams away. Then don fresh
powdery gloves, and with my left hand I adjust my surgical mask and open the car door, step out, let my lungs
and eyes adjust to the Stench. Hit the power lock on the
vehicle, and shuffle left to the corner. Then it's a strict left
across the street, and another left back to the entrance of
154 Hester. Recall, prior to 11 a.m.: left turns only. That's
System 101.

Dos gets it. Gets the System. The man thinks systems
too.

I move past an abandoned FedEx vehicle, within which
I note stacks of boxes, mostly Amazon debris. Useless.
Kindles and shit, no doubt.

Gazing high as I approach the door here, I see two
closed-circuit cameras, no obvious weapons, concealed
explosives, or bear traps, but in truth you're a fool to make
assumptions when it comes to Dos Mac.

There's a button with a simple *A* and an aged sign un-
derneath in Mandarin that reads, *NO MENUS/NO CLONES.*

I grin at that, vintage Dos. Depress the button with my left thumb.

No response for the time being, but that's no shock. I remove my new hat and stand for about twenty seconds under the camera, rotate (left) so he can scope me should he be paying attention. It's pretty clear I'm strapped, the suit is cut a bit close and you can almost see the shape of my pistola under the jacket.

Burst of feedback from the intercom.

"Librarian." Dos must be using a voice scrambler, or one of those old Kanye autotuners. Probably just for the fuck of it.

"What's good, Dos?"

"Clearly very little, if I got the Librarian wanna darken my door. You must be one desperate motherfucker."

"My man," I'm maintaining casual. "Who's saying I wasn't just in the neighborhood?" Spread my hands, slow, mellow, no sudden moves now. "Woulda brought croissants or something, but Balthazar was closed."

A long pause. Uncomfortably long. Just a hair.

Decide to goose him a bit. "Still got my pistola, kid?" Knowing damn well he lost that thing.

Then: a pitched robotic trill, probably Dos simply letting out a long exhale. Then: "Just push on it, brother."

Dos buzzes me in.

The reinforced steel door hinges open, revealing absolute darkness. I hesitate at the threshold.

Maybe this was a fucked-up idea.

Maybe I'm fresh out of good ideas.

Proceed inside, hands in the air. "Dos . . ."

The door whispers shut, me thinking I deserve whatever I get in here.

What I get is a faceful of high-wattage industrial light. Reflexively, I go to protect my face, straining to keep my movements mellow and obvious.

"Letting you know I got a shotgun on you, so just stay put," says Dos, slightly to my right, pretty close.

I know better than to respond.

"Running a quick scan. If I read you as a clone, I'm gonna send you back uptown in a whole bunch of plastic bags. Try to hold still."

I'm trying, but I wanna loosen the vibe. Say, "'Fraid I'm gonna disappoint you on the clone thing, Dos."

"I sincerely hope so, now just hold still."

Don't need to be told twice. Another minute with the light in my face, there's a fluorescent-sounding hum, and a buzz not unlike an electric shaver.

"Okay," says Dos quietly.

The overheads come on, we're in that cavernous space I remember, which despite its size manages to feel cluttered, in constant upheaval.

Dos is blinking at me, no sign of a weapon on him,

bit disheveled in a dirty white Adidas tracksuit. He's lost weight. Who hasn't? Hair longer, natural, nappy. I know him to be forty-five but he could be anywhere from mid-thirties to fifties, you just can't tell anymore. Big thick glasses, which I reckon is just a look he cultivates, not cause he needs them.

"I was bullshitting about the shotgun. And man, I never did apologize but I'm sorry about that nine, Librarian. Force majeure. Was just making coffee, you want some coffee?" Already with his back to me, busy with this and that.

The machine he had trained on me looks like one of those ancient overhead projectors we had in school. He's got it on wheels and is maneuvering it into a corner, the device making clicks and whirs.

"Looking trim, Dos. How have you been holding up down here?"

Dos scoffs. A single bark.

"I look like fucking death. Feel like death. You look like ass too, player. Somebody go buck wild on your face? Step all over your hand?"

Dude starts fussing with what looks like a homemade percolator.

"Yeah, a Korean chick kimchi'd my shit."

Dos makes a face. "Those people are loony toons. Run a tight grocery though. Unlike the motherfucking Dominicans, man. Twinkies, pork cracklins, and shit? I like me some kombucha."

"I never got that kombucha thing. Rotten-ass tea? Fuck that," I say. "But hey, for real, Dos, you look all right. Fuck it, man, it's hand-to-mouth, yo, it's no joke out here. To state the obvious. You're holding down your zone and that's doing pretty good in my book."

Mac grunts again, says, "Want the good news or the bad news first, Librarian?"

I laugh. Dude is a cut-up.

"What kind of fucked-up question is that? If you got any kind of news, just come with it."

"So good news first." Starts singing a variation on that old MJ ballad, in a striking falsetto: *"You are not a clone."* Grins wide. I'm stunned. My boy sounds *good.*

"Damn, Dos, you may have missed your calling . . ."

Him saying, "And the bad news. You, sir, are one popular nigger. Every law enforcement and government operative with a radio is talking you up. You jumped from under the radar negative to nation's most wanted, public enemy number one. Crazy-fast rise to the top. Give any man a nosebleed. But don't forget the little people, get all cocky on me, cause I knew you when. All I got is creamer. Want creamer?"

I'm processing. That was fast, again no surprise, but speedy with the APB.

The coffee. "Naw. Yeah, black is fine."

"Indeed it is," says Dos, eyeing me. I see him flash on my gun. Get a whiff of something, what is that? Smells like fear.

Good. Be afraid, Dos.

He pours two cups, hands me one.

"Thanks. Mac, check this," trying to vibe breezy, put the boy at ease, "I gotta be straight about—"

He holds up a hand. "Before we get into that, before you explain to me why you'd drag my ass into your nightmare, I owe you the balance on the bad news. If you wanna hear it. Some folks, they don't even wanna know. Might not make any difference whatsoever."

I sip at my coffee. Scalds my smashed upper lip but I don't flinch.

That he would even hesitate to drop it on me, this is concerning. Dos doesn't generally give a shit.

Fuck it, he's either gonna tell me I got cancer eating my heart and moments to live, or confirm some such suspicion I've had for ages anyway.

"Well goddamn. Since we're chatting like this and we got a minute or two, let's have the whole nine, Mac."

Dos is watching me over the top of his glasses. Sets down his coffee. Rubs his forehead, sighs.

"You're absolutely riddled with implants, Librarian. I don't think I've ever seen anything come close."

Ever gotten a niggling suspicion you always knew to be all too true independently confirmed? There's that satisfaction, see I TOLD y'all, and the pure horror of the thing itself.

Two fingers shoot to my throat and I hold them there, feeling my heart accelerate.

"You okay, Librarian?"

Swing my peepers here and there, looking for a place to land them . . .

DA Rosenblatt. "Decimal. Your file. The stuff they did . . ."

All this time, all this pain, all these fucking questions, all these blurry brain snapshots, and I'm closer to an answer than I've ever been. I am near tears.

"I just . . . ah."

"Yeah, boss," sighs Dos Mac, sipping his coffee. "Them's the breaks. They got you good."

Now I focus, and take a nice long look at Dos Mac. How well do I really know this man? Certainly anybody could be employing him. Just as anyone could be employing me. Circles within circles.

My body is misbehaving. I go to set down my coffee and miss the table. My cracked mouth is numb. My voice is not my own and emanates as if from across the room.

"No doubt there's . . . surgery. Surgical procedures."

"Hey. Hey, man," says Dos, looking concerned. He laughs uncertainly. "Just playing, brother. I know you had hang-ups, but damn. Librarian, I'm just fucking with your head. You're clean, you're good."

Relief and solid fury have a brief wrestling match in my throat. Relief wins.

Dos picks my coffee cup up off the floor, then wanders over to the homespun machine and retrieves what looks like a transparency, or an X-ray.

I'm trying to reestablish my ability to speak, and Dos adds: "Clean except for that big motherfucker at the base of your skull, of course. Wrapped around your, what's that called . . . your medulla." Peers at the floppy sheet closer. "Got like tendrils going every which way, very very fine threads, my equipment's not sensitive enough to register all of them." Slaps down the sheet of celluloid. "What is that nasty shit, some sort of pacemaker? Whazzit do for ya?"

Looking through and beyond Dos again. I bring my hand, gently, to the nape of my neck. Shortly I smile and begin to nod my head, up and down.

Now is not the time to take this one on.

"Yeah. Like a pacemaker," I say. "Dos, lemme tell you why I'm here."

Goddamnit if Kathleen didn't come around almost as soon as I hauled her up and out of the backseat of the e6 and slung her over my shoulder. Goddamn if the woman didn't start bronco-bucking, cracking her own head against the doorjamb in the process. Her knee glanced off my cracked knuckles and I nearly passed out. Bitch screaming and whatnot. Were it not for the rag I shoved into her mouth she would've undoubtedly been clearly audible for blocks in every direction.

Not that anybody would've particularly noticed. Chinatown isn't all negatives, baby. People drifting around, urban tumbleweeds. See no evil, hear no evil, that's the way they do and that suits me down to the dirty ground.

Now. Dos and I met under somewhat sensitive circumstances. Without belaboring it, some Kuwaiti power broker/construction magnate had his boyfriend go missing. The DA sent me after the kid, and that led me here, where the young man and Dos were cohabiting in what struck me as a completely consensual manner.

Hey, I am many things, but I am most assuredly not a moralist. Each to his own hustle, and these two gentlemen seemed genuinely okay.

So I buried the thing. My report said the kid had fled the country, and I had documents made up to prove it. My findings were never questioned. Nobody had really wanted to juggle that hot potato anyhow.

More recently, the boy borrowed a 9mm off of me, and

promptly shot himself with it. Not on purpose, mind; so to spare him embarrassment, I'll leave that one alone. Wasn't really my gun anyhoo.

Like I say, I am all for kicking it laissez-faire, but while investigating him, I couldn't help but discover that Dos dug it a touch kinky. My man got physical. All within the realm of acceptability, which is to say nobody ever got, like, irreversibly hurt. Or so I was assured.

One of the features my brother rigged up, devoted exclusively to libertine pursuits, was an isolated, underground S&M chamber (he calls it a "soundstage") set up with microphones and cameras and whatnot. Beyond the fact of it, I didn't push him on this, but I assumed it wasn't just for personal use; the setup was expensive, and professional-grade video could be generated therein. Resulting material, of course, could be sold or traded.

It was this room that must've got me thinking last night, with respect to ol' Kathleen.

Yeah, the whole issue disappeared with the Kuwaiti, and from more recent encounters I know that the boyfriend has hit the trail as well . . . but one thing you don't want is to be on the bad side of a jilted lover with a pile of cash and access to all manner of manpower and guns. Though I would never be so gauche as to articulate it, this allowed me a certain leg up on Mr. Dos Mac.

I suppose what I'm doing right now is exploiting the relationship a hair, but hey. It is what it is, y'all.

First thing Doc says this morning when I start talking about Koch is absolutely no fucking way. Tells me to take my drama elsewhere.

I just need to look at him. Mac moans and kicks something over. Knows he's got no choice.

Dos Mac. The Dos and the Mac, to demonstrate that the PC-versus-Mac argument was based on snobbery and packaging. The man is comfortable on both platforms. It's all x's and o's and the rest is lifestyle shit, like designer coffee, office chairs.

Another thing I dig about the guy: he doesn't give two fucks about the Internet as a tool of worldwide unity. The lie of the "Global Village." His interest is in strictly localized systems, area specific. Subways. Traffic flow. Urban layout. This slots right in with my own System.

First thing I did was drop all the CDs and the hard drives on the man, he took a quick look and confirmed that for the most part they are data discs holding video. One or two are audio CDs. We'd get to all that; meanwhile, we got lady Koch comfortable.

Row of old computer monitors stacked willy-nilly on top of one another, Dos is fiddling with a universal remote, frowning. Half of the monitors are working and display different areas of the building, the street outside, the mouth of the Holland Tunnel, Times Square, the doorway, etc.

"Oh, here we are. Haven't, uh . . . used this thing in ages," says Dos, with a pretty good approximation of cool.

Fat old iMac hums to life, as the screen warms up we're looking at a black-and-white image of the mummified Kathleen, taped to a chair.

She's been down there in Mac's aforementioned "soundstage" for a good twenty minutes, and I can report now that she has stopped struggling.

I realize I gotta speed this whole thing up. No clue as to what's doing with Cyna-corp, and as things drag out it's looking progressively worse for Rose Hee . . .

Lean in, say, "Do we have audio?"

"Affirmative, boss, just gotta turn it on."

"All right, well, before we do, enjoy your last moments of peace, man. Woman likes to hear herself speak."

"Yeah, so I understand. Hey, you're for sure gonna get me killed. Look at this shit," says Dos.

I hook him up with two sticks of jerky and he rips into one. Eyes nearly flip into the back of his head.

"Motherfucker, I forgot how amazing these things are. Why didn't I get down with more of these joints back when?" He looks at the package in wonderment.

I'm exploring the flesh of my neck. Methodically. Trying not to think about it. Say, "It's relative. Water to a drowning man. I thought you were like a vegan, cousin."

"Ha, that's a beautiful record. Or is it 'Water on a Drowning Man'? Yes indeed. Naw man, the vegan thing went out the window way back. Gotta get some protein up in here. Librarian," he says, shifting his eyes to meet mine, "you know why I have all this security, this precautionary jazz? Cause if any of those contractors knew I was down here, they'd be on me in a second, trying to suck me into their shit. Making me offers I can't refuse and whatnot. I'd rather be drawn and motherfucking quartered than work for those thugs."

It's true. Anybody the least bit interested with infrastructure would be all over the Mac if they knew he was on the scene. His designs build themselves.

"As it is, they're just aching to clone me. All they need is a clean scrape of skin, a couple hairs. Never, fuuuuuck no."

I don't know about this whole clone jive. Dos takes another bite.

"Word is, they got something big going. Like, big-as-a-motherfucker big. They're dragging in everybody, especially folks who worked with the City, civil engineers and shit . . ."

"They, who they?" I ask. Thinking, as much as I find this fascinating, I need to get things moving . . .

Dos laughs. "They, like you know, man—all of them. Can't tell them apart. Private, government, contractors . . . Chinese, Middle Eastern, white motherfuckers from all over, CIA, former Blackwater, CACI, Titan, yada yada . . . they're all in the same gang. Want no part of it. Don't wanna know. It's too much, man. Oh yeah. Looking for me. They even got a bounty out for anybody who can get Dos Mac to come in. No, fuck no. Never."

Dos snaps his fingers as if he's just remembered something important.

"Yo, you of all people will appreciate this shit, Librarian. Wanna show you what I'm working on."

Digs around in a desk drawer and pulls out some sort of smoky black pad–type deal, flips it on, and hands it over.

Torn, I'm looking at the time, yet fully aware that it's an honor to be getting a peek at this man's work.

His pad comes alive, an elegant tangle pops out in the 3-D, multicolored and layered. It's exquisite. It's beautiful. My heart goes straight to my throat.

"Am I looking at what I think I'm looking at, Mac?"

He leans back and wags his head, grinning. "I improve on the shit a thousandfold here. It's self-sustaining in every respect, self-cleaning, and the best part is it requires very little actual construction. Look, man, we're using the old physical stations."

Of course, I'm looking at a speculative map of the New

York City subway system. It is truly a thing of wonder, and I say so.

"This is, this is amazing, Dos. This is for sure the future if there's gonna be one."

Dos nods again. Proud. As he should be.

"Hey, brother, it's my theory that urban planners, engineers, we've been looking at shit all wrong. Looking at existing train/road systems as a starting point for new designs, et cetera. But it's not like that. We should be applying biological models. I'm talking about looking at the human body. The circulatory system, the nervous system. We're nothing but overlapping systems ourselves. Exquisite models. So if you're moving blood, energy, vehicles, anything, it's the same shit . . . you just need the right channels, channels that complement each other."

I see it. I don't understand it, but it speaks to me. It's like the System, my System. In order to fully manifest it, I need to internalize it. I'm not there yet, but . . .

"Dos, I'm telling you it's incredible work," I say, meaning it sincerely.

Bright-eyed, he stabs the screen with a pinky. "Years have gone into that design, man. It's far superior now, but I've had this sketched out for ages. Way back, Bloomberg wanted to implement it but we ran out of time and it was kept on the DL. Now, shit, now I'm happy about that cause if the motherfucking Reconstruction people got a load of this tech? It has mad applications elsewhere, of course. They'd be all up in my business. They already are, you know. They suspect I got something like this. They know me. There's rumors . . ."

He's suddenly nervous. Takes the pad from me, shoves it back in the drawer. Shuts it, and pointedly locks up.

"I'm not, hey man . . ." I say.

"Oh, I know, shit, Librarian. Listen, I just . . . you can't be positive what to think about people anymore."

Dos returns to his jerky. End of subject.

I would love nothing more than to get into it, but we have to move, and Mac waves the compressed meat baton in the direction of the screen.

"So, for real. This is the bitch who got that fence built around Texas or whatever it was? To keep out Mexicans?"

"'To protect American jobs.' This is the very shorty, squire. She ran for fucking president, Dos, where you been?"

But I know very well where he's been. Down the rabbit hole, like me.

"This lady," I say, "we may reckon her a clown, but this lady is straight poison, Dos."

The man is shaking his head. "Hell, I know that much. Can't really get my head around it, this is that same bitch."

"Well, she's obviously out of context but it's her all right."

"We should fuck with her mind a bit, Librarian. Tell her we're some Muslim faggots snuck over the border, gonna marry ourselves right in front of her unless she—"

"Oh, I'm sure that's along the lines of what she's already thinking. That's her paradigm."

"Huh," says Dos, ceding the point.

We sit for a moment. I'm trying to get myself moving. Looking at the screen, her slumped form. Dos says, slowly, deliberately, "I'll admit it's a . . . diversion, you just showing up with all this, and not totally unwelcome. But this kind of . . . Damn, Librarian, I'm telling you, you have everybody with a communication device in the tri-state in a motherfucking tizzy. You're like, who was that cat bombed the Trade Center the second time?"

"Dick Cheney?" I deadpan, earning a fist bump.

"Deep," says Dos. "That's real. But you know I mean the Saudi motherfucker those arrogant-ass Seals capped in Pakistan, dude who took the rap for the whole caper . . . Seals. Navy Seals always rubbed me wrong, can I get a witness?"

I nod. Navy Seals are famously a bunch of self-righteous pricks. Which matters not in the least.

"Then they cap the Seals, and they cap the dudes who capped the Seals, and cap *those* dudes, so what do you got left?"

Dos looks at me as if I have the answer. Wild-eyed. Making me nervous. I chuckle, shrug. Say, "Well, listen, this be a crazy fucked-up world, Dos."

He shakes his nappy head like a dog shaking off water. Continues: "Straight talk now, we're having a time and all catching up, but outside? You got yourself lots of very angry riled-up men and women with big old guns looking to fuck you up bad, Librarian."

I'm very aware of that fact. I appreciate his concern and tell him so. Dos raises his eyebrows, drops them, polishes off one stick and tears open another.

"I feel you. You hard rock. Lone wolfin it. But this level of static . . ." He waves his jerky. "Hey, what can I say? First heard the chatter this afternoon, always gotta keep an eye on these lunatics, but wasn't really paying attention till your description went out, thought to myself, that can't be but one man in the whole of New York City. Then they started yakking about the library and I thought, shit, you are in a very tenuous position. And me just jumping in bed with you, man, I should just go hand myself over, let them hook me up to those machines they got. I must be crazy. Cause I like where I'm at. This is exactly what I do not need in my world right now, Librarian."

I give him the look again. Subtext: he owes me, he knows it, I don't even need to go reminding him. Would I do it? Would I hand him over? Does he want an angry, murderous Kuwaiti with unlimited resources up his tract? Not likely, but who can say for sure?

Dos Mac digs this, sighs. Busies himself with the remote again. Leans over and starts tickling a beige keyboard.

"Lemme get that audio hooked up," he mumbles. "And then what, boss?"

I hate that Dos, such a brilliant and fundamentally decent brother, has gotta feel like I'm holding past bullshit over his head, but time doesn't allow for more sensitivity.

"You can get a feed going, right? And you can roll it out on a frequency so anybody monitoring video is gonna pick it up, am I right?"

Dos flutters his eyes impatiently like this is the most elementary jazz he's ever been consigned with. Take that as a yes.

"Hot," I say. Look at the screen showing Times Square. Military vehicles amassing. My stomach drops, I glance quick at the front door. Getting paranoid.

"You absolutely positive none of that computer shit is traceable back to this here address, Mac?"

Dos nods his head. "Yo, I wouldn't be doing it otherwise, even for a good friend like yourself. Got it directed so that if you pulled on that rope you'd find yourself somewhere outside Kuala Lumpur, then pinging back to a spot in San Juan. So no worries."

Nodding, I gingerly prod the back of my neck again. Think about putting some Purell™ on that very spot, but what good would it do?

On the other hand, what's it gonna hurt, so that is exactly what happens. Dos just surveys me, no judgment there. After I've swapped out gloves again, and done up my hands, I rub it in there thoroughly.

"We do this," I say, "and then I'm gonna need you to sort though that video I brought by."

Dos inclines his head.

Pop a pill. Just to maintain. Need a fucking painkiller, my shattered claw throbbing.

Grab that Paul Smith box cutter.

"Lemme have a couple minutes with her first. Then I'll give you a signal, and we'll go ahead, go live with this jammie."

Dos has his eyes half closed and doesn't respond. That's his work mode. Man'll do whatever I need him to do.

Head for the soundstage, removing my jacket as I do so. Don't wanna stain that smart shit, not so soon anyway.

She hears me enter, blindly snaps around, and just launches right into it. Unreal. Comes muffled through the plastic: "Oh jeez, this is a fact of war on American soil. Ya cannot deliberately hold an American citizen against his or her willingness, in accordance with the old Michael Mann Act of 2001. Homeland Security—"

"Ma'am, I'm going to take this off your head. If you move you'll get cut and that will be your fault, not mine."

"Oh Lord, let Yer mighty hand cast this terrorist Devil outta Yer servant Senator Kathleen Koch, so this freedom-hater may no longer hold captive this person whom it pleased Ya ta make in Yer body image—"

"That's absolutely right. Move and you'll get cut."

I run the box cutter up the side of her head as she blathers on, very cautiously of course, she yelps as I inadvertently nick her cheek what with all her twitching around. I'll admit my hand slipped a little.

"Uh-huh. Told you not to move, lady."

Tear the remaining plastic off with my gloved hand, stray tape pulling out some of her hair in the process. Another indignant noise, but she's trying to not give me the satisfaction.

What does she see? A concrete room. A wraithlike, dark-hued mongrel of a man in a nice suit, wearing a surgical mask, gloves. Holding a semiautomatic and a box cutter. Behind the black man, a wall full of deadly looking dildos, whips, unidentifiable leather objects. A cheap card table is all that separates her from the evil-looking gentleman.

I'm pretty sure it's scary.

Set down the gun, and crouch so I'm level with her face.

Points for moxie, she's aiming for stoic but it's clear she's shitting in her Jackie O. wear, terrified, seemingly only now grasping the reality of this situation, Kathleen squawking: "You are Holy Gosh WOW so damn dead, mister. Kill ya! Capital offense already. My team'll find ya. Oh yeah. America's best, heroes . . . Not that, ah, maybe there's a some kinda deal thing we could get going for ya. I just have to make a call. But you wanna play this the wrong way, you . . . insurgent? My team will getcha. Getcha good . . ."

And so on. I let her exhaust herself. It takes a minimum of fifteen minutes. I consider her mouth, her hair, the whole construction. Highly engineered. To a particular purpose, this is a woman who is considered irresistibly attractive to a certain segment of our old society.

It strikes me that there's something creepily robotic about Kathleen Koch. She's exactly what a right-wing money person would build for themselves, not just as a sex partner, but to send out into the world, get through doors they otherwise couldn't penetrate.

After this period of time, I note she has stopped speaking and is just bobbing her head silently. I clear my throat, and say calmly, "Kathleen Koch. You are in an extremely unfortunate position, and I want you to understand where you stand very clearly. Are you listening? I need you to listen and not say anything."

I pause. She appears to be unresponsive. Rocking back and forth. She has begun weeping. Good. I carry on.

"Can I call you Kathy? Great. Your reputation is that

you are not very intelligent. I'll give you more credit than that and speak to you like an adult. Kathy, this is a one-way conversation. I need no information from you, so you are useless in this respect. That's number one."

She starts mouthing something. I can't hear her and don't care either which way, so I continue: "My constituents and I have no allegiances to any organized group, construction firm, corporation, or country. We have no associations with state or private military, nor is there a political dimension to this."

She's fucking praying aloud. This is rich.

"The Lord is my shepherd. I will not want," mumbleth Kathy. "He feedth me from fine pastures and delivers us from the axis of evil . . ."

Wow. Almost artful how she mashes up texts.

In my estimation she's playing at crazy. It's strikes me as completely contrived and therefore not even pitiable. I can't help but say it: "My personal belief that you are a charlatan, an opportunist, and a sociopath has bearing only in the sense that there is no part of me that is the least bit concerned for your continued well being. You are here as a hostage, not as a guest, and you will not be allowed basic comforts such as food, or trips to the ladies' room, et cetera, so there's no percentage in requesting for such luxuries."

". . . don't negotiate, never surrender to servants of the Islamist Illuminati . . ."

"You are alive only because your husband and his business associates have wronged my associates and me in a profound way. You're just a bargaining chip, and if it doesn't work out, it's no sweat cause we have other angles. Look here, Kathy, I will indicate two cameras: one there, and one there."

I point them out but Koch doesn't look up. She's making shapes with her mouth. Wacko stuff. I won't lie, I'm enjoying this.

"Shortly we will make sure your husband and/or one of his representatives sees you. Your only function is to be seen. You may say two things and two things only, which are, one: that you are relatively unhurt for the moment; and two: if the senator does not cooperate, I have assured you that I will kill you at my whim."

Kathleen is tripping out. She commences gnashing her teeth, rolling her eyes, etc. It's a lame act and it's pathetically transparent, so again I ignore her behavior.

"Do you understand what I've just told you?"

Kathy is now speaking in tongues. It's some snakehandling kind of shit. Spit fills the corners of her mouth. Her thickly applied mascara streaks her cheeks.

Sweet Jesus. But it's good. She is appropriately fucked-up looking. But what bullshit, all these cheap-ass theatrics.

"You need to believe that I will kill you Kathleen. Do you believe that?"

More spittle, more nonsense. Please. Basta. I pick up the pistol and fire just to the right of her ear.

That shuts her the fuck up quick-fast in a hurry. Booya, Kathy.

Let her digest what just happened, and repeat, "Kathleen Koch, have I succeeding in conveying the speed at which I will kill you should you not participate? If not, let me simply say I'll kill ya slow cause I'll be having a good time doing it. Believe me?"

She flips her head around. Gets coherent.

"I . . . peed. On myself," croaks the senator. "If I could get just, ya know. A towel."

Aiming a bit tighter in this time, I fire just past the other ear.

She starts shrieking like this particular type of monkey I saw a show about on an airplane going to or fro some hole of Hell. The lady has a little seizure.

Again, I let this settle down and it resolves itself into deep sobs, which strike me as much more authentic. More good stuff.

Among other things Kathleen says is that she cannot hear anything. Which is fine too.

I step forward and lean in a bit. "Again, you just need to be seen. We're turning on the cameras," I say, louder than necessary. "And again, I think you're smarter than your image would suggest, so I do hope you follow the guidelines I've laid out. I suppose we'll see exactly how much your husband values you, Kathleen—that should be informative, if nothing else."

I signal Dos. Slide my metal chair back out of frame.

"I'll be right outside," I say. "Just play it natural and you'll maybe get through this. Remember that I am not invested in you in any way, and would gladly have the next bullet go in your mouth. M'kay?"

She wags her head, eyes darting between the cameras and my gun. Her teeth are chit-chattering audibly. Christ, she fell apart pretty quick there. I had thought she was a warrior, a proper tiger.

"Hey, Kath." She's spacing out. "Kath," I repeat. Her eyes swing in my general direction. She vibes drugged but the terror is still there too. "Kath, just since we're chatting, curious about that seven-hundred-dollar nail job they rattled on about a couple years back. Where you got . . . what was it, diamond-encrusted American flags . . . ?"

That rouses her a touch. Kathleen seems like she's trying to regain some dignity. But it all reads android to me. I wonder if we have that technology. The ability to build something like her. That would be some deep tech.

She serves me the schizo boilerplate on this one, it's like she's reading off cut-up cue cards, her voice monochrome.

"Fair use of American tax money. Ah, I successfully litigated five lamestream journalists 'bout that, see, cause which is a matter of public record, so I have no comment. Aw jeez . . . aw jeez . . . my head is . . . I get migraines, bad ones . . ."

She trying hard to stay on message, but even at her most coherent, her message is a whole tangle of mad crazy. So it's hard to tell when she's losing it. Blame it on the migraines, that was her mantra as she exited the presidential race, the headaches, the headaches . . .

Jesus, but she's tacky as fuck. Can't contain myself, say, "Well, who said white-lady politicians couldn't shine on? Blingtastico. Ghetto stuff, the nails. Showing anybody can be a hood rat. It's inspirational. And another thing you've driven on home, Kath. Genderwise. You sure enough broke the glass ceiling on being a fucking scumbag. So congrats on that, Kath. You're a nasty piece of trash like the rest of us."

Senator Kathleen Koch, encased in a plastic bag and duct-taped to a chair, commences weeping.

Doesn't take long, Dos saying: "Yeah. Skype account I have tied to this feed is blowing up already. How do you wanna handle this, player partner?"

I don't think I know exactly what Skype is . . . damn, that Internet thing was a bunch of bullshit. One big advertisement for itself, and somehow you paid to watch the same ad over and over.

"Skype, is that text-based messages and whatnot?"

Dos considers me. "How old are you, my mellow? Text, yeah, if you want. Or video-conferencing kinda thing."

"No, let's do it like text."

Dos taps a couple buttons, has a look. Starts whistling something.

"All right, here we are. Lemme just filter out . . . We could make some money here, Librarian, we got folks offering real cash for this video. People making suggestions as to what we do next . . . Ha. I'll bypass those." Dos nows starts singing under his breath, "*Till you just can't boogie no mo* . . . Okay, this looks like something. Oh, I'm singing that fuckin song! User name is *BOOGIE_OOGIE_OOGIE_MAN_2—*"

My stomach drops. Cut him off: "Lemme read it." Peer at the screen.

In a little yellow bubble I dig:

DELUCCIA HERE. LET'S DO THIS WITH SOME CIVIL-
ITY. ROSE HEE WILL MEET AN UGLY END IF YOU
DO NOT HAND OVER SENATOR KOCH UNHARMED.

KINDLY ESCORT THE SENATOR TO THE STATEN IS-
LAND FERRY WHITEHALL TERMINAL, SECOND
FLOOR, AND AN EXCHANGE WILL BE ARRANGED. BE
UNARMED AND COMPLIANT. 12 NOON TODAY. AC-
CEDE AND WE GO EASY ON YOU. RSVP.

"Does that seem legit?" comes Dos.

I look at the clock on his computer. 9:18 a.m.

"Yo, Dos, help me out, how do I do this?"

Dos again peeps me askance. "Just type the shit in.
How did you miss the fundamentals, man? My kids were
doing this by the time they were four."

Hate to touch the keyboard but I'm typing. I'm a single-
finger kind of typer. Painstakingly, I manage to eke out:

AGREED 2, W CAVEATS. 1) I WILL BE ARMED, + 2)
WEARING BODY BOMB ATTACHED 2 EKG SO IF HEART
RATE DIPS BOOM. U R FOREWARNED. I WANT 2 C U IN
TH FLESH, ALONE, NO FLUNKIES, I SPOT A FLUNKY
DEAL'S OFF. SEE U @ NOON.

"That's . . . kinda thin, yo," comments Dos.

"I'm under duress, man." He's right though.

Dos shrugs, I make jazz hands at the keyboard.

"Then what?"

"The computer? Press *Enter*, prince. Jesus. What up
with this bomb jive?"

There's a silly sound, a digital bubble, as I see my message appear in the main field.

"Suicide bomber, it's a straight classic. Never watched
24?"

"You are solid old-school, holmes."

"I am that. Message sent, right?"

Dos exhales. "Yeah."

"Then that's me jetting," I say, reaching for my coat. "Kill that video feed. Gonna move Koch. Can you slap me together something that looks . . . bomb-ish? And if you could have a go at that data I brought in . . ."

The Mac bobs his head.

"Hey, for real though, you're a peach, thanks a million, Dos."

I'm legging it toward the basement door. Dos calls after me: "Yo, Librarian. You're gonna die young, soldier. But just in general, you know I give you an A for effort."

Aware of the deep need for speed, I resecure the jabbering senator, who almost manages to bite me in the process, and bundle her into the trunk of the Chinese car. Woman yammering about a migraine.

Guess the Rohypnol (Dos very casually mentioned he had "a couple lying around somewhere") hasn't kicked in yet.

Praise Jah for duct tape, which is a gift directly from the gods.

Milky, foul-smelling rain falling . . . hard to tell what's airborne toxin, floating industrial silt, etc., and what's old-fashioned cloud-cover anymore. I suppose there's no difference anyhoo, as it's all rolled up into one big discolored mass.

The light is a dirty yellow and the air pressure feels thick and headache heavy. Leg giving me grief which generally means a coming electrical storm, but who knows?

Trust the System to keep and guide me. Stick to the rules, this is the word.

Despite the shower of piss, a group of older folks are out, conducting tai chi practice. As I hump the body-shaped bag into the vehicle, they pause to watch my efforts, expressionless. Other sets of headlights eye-fuck me from windows. A Mao-jacketed man floats past, ignoring me. And I blank them all. They don't matter.

Limp around to the driver's side, thinking left, left, left, heave my corpse in. Check under the passenger's seat: the senator's file in place. Stupid of me to leave the shit in the car, and relieved to see it untouched. Sloppy work, Decimal. Like I told Dos, I got stress.

Fire up the vehicle in that unsatisfying, hushed manner of these electric jobs, and jump on it.

Now, as the dashboard clock is reporting 9:37 a.m., I will adhere to System dogma with respect to navigation. On foot, we simply stay mindful about those left turns, but via car there are more advanced guidelines if you really want to get some extra credit, having nothing to do with direction, but rather the name of the street or avenue itself. These are the rules behind the routing I take: When in a vehicle and traveling on lettered streets, it's essential to move in ascending alphabetical order. Likewise, we ascend on the numbered streets. This reminds us we can never go backward in time and must live in the present, always moving toward the future.

So: Hester Street to Ludlow, traveling north across Delancey and straight across Houston to 1st Street, taking it west to Second Avenue, whereupon I swing north (in theory against traffic), exiting Chinatown at about 6th Street, passing the Ukrainian Social Hall on my right side, which gives me an Iveta-jolt, hanging a right on 14th Street and east to the FDR, whereupon I swing north, clipping a concrete barrier as I climb the ramp to the drive.

I slow-up close to the Midtown Tunnel (flooded and impassable), anticipating a detour, but recall the bombed-out area near the UN has been repaired . . . bounce across the wooden bridge (wood!) that's been thrown together, the black hole in the concrete yawning below, and from here allow myself to floor it.

"Flooring it" is a frustrating action in an e6, but I work with what Allah provides.

Exhaust the FDR, take the Harlem River Drive to the Willis Avenue Bridge, hop on the 87 . . . it's always been lucky exit 13 off the Major Deegan, and that, people, is Gun Hill Road. In the much maligned borough of the Bronx.

See, I got a little hideaway up here in the broken jungle gym of my youth. A pied-à-terre, if you will.

Do a half donut into the dilapidated parking area when I reach the Gun Hill Houses. By "Houses" what they meant was "Nasty-Ass American Housing Project." A rose is a rose is a rose.

I note an old fossil-fuel Honda, stripped of its tires. A NYPD Dodge Challenger, looking relatively untouched. Maybe three other vehicles. Otherwise the parking lot is all but empty. This emptiness is palpable, huge, a crushing gravitational force.

The rain has picked up again, and I pop the trunk. Lean over and get that file, stuff it down the back of my trousers as I exit the Chinese piece of crap.

Move move move. I'm playing it like I'm unobserved and unaccounted for, but with Cyna-corp that can't last . . .

Nobody lives here anymore. Amendment: nobody *ever* lived here. You can't call what folks did here living. Folks maintained. Folks slept and ate and survived to get up and do it again the next day.

The Honorable Kathleen Koch is noodle-limp, playing possum or genuinely unconscious, seems like the drug has taken effect. Toss her over my shoulder like a bag of cement and head for the huge, hateful building. There's a reason some described this as "Brutalist" architecture. It's brutal. And yet it's my home away from home. Once my home, period.

Quick stagger across the cracked concrete of a playground, sad white plastic-swing akimbo, the usual urban tumbleweeds, yellowed with age now, the chicken bones, the forty-ouncers, the empty Newport boxes, yada, yada . . . future archeological material, describing how we as a tribe numbed ourselves to our fucked-up reality.

Bang through the doors and into the foyer. Depress the elevator call button . . . the electrics intermittent up in this spot.

I wait. I listen at the metal door. Zilcho.

Gonna have to hump it. That's a bitch, but I'm spared the unpleasant ride up, more stress I don't need. Very short on time here. I lower my mask, spit, replace it, and head for the stairs.

Another dark stairwell. I'm either headed up or down, but there's always another stairwell.

Winded is hardly the word as I gain the ninth floor. I'm quite sure my knee is forever fucked, and my gut has moved to my throat in preparation for me to puke it out.

But there's no time. Shakily I make my way down the hallway, shifting Kathleen to my right shoulder. Hands quivering as I dive for the key in my new pants pocket . . . withdraw it, key wavering hither and tither, and finally inserting itself into the lock, which I turn without a problem.

An apartment with no identity or furnishings, save the futon on the floor of the bedroom. The air is musty and stagnant, but with a quick peep around the joint I'm shocked at the halfway decent state within which it's kept itself.

The windows are shut tight, as if they can't bear to look. The only light I have to work with pokes anemically from between the broken slats in the crappy venetian blinds.

I dump Senator Kathleen Koch, who remains slack, on

the mattress. Time is falling away but I prod at her with a new shoe (happy to report they're breaking in nicely). I am sweating, y'all. Take a second.

"Kath," I rasp, panting. "Hope you don't mind the sheets, they've only been used a couple times."

KK gives a muted cough. Eases my mind a smidge. She seems to have given up entirely.

Almost out of tape, but I truss her up once more.

Mummified, one female eye rotates around the apartment.

"Hang tough, okay, Kathleen? I'm back in a jiffy."

No response. Fair enough. I drop a couple jerky sticks and a bottle of water on the floor near her head. Think again; lean over and cut one hand and her mouth free cause I'm basically a decent guy.

On my way out: see the square-foot dark patch on the floor. I squat, put a hand on the carpet. Run my fingers over the crusted fibers. Always imagine somebody's gonna scrub this down, but then I'm the only one with a key. I think.

In the bathroom I step up on the nonworking toilet to remove the vent cover. Slide the senator's paperwork into the shaft, replace the grill. Do it quiet.

Check the windows: painted shut. Shake out a pill and swallow, take a second to disinfect with Purell™, swap out my gloves.

Getting realer by the moment.

Make sure the door is securely locked from the outside as I've rigged it, and I ghost.

Ditch the bullshit BYD in a particularly overgrown area of Battery Park and lurch forth, doing my lopsided version of a jog. 11:24, I'm good for right turns. Rain coming down pretty steadily now, dismayed to be planting my nice brogues in the mud and tall grass. Good thing they had a brownish tinge to them from the jump. Happy as well to have snagged that overcoat as it's serving a brother well now.

Run a quick inventory check: in hand I have my CZ-99. My pockets are stuffed with rubber gloves, a pill bottle, Purell™, my key, one stick of jerky, and the box cutter. Strapped around my ankle rides the Sig Sauer P290, and I dig the comfort of its weight.

As I come out of the park onto State Street just near Pearl, I kneel behind a rusted-out moped chained to a telephone pole. Beneath my coat, the thrown-together "bomb" wrapped around my midsection pinches the skin near my rib cage, causing me to wince.

Peep south at the Whitehall Terminal, the words *Staten Island Ferry* quite clear from my vantage.

I'm ahead of schedule up in this piece, dirty early-bird looking for the worm, but do I pause? No sir, it's all move move move.

Lean into a stiff jog, let's go. Here, straight ahead and due south. What am I looking at now? There's a cluster of dead-looking yellow taxicabs further down State, describing crazy angles, blocking my view of the street-level entrance to the terminal. Maybe twelve, fourteen cars in all.

Check the CZ-99 and make sure a bullet is in the chamber. I motor south. What up with the taxis? No choice but to dip in and out of the dead vehicles, serving me well as cover. Chassis like sleeping kittens, all piled up together for warmth. Some of these cars, the only way to explain the manner in which they overlap is to imagine them dropped from overhead. Which I wouldn't rule out. Crop-circle shit.

Note Port Authority cops drifting around, not saying much. Sanitation workers, other uniforms I don't recognize, a couple civilians. Not shit they can do about this pileup, it'd take a crane or three to clear this clot. Two or three folks grit on me as I slip by, but if they clock my weapon they don't intend to do anything about it. Worn-out men and women, threadbare clothing tatty and mismatched.

The vehicular tableaux is disconcerting, but just one of thousands of such inexplicable phenomena one trips over every other block in this town. You don't ask how or why anymore. You take what you can use, and ramble on.

Which is what I do now. Stomach flipping, anticipating Nic Deluccia. How am I gonna react when face-on with the man himself? Why do I prevent myself from looking directly at our past relationship? I know not to try to answer that question. Keep my hustle on, face cameras wide open. Move.

My nose is adjusting to the stench of the river. Like the broiled plastic of our everyday environment, I suppose in time one would get used to it, but I find myself gagging slightly. Odd, though, this odor is way more evil farther north on the West Side, less so on the East.

Park myself about fifty yards out from the tall, handsome entryway, on my haunches. Always liked the new terminal, not big on modern structures but this one was well done. This and the New Museum on the Bowery, I groove on both buildings. February 14 left it untouched, so it sits, ready for a massive wave of commuters and tourists that will never come, rendered useless.

A few Transit Authority cop cars and a smallish bulldozer out front of the terminal, otherwise nothing catches my eye. The spot is like one big crystal decanter so there's no viable way to creep on it. I don't bother trying.

Pocket the CZ, commence my signature lope across the plaza toward the main doors. Gust of nasty wind comes off the water, I have to hold my hat and turn my collar up against it, gut churning, feeling as wired-up as I've felt in a long while.

My plan is extremely simple, people.

Dig: I secure Rose, and then kill everybody else, most especially and most thoroughly Mr. Nic Deluccia, and the senator if he pokes his head in.

Get this whole episode behind me as quick as possible. Make a return to what I suspect will be a long rebuilding process with respect to my books. Start over from null. Whatever.

Maybe Rose wants to hang around. That I wouldn't mind. But whatever, yo. I mean, we just freakin met. But you know how that goes. You catch a vibe off people . . .

But all that would be icing. Getting ahead of the moment, and the System doesn't respond well to daydreams and flights of fucking fancy.

The primary goal: gotta sort out these various folks who believe they have a line on my past movements. That is a vibration I cannot have in play. Seems like the moment I take care of one situation, another joker pops up alleging foreknowledge of yours truly, with accompanying documentation.

It's a nightmare. And I won't have it.

Move. The double doors that line the face of the terminal, the whole wall's worth of them, are standing open . . . this in itself is a bit freaky but I don't see how it could make the scene any more charged than it is.

You might call my plan elegant in its simplicity, were it not for the fact that I don't really have a proper motherfucking plan.

I slide inside the entry hall, which retains most of its former grandeur, the eighty-or-so-foot-high ceiling now sporting enough holes to allow in the rain, creating opaque, whitish pools here and there on the stone floor. A massive American flag hangs heavy over the wide stairs and frozen escalator banks, waterlogged and beat. It's a nice metaphor but I don't linger. Move.

Take the double-wide stairs in pairs up to the mezzanine . . . halfway up I glance over my shoulder through the soaring wall of glass and get a load of the monumental waste that is the Freedom Tower, partially obscured by clouds. Hate that fucking structure.

Make the second level, squat up against one of huge columns, and have a gander at the old waiting area, let my lungs catch up with me. The open-plan design is such that I can pretty much see everything going on in the building from this spot.

On the b-side, pretty much anybody who's looking can see me. No margin for stealth here, y'all.

The rain has brought a fair bit of darkness with it even at this early hour, so it's not a complete cinch to spot everything on this level, despite all the windows. Thus far I spy exactly nobody, which doesn't bode well. The mezzanine silent, abandoned . . .

No, hold up. Seated on one of the granite benches back toward the gates I make out a figure. My gut flippy-flops. Could be a random citizen. Highly unlikely. Squint: they're facing the other direction, away from me.

I hear a helicopter. Nothing unusual, but I listen for it to pass overhead. Headed uptown.

Fuck if it's not another neat setup, as no matter what kind of rock and roll shapes I throw, I'm totally exposed. Any eight-year-old with a rifle-mounted scope could take me out sans problemo. So fuck it.

I pop a pill, bring myself to a standing position. Get to crunking across the floor toward the only occupied bench. Trying to manage my limp, and vibrate strength. Holding my dead hand to my side, so it's not completely obvious that I'm one impaired motherfucker. Move.

I'm checking side to side as I close the gap, seeing nothing notable, hearing and smelling only the rank water, and remote construction cacophony.

Reckon I'd better be prepared for dramatics so I raise my 99. "Hey there," I call out. "Be advised I'm armed."

No response from the seated individual.

"Gonna need you to identify yourself, right fucking now."

Still nothing, though I'm close enough to read the person as female . . .

Rose.

I stumble around the column at the end of the row of benches, looking left and right, gun extended. All a bit of a charade as my shit is wide open.

NB: out the exit doors directly in front of us I can see the dark water, and a small Coast Guard Defender–class boat, engines idling. Assuming it's manned. Its military function announced by the large aft-mounted machine gun.

Rose Hee is sitting stiff-backed straight, dressed in orange prison garb, her hands behind her back, mouth sealed neatly with black tape. Her hair is down. She's got metal shackles around her neck and legs. Makeup a clownish smear. Gaze stunned, attempting defiance. Her vast, shiny peepers track me as I come up on her.

"Rose."

I kneel down, digging the white plastic leg shackles. Rose is making a squeaky sound, attempts to kick me. Eyes wild with frustration, fear. Points her chin at . . . orange nylon rope, attached to both leg and neck restraints, leading—

Turn around. The ropes thread under the doors, out to the water . . . I move forward, tracing them out the window, down the slipway, and onto the boat. They must spot me now, cause the Defender guns its engines, and kicks up foam.

So Rose is tethered to the boat. Fuck me. Cute.

Spin back toward her, and there he is, hand on her head.

Early seventies, but military sharp despite the jowls. White mustache and an NYPD baseball hat. Bomber jacket. My head goes whiz bang, and I see him clearly, turning toward the child that is me several decades back, a spray of camera flash.

"My two favorite kids," says Nic Deluccia, showing us his teeth, his fine dental work. "Who'd a thunk it?"

My tummy in a twist, I raise my pistol. It's a thick

New York brogue he speaks with, and I recall it well.

"Nic," I say. "Correct?" I'm all kotted up, smooth talk eluding me, so I do the safe thing and rock it dumb.

He gives a pained, off-kilter grin. "You gonna make like you're not sure it's me? Listen. I dunno what's the idea with this amnesia bit, which I find kinda, well, kinda fucking insulting, given all I've done to help you better yourself, son."

"Don't know what you're talking about," I say, froggy. Realize his voice has never left me.

It's my intention to stick with the plan to claim ignorance, floss stupid.

Nic snorts. "Really, you're gonna play this thing out all the way like you don't remember old Nic Deluccia? Goddamn if I haven't known the both of yous since you were nothing but tadpoles. All but raised you, son. This is like a family fucking tragedy."

"Let's just do this and cut out the fat," I counter. Won't look at him, no, not directly. "Say what you want, guy, I don't know you, so there can be no head-fucking. I'm immune."

Nic examines me, shrugs. "Well, hell, it's not important, I suppose. Cause I know you."

Now I look at him. Eyes. Blue-gray-flecked headlights on the man. I'm twelve years old. I want him to be proud of me. Shudder, wanna shuck this sticky feeling.

Him saying, "And the fuckin thing is . . . none of it makes a lick of difference now. Cause you kids . . ."

He laces his fingers through Rose's hair. Her eyes are locked on mine. Nic now shifts attention to Rose. I scan the man's torso for a clear shot. Dig me now: it's gonna be difficult to bring myself to pull the trigger on this man.

"And I'm most disappointed in you, my dear. Such a

smart and well-behaved woman, always toeing the line, always helpful . . . What happened to the young Rose I know and love? The world was your oyster, my sweet Rose."

Since Rose can't respond, I do.

"She grew up, pal. So give and let's all just skate home, happy as clams."

Nic checks me again. Contemplates my damaged face, my split lip, my gimp hand, my many open wounds, ropes of scar tissue. I'm no beauty, but if I didn't know better I'd have the impression he was actually glad to see me. Glad but disappointed.

"You," says Nic, directing his mouth at me, not without affection. "Willful as all get out, you were. Are. Apparently few things change."

"Let's wrap this up, dreamweaver. Tick tock." Tough stuff, heart thumping in the back of my throat.

"That's right, son," says Nic. "Game running down on you both. Now listen to me, and listen good."

I swallow. Something of the scared child turns in my chest. That voice.

Saying, "You kids have succeeded in inserting yourselves into an affair that is very fucking serious business indeed. And a soft touch I may be—"

Twists Rose's hair, hard. She audibly inhales, tenses further. A single tear ambles down the side of her face, trailing black mascara.

"But I don't allow personal histories to complicate matters when I'm in the field. Business is business. You kids. Fucking around with my golden goose. Money is money. This kinda thing though? This is tough on me, don't doubt that. Even if you wanna fake like I'm nobody to you. Like I said, I'm fucking insulted."

"Back up off of her, Nic." My voice hangs there lame, like a shitty joke.

He shows me his teeth, and they disappear quick. Directs his chin at me. "I see your gun, son. That's a pretty gun. Sure. I'm not backing up anywhere. The very second you get a shot off, you'd better hope and pray it's a winner. Which is neither here nor there, cause either way the lovely Rose goes waterskiing. Hell, it'd be a shame to see such a beautiful lady meet such a ridiculous end. So come with it."

"Kathleen Koch is nearby," I say, not sure what I'm doing anymore, waving the pistol vaguely, pressing forward, all I know is I gotta press forward. "She's unharmed. She's close. Rose gets cut loose and you get her, no fuss, no muss."

"How about your bomb, son?"

That doesn't track. I blink. The reappearance of Nic Deluccia in my zone has succeeded in throwing my normally verbose ass for a loop.

"You don't mean to tell me you forgot to wear your handy body-bomb thingamadoodle? As promised."

Goddamnit. Spacing on key shit . . . If I could just back up and do this again, but that's not the way the world turns . . .

I open my coat with my smashed hand, say, "Take a look, motherfucker. That's right." Halfhearted. It's not gonna float but I gotta go through the motions.

Nic doesn't bother moving his eyes from mine. "I won't push ya, son. And I truly hope we get the chance to all walk away from this thing friends, healthy and happy."

"Cocksucker, nobody walks out of here at all, dig? Unless you let Rose, unless you, unless you get your fuckin hands off . . ." I'm stumbling over the words. Something in my mouth. My tongue, my tongue in my mouth, lumpy, a hunk of fat.

Nic shakes his head. "You're a mess. Hard thing to see. Lookit here. Think about what you're saying, kid. Really. If you had a bomb, a real bomb, would you want to blow up yourself and your girlfriend with you? For what? Just be clear, there's no bomb, and you've welched on the arrangement. Madame Senator is not here. Which means you're not respecting anybody's *time*. You're not shooting straight, son. Giving me an ulcer. After all I gave to you. Listen up. The senators, particularly Senator Howard, are some of my best clients. You'd better believe if I was running security for Senator Koch, you, son, would not have gotten near her. Unthinkable. Now, all right." His tone gets sincere, sympathetic: "Business aside, we can help you out, honest we can."

I almost buy it as genuine sympathy. Maybe it is genuine.

Nic continues, "Son, I've seen soldiers . . . I've seen men and women come back from even the most devastating circumstances. I've seen 'em come off the edge of that cliff, rebuild their lives."

He speaks softer still. It's like it's just me and him.

"That's a big part of the Cyna-corp family, why I started it up in the first place. You know what I'm talking about, cause however you slice it we've had this conversation before. My organization, it's somewhere to go for people with a . . . what? With a very special skill set, who might otherwise find themselves spurned, ostracized. They send you out there, and then, hell, nobody wants you back, am I wrong, son? Unsure about what's next for ya? Nowhere to go to do what you've been trained to do. I've been through it myself, God knows. Hell, you were part of my outfit, once upon a time, son . . ."

My vision goes a little wonky . . . spiky ticklish pain, as if insects are attempting to gnaw their way out of my eye sockets. A bomb, a real bomb. See the mystery chest, deep in the guts of the library, overflowing with explosives . . . why . . . ?

Reflexively, I put my hand to the back of my neck, to the small machine that waits there under my skin. Does it shift, push back a little?

Get it together, Decimal.

For Rose. For Rose, insists the killer in my head, I have to rally. I must overcome. Okay, the body-bomb thing is a bust. I fumbled there, and that's my badu.

Aware that Nic is talking. I keep the gun trained on him and think very carefully, from the ground up, about how exactly Rose is secured.

"Like I said. Hey, we'd love to have you back. You were part of the team, but I can't ignore you didn't execute your job up at the library. No follow through. Maybe you just got confused, like you're confused now. Trying to say that's okay, kid, we can move forward in a new—"

She's not lashed to the seat. Okay. Set it off. I shoot Nic in the chest.

He gives a surprised snort, steps back, and catches his own foot, collapsing behind the bench.

Step lively, Decimal. Unseen snipers cut loose with gunfire but I go to work, yes I'm moving, I hug Rose and swing her around do-si-do. Bullet knocks my hat off and I'm shoe-slapping full bore toward the slip, bang through the doors, hot sting on my shoulder as I'm hit but it doesn't slow me down much, Rose under one arm, gun in my floppy left hand, firing on the vessel with my ring finger, maybe twenty feet out, the guys on the boat panicking, one of these geniuses makes for the machine gun, realizes he won't be able to spin it around without spraying the cabin, so both turn and return fire with sidearms, then (go go go) one of them gets smart and hits the gas a bit too energetically.

As the Defender slides sideways toward the dock for a moment, I throw myself and Rose at the boat's rear, trying to turn in the air so as to land on my back in the manner of the pole-vaulter, but an athlete I am not . . . sickeningly I'm looking at nothing but water, yet we bounce off the twin engine hulls and come down hard on the boat itself. If the Defender hadn't slid sideways at that moment, we wouldn't have made it. I don't dwell on this.

One joker is barking at the other as the Defender shoots out into open water, with us hanging halfway off its rear runner. As we come out from under the shelter of the terminal, the rain douses us, and I get on top of Rose, the pile of nylon rope slack, trailing harmlessly off her legs and neck into the river . . . goddamn. As I eliminate one source of fucking stress, a whole slew of new problematics come bopping in.

Copilot is letting off a volley of close-range shots that are going embarrassingly wide. I get up on my elbows, hurting. Take a deep, peaceful breath as I focus on his dome, squeeze that trigger.

There's a burst of blood from atop his shoulders, and the man I just killed shimmies off the side into the river.

Skipper seems to be trying to decide between steering the boat and protecting his neck, and in that moment I shoot him too through the back of his skull, he collapses neatly, I daresay a fine bit of left-handed gunwork on my part considering.

Rose is moaning and groaning, her hands and feet immobilized as they are. Gunmen on the roof of the terminal are letting us have it, and I'm trying to drag the lady into the tiny cabin, munitions pinging and ponging off the boat, I'm praying they don't hit the engine, and then it occurs that the most pressing problem is the fact that nobody's steering the ship. Move.

As I pivot to seek out the wheel of a fucking *boat* for the very first time in my tragicomic life, we glance off the listing wreckage of a Circle Line ferry. With a horrendous scrape, the impact knocks me over, sends my gun skidding down the length of the boat . . . I'm crawling after the 99 and simultaneously attempting to crane my noggin around to see what's doing, and we smack into the looming Circle Line hull again, this time causing us to spin all the way around, effectively killing our engines.

There are two advantages to this development, one of which is my gun slides neatly back into my hand, the other is that we are effectively shielded from fire on the Whitehall Terminal roof.

A pause in the action; the Cyna-corp grunts holler and hoot at each other, scrambling to put Plan B in effect. We've come to a very unsteady stop against the sloping side of the far larger shipwreck, face-on with the ferry terminal.

Rose is prone, kicking the aluminum paneling in the ship's cabin.

A bullet zips past my ear and cracks the glass behind me. I get clever, get my head down.

Very cautiously I withdraw the box cutter and start sawing at Rose's armcuffs. What I need is some kind of wire clipper . . . It all but breaks my cutter in two but after a fair bit of struggling I'm through the cuffs, which come snapping off Rose's chafed and bleeding wrists. Go to work on her legs . . . same story here, I get about half-way through and my box cutter snaps like a stale pretzel, though I'm able to pull the remaining plastic off with my hands, gloved as they are.

Rose is coughing into the tape around her mouth, and I peel that off, again being cautious not to hurt her in the process.

I wanna be clean, lather up with some sweet Purell™, but the situation doesn't allow for it.

After an impressive coughing fit Rose recovers to the point where she's able to speak: "You *know* Deluccia? You used to fucking work for him?"

My head feels hot, me saying, "Just give me a minute, Rose, this is not—"

"I knew something was up. What fucking gives, Mister X? He was more interested in getting you back on his team than in . . . Oh, and thank you for saving my life, or rather, for making my death more drawn-out and complicated—"

"Shut it for two seconds. Lady, what gives with you shadowing me to the library in the first place? If you got an organization to run, you're not doing your peoples a favor, putting yourself at serious fucking risk for some fucking outsider, or am I missing some shit?"

"Mister X, I *needed* to go with you. Don't you see? I needed to disappear too."

"What the fuck are you talking about?"

"They would have found me anyway. Why not just walk into it? Less people getting hurt. It makes less sense now that I say it. Made sense at the time . . ." She trails off, looking at my shoulder. Goes white. Looks around the cabin wildly.

Swaying slightly. "Rose . . . okay now, what are you doing?"

She's hunched over the dead guy, pulling off his bulletproof vest, and working off the dude's black polyester shirt. She comes up with it, presses hard into my shoulder, a move which is so excruciating that I very nearly black out.

"You're bleeding." She sounds scared, which in turn makes me nervous. "Hey. You're bleeding really fucking bad."

Pressing on the wound, I don't particularly want to but I look down, rotate my arm forward, and dig with some relief on a clear exit point. My brain pounding, flushed with liquid.

"In 'n out," I say, cause that's what you're supposed say, like it's great news. "S'fucking nothing." Give her a grin, aiming for something reassuring. "Thanks though, darlin."

Calculate the shot is high enough so as to not present any problems. If an artery had been hit I'd be bled out already. I might be tilting a hair, but this boy still got that PMA, see? Takes a fair bit to slow down my grind. Lightheaded as a motherfucker though.

Rose's mouth moves but I seem to have momentarily lost my hearing. Try not to be overly concerned about that, distract myself by having a look at the boat's control system . . . a wheel and a throttle. It seems simple enough but I like to observe the old maxim: when drinking or bleeding heavily, avoid operating vehicles or heavy machinery.

". . . a fucking communications major," Rose is saying.

"I may have been involved with some bad stuff but never in my life have I been near . . ."

No, rather I have a look at the window on the ferry we're nuzzling . . . not quite level with our position, we bounce about two feet below it, but it seems far more realistic than trying to figure out how to skipper a boat, especially in my condition. I know we should be trying to put distance between ourselves and the Cyna-corp people but I reckon at this juncture it's all the same.

Peel off my overcoat with some effort, as it's heavy with water and blood, not to mention I'm doing everything one-handed. Strap on the dead man's vest. Cause you never know. I also snag a nasty-looking diver's knife he's got strapped to his belt. With reluctance I shoulder my shot-up coat back on.

". . . gotta keep direct pressure, what the fuck are you doing? That's a serious . . ." Rose is saying, shrill.

Fuck this, I gotta move.

"Rose," I interrupt her, "can you . . . shield yourself somehow, okay . . . gonna just . . ."

Duck out of the cabin and the rain greets me, tepid and nasty. Rose calling to me but I'm out of range, crab-walking out onto the front of the boat, toward the machine gun, my new leather-soled shoes slip-sliding all over the wet surface.

Those gentlemen on the terminal roof get excited and commence firing again, but it's a tougher shot now, we're far enough out to make it challenging . . . doesn't stop them from trying. Good boys. Peripherally I note a Coast Guard boat of the same make as ours, another longer vessel, even a couple hot shots revving jet skis.

A chopper loops over the terminal, and this breaks my stupor. Fucking choppers.

Do it, Decimal. Take ahold of the big gun, have a quick peek at its mechanism, slip the safety off.

Breathe, on an exhale I spray the terminal from east to west in a slow deliberate movement, then shift the barrel up and give the heli and the guys upstairs a little. I don't think I hit much of anything but my point is made.

This latest Dewey Decimal appearance seems to have given the boys cause for a rethink, everybody seems to back up a step, engines drop a gear, all positive stuff for my purposes. Chopper cruises straight over my head, out onto open water. I don't need to look to know it's banking around for another pass.

Take this opportunity to rotate the gun and train it on the ferry window, call again for Rose to cover herself, press and hold the trigger, chewing up the hard clear plastic, one eye on the helicopter . . . After what seems like an age, considering I have my naked back to a lot of men with weapons, the window folds and collapses out of its frame.

Go low and scuttle to the cabin just as the helicopter lets loose its guns on us, Rose shrieking, once again I do my utmost to cover her with my body. Give it a second and as the chopper passes I snatch up the lady, hoist her through the hole I've created, and into the ferry. Pain. Hand, hips, and leg calling mercy, mercy on a cripple.

Bullets and dirty rain slap the surrounding area, but I pay this no mind as I grasp the sill and haul myself up, thankful that I'm a scarecrow-assed motherfucker. I come up over the side and put my legs down on a wood bench, then tumble forward onto the floor of the ferry.

Rose is crouched next to me. Talking again. ". . . so fucking scared. I am so fucking scared."

So am I, Rose. But that's not the part of me in control

at the moment. I rarely let that pussy drive. Drives scared, and that gets you dead.

Move. We're up, swaying toward the stairs. This particular Circle Line boat probably dates from the 1960s, an elder in their fleet, and the deck slopes at a thirty-degree angle. Noxious rain and river water has pooled up on this side of the boat, as well as soaked cardboard boxes of Cracker Jacks and M&Ms and a large number of various floating soft drink bottles, bobbing in the shallow lake.

I believe it's one of those triple-decker affairs. Rose goes down and I manage, only just, to catch her by her forearm, which feels childlike, insubstantial. Vaguely register her protestations but I'm getting progressively dizzier, motherfuckers, I need to keep hitting it while I'm still capable of movement.

Find the stairs, everything at fun-house angles, attempt a quick look back at the terminal but my vision, my vision is . . . dim, things seem to be contracting like the end of an old film as the curtains move in from the sides. Gotta hurry this up.

Two flights up and we're out in the open again, the rain pelting the deck and tickling my hot skull. Rose slips and falls onto one knee, I haul her back up, she slips again. I'm blinking, blinking against the wind and rain, again I steady Rose and we stumble forward, slipping and sliding on the oily surface of the deck, and in due course we are at the plexiglass railing, with nowhere else to go but straight down into the river.

Fuck me. All indicators pointing to an ugly resolution here.

"Hey yo!" calls a vaguely familiar voice from behind us,

only just audible over the drumming of falling water on metal. Or maybe I'm imagining it.

Wearily, with scarcely any air in my chest, I turn to face a masked Cyna-corp soldier. And more to the point, I am looking down the elongated barrel of a Colt Python.

I've had it. This has to stop. I am smoked out, people. But my body, on its own accord, has brought my CZ level with the soldier's bug mask.

"Do what you gotta do with me here, we gonna tussle, whatever. But the lady walks," I wheeze. I am not sure if I'm heard.

The Colt is partially lowered.

"Bitch-ass nigga," says the soldier. Sounding triumphant, and very familiar. "Stuck-up motherfucker, look who's shining now!"

"Kim!" snaps Rose, launches into a Korean tirade that my spent brain doesn't decipher straight off . . .

Kim, peeling off his headgear. His black hair plastered to his scalp by sweat. Stupid handsome, he wears that dumb grin, nodding at Rose.

Tune it in . . .

". . . gonna walk us out of here right now, Kim, you have some fucking nerve."

Still nodding, showing us his healthy chompers, the young Kim speaks in English. "Word to God. Miss Hee, with all respect to my *shateigashira*, you gotta speak a little more respectful to me. Situation done changed, yo. Up in this bitch all ninja, drop it *Mission Impossible*–style." And turning to me again. "Hey, how's it feel . . . ? Hey yo, lower the heater, faggot."

I don't do it. I don't think that would be wise. Never did exactly trust this kid and now I sense I'm getting confirmation of his shifty-ass loyalties. No soul.

Kim laughs. "Are you crazy, dog?"

Rose saying, her arm on mine ". . . here to bail us out, that's not a very gracious . . ."

"I get it now, so you gonna save us, Kim?" I say. "You gonna fly us home all magically delicious?" Finding a little oxygen, a little booster for my blood, emergency stuff I must've had on reserve. "You the real big boss here, you the hero?"

"Got some nerve, black, I will say that. All backed up against the wall and still beefing—"

"Not putting my gun down, Kim," I say, eyes flapping at the rain, wishing I could see straight. "So make your move if you got one, hot stuff."

Rose is jerking her gaze back and forth between us like she's at a tennis match.

Kim's big dumb grin twists itself into a hard leer. Rose starts to put it together.

"Don't fucking tell me you're . . . *working* for them, Kim," she says.

The boy jerks her into his chest, she lets out a short scream. The Python is back up and directed at me.

"Oh, don't sweat it, Miss Hee. Ain't nothing really changed."

I try to get sensible on the boy: "Don't be a fucking dumb-ass, Kim. Let her go. This is the wrong route, brother, I'm telling you. These folks have nothing for you."

Rose is vibing pissed off and brave. "I'm your family, Kim, and you want to fuck that up?"

"Listen to Rose, Kim. She's making some sense," I say. My gun hasn't moved out of his face. The better part of me hopes he doesn't make me do it. Feeling stronger. Don't know where the extra energy is coming from, but Allah knows I need it.

Kim laughs again, and it's a nasty sound. "This nigger."

"You don't get to call me that, Kim. Now let's back this up and do it right, there's still opportunity here to do the proper thing. No sweat. Let's just rewind this shit."

Kim is squinting, eyes hooded, and if he's wavering, I can only tell by his voice, which oscillates only ever so slightly. "Naw. Jal ja, bitch."

Me and Kim. We fire our guns at the same time. Doesn't please me in the least and I think of his asthma inhaler, his basic humanity, but I put one in his eye, or at least I'm pretty sure because in short order I'm distracted by the force of the .357 caliber bullet hitting my vest like an anvil, emptying my lungs, and knocking me back just enough to compromise my footing.

I slip and go backward over the side of the boat. The foul water comes hustling greedily up to meet me.

Despite everything that's transpired, I'm blowing taps, and mourning yet another perfectly good suit. And thinking this Kim kid wasn't the sharpest tool in the shed, despite his drive. The punk put his money on the wrong horse. So motherfuck him.

Hit the poison river like it's concrete, and the darkness that's been loitering takes the opportunity to pounce. And consumes me.

At the precinct, seated at a metal table. A coconut Yoo-hoo and a set of Reese's Peanut Butter Cups are placed in front of me. It takes my twelve-year-old brain a bit to come to the understanding that this bounty is actually mine to do with as I see fit. To date, it's one of the kindest things anybody has ever done for me.

But shit. That bar was set pretty low to begin with.

The cop with the mustache and the gentle voice straddles the chair across from me backward, like Rog from What's Happening!! His mustache is salt-and-pepper, brown with some gray in it. Kind of like my dad's beard looked just before he finally gave up, let it all go.

"Son," he's saying softly, "there's a lot of things we could talk about. We could talk about all the junk you and your friends have done in the past, the spray paint, the trespassing, the switchblade here, all that, and the trouble you could be in right now. But we don't have to do that. You know why? Because you're helping us out, in a really big way. Helping out each and every person in your neighborhood. Especially boys your age. Do you understand that?"

I nod. I understand.

"And you understand the difference between telling stories that aren't true, just cause, you know, it's fun to make things up; and then telling stories that are true, about things that really happened. You get the difference, right? I know you do."

Again I nod. I understand.

"So when I show you those photos again of all the different men, are you gonna tell me the same thing?"

I nod. "Yeah. He's not in there."

"No?"

Shake my head. "Nobody believes me."

"Well, I believe you."

He believes me. I look at him. He says, "Then maybe you can tell me where he is, if he's not in there."

So I tell him. Finally somebody asked the right question.

I tell him about the man, the super at the Van Courtland Houses. The Boogie Oogie Man, who took me to that building on Crotona with the other kids. I told him what I saw and what he did. Pretty soon there's a couple more cops in the room, somebody taking notes and glancing anxiously at the clock above my head. People go outside to talk into telephones or radios. I hear people running out in the hall. I get scared, but all through it, the cop with the mustache holds my eyes and says, "Go on. It's okay."

And he makes it seem like it's okay.

I get sleepy and close my eyes for a second and now the cops are gone. The sounds are different and it's extremely bright. I squint and look down. No longer a child, I wear a black uniform. See my boots, black as well, beat, a soldier's boots.

The cop with the mustache again, grayer, thinner, but the same man. He's not a cop anymore and wears the same clothing I wear.

"All right there, son? Lost you for a minute."

I nod. He slaps me on the shoulder.

"Yeah, yeah, we're all tired. So let's do this fucking thing and go back to the hotel, huh? That's my boy."

I nod. He's moving off across an area covered in a light dusting of sand. Me standing there in military regalia, assault rifle in hand, sand camo, turning now to address my crew, mouth open, and our orders are . . .

Get sleepy again, close my eyes for a moment, and the light is different. The sound . . . muffled music nearby. I'm in a complex with many small rooms. Next to me is a beautiful girl. She could be Japanese, but I don't think so, and she wears a black silk dress with a dragon print.

Her long hair is in a single thick braid that lies across her right shoulder, covering her right breast.

"Song Ji-Wong?" I'm positive it's her. It's got to be her. I need it to be her.

She leans into me, giggling with her mouth covered. "So cute! I told you my name, it is Kiki." She knocks on my head like it's an empty shell. "Kiki Oda. Come on, we sing a song!"

"Okay," I say.

"First I sing you a song?"

"Okay," I say.

She claps her hands together, snatches a black cordless microphone off a glass table. There's a small bowl of lychee fruit, and another of those Japanese crackers. Two martinis. Mine is cloudy, hers is not.

I am smoking a cigarette, a menthol. The box is on the table as well, the brand is called Zest. I stub it out in a nearby ashtray. Don't like menthols.

Music starts, and on a large flat-screen TV an '80s-looking video, a white couple with big hair enter a glass elevator in a huge hotel, turn to each other with dreamy expressions.

"They say give you this too. Okay?" She looks at me shyly, holds up a folded piece of paper, kisses it, and hands it to me. "Now I'm gonna sing."

Okay, I think. She sings and it's achingly beautiful, I want desperately to keep listening and just fall into it but the sound fades as I smooth out the paper on the tabletop.

Her lipstick marks the corner. The sheet comes into focus and I recognize it instantly. It's a faded Xerox of the floor plan for the New York Public Library. The number 18 is at the top of the page. Small x's are drawn in throughout the building. Evenly spaced. Placed next to . . . placed next to exits. Next to supportive, weight-bearing columns.

This can't be right, I think.

I hear the voice of the cop with the mustache saying, ". . . can't overstate the importance of this job. It's historical stuff, boys. We can only be honored to . . ."

Song is shaking me. Smiling her geisha smile.

"You fell asleep. Maybe drank too much. Don't fall asleep here. No sleeping. Wake up. Wake up, mister."

I look at her face. Her smile disappears. She's simply staring at me. I am watching her true face, hard but warm, hardened from exposure to horrors I couldn't even come close to imagining.

"Wake up," she repeats. And I do.

V omiting thick cloudy water into thick cloudy water. Another wave comes sideways and smacks me in the face. Gargling, choking on the taste of it, which is indistinguishable from the stench of it, I am suspended in viscous liquid waste. This, the most irredeemably polluted river in the western hemisphere.

The temptation to panic is great. Won't bullshit. In the best of times I am no great swimmer. I kick at nothing, mouth going under, back up, gasping, hacking up liver cocktail and rankness.

To call this seething mass "water" . . . opaque wetness with the awful complexity of wine, I detect meat, some sulphur, mercury, and an iodine/pus finish. Like sipping a liquefied corpse. I am made a cannibal. All of my precautions for nothing. Sliding in and out of my wounds, filling my lungs, my stomach, my skin absorbing its contagion. No sea life can survive this, let alone us land mammals.

No. Only microbes. Bacteria. Amoeba. Carcinogenic particles. Single-celled parasites, seeking out my heart, my stomach, where they might grow larger and stronger until the day they begin eating their way out.

The temptation to despair is even greater than the temptation to panic. I struggle out of my suit coat, my head going under again a couple times in the process, remove the vest that certainly saved my life, my mouth an "o," trying to keep it above the river. Lost my face mask. I push my right shoe off, can't manage the left.

The System doesn't have much to say about travel on or in water. I look for help there and find none forthcoming. So I flap my arms like the shitbird I am, try to orient as best I can just eyeballing it.

Pick a point onshore and focus, get to chilling myself out. I float about fifty feet from the island, apparently having drifted north a good stretch . . . I see the remnants of the Seaport, Pier 17, and what I reckon has got to be the rear of the old fish market. The mast of the sunken *Peking* is just visible above the waterline.

Watch a chopper bank east, headed north. Black, no markings I can see. As it slides out of view, I observe myself as if from above, I am granted clarity.

Yes, clarity. I chill, I let my muscles slacken. Stop my thrashing. Just float now. Observe the rain hitting the oily, almost gelatinous surface of the water, blinking slowly, allowing myself to be calm.

In a sense I am relieved. One of my greatest nightmares, being submerged in this river, has now come to pass, and as of this moment I am still kicking back. I still possess the will to continue. Disease may overtake me but I will push on until I can go no further.

Been treading water for many many years. To be literally doing so now is, strangely, a kind of release.

Faced down worse than this poison too. Flash on it all: Stress positions. Sensory deprivation. Drug-enhanced interrogation. Probes of all kinds. Injections. Psychic assault. Countless surgical procedures, serving unknown purposes. Niggers sloshing around in my brain. Removing things. Substituting things. *Adding* things.

But more than this assortment of tortures, far heavier than my saturated clothing, far more painful than any bullet wounds or broken hands, far more noxious than the water I tread, is the dawning understanding of what happened here, in this town. What has been done to my city.

And I've know it all along.

My head skyward, mouth agape, cause however tainted, the rain tastes better than the river. Droplets prick at my face.

I can now say with some certainty that I have been re-awakened to the facts surrounding February 14. Almost as if impact with the river itself has jacked open the crypt in my skull within which this information was interred.

Why this happens now I am not entirely sure, but the man known as Nic Deluccia's reappearance in my sphere has, very likely, much to do with it.

I can now face the fact that I myself am complicit in the actions carried out that day. I can live with this, only because I now understand that I did not follow through with my portion of the assignment.

Yes, I have a very good sense of what happened here, and yes, I've known it all along. This understanding is so vast that I cannot look at it directly.

What I do not understand is *why*.

But I have a couple of pretty solid theories, y'all. Confimation of which requires keeping myself alive.

So. This simple decision to live obliges me to perform a slow, zigzaggy doggy paddle, my only dance move when fully submerged. Head toward shore, the rain not slackening an iota. Have the impression that every drop is aimed at my hatless noggin and, as I struggle toward the embankment, that the river wishes me dead, is actively trying to murder me.

C oming up on seven p.m. by the time I'm back at 154 Hester, popping a pill, propped up and patched to-gether. At this hour the street action is heightened a touch, as the work shifts change and folks are either headed home or to their respective job sites.

There's just enough bustle that I allow myself to fade into the background, parking myself on the corner of Mott Street in front of a former optical store, now stuffed to the gills with dried fish, vegetables, and herbs. Used to be the smell of such a joint would be enough to make me gag, now the Great Stench overrides everything and renders all neighborhoods olfactorily conformed.

Spent some quality time with my Dr. Feelgood, who has his base of operations over at the old NYU Hospital Center, since renamed Petraeus Memorial.

Don't have the luxury to sob over the loss of my Paul Smith kit. After tossing a J. Crew near the Seaport for some fresh gear (desperate times, yo . . . the simple gray suit will suffice until I have the luxury of doing some proper shop-ping), I got up to the hospital having commandeered one of those Chevy Volts down on Front Street. It's that puke-generating neon-rust color so popular pre–2/14.

At Petraeus, I park in the *AMBULANCE-ONLY TOWAWAY ZONE*, and I'm whisked past a teenaged Russian girl with a crushed foot. Stitched up in no time. Clean shoulder wound. Painful tetanus shot there. Would've stood for a tetanus enema, a bleach bath, after that dip in the river.

Hand is set in a plastic brace, wrapped in gauze.

Broken rib from that .357 shot, nothing to be done about that. They ask no questions but I get the usual rap: stay off my feet, blah de blah. Lucky to be alive, blah de blah, et-fuckin-cetera. Do I need anything else?

Moi? Well . . . sure I do. Drugs.

J. Crew was also good for something in the murse family. I have to be realistic about my world now, can't go carrying everything in my pockets. Black fabric sort of bike-messenger bag. Stuff it full of pills and Purell™, grab my two pistolas that a nurse dried off for me, and bounce.

Dr. Feelgood doesn't even protest anymore. The man is terrified of me, and I don't do anything to dissuade him in this respect.

Back in the Volt, zoom downtown, return to the swamp that is Chinatown. Kathleen will be okay for another couple hours. Probably.

I watch 154 Hester for a good twenty minutes. I watch for others watching. Trade a bottle of Percocet (keeping a couple for myself) for a pack of Lucky Strikes and a shitty Chinese electric zippo, and with one stroke I am a heavy smoker again.

Kill four cigarettes end to end. Nobody looks at me twice. Purell™ up no less than six times. Tap out yet another pill. The wrapping on my hand filthy already.

Choppers overhead, moving uptown. Always, always with the choppers.

I figure it unlikely that a) anybody would have traced action down to Dos Mac's hideaway, and that b) they would have been able to gain access, Cyna-corp or not. So what the hell.

Make my way down the street and casually lean on the

A button (*NO MENUS/NO CLONES*). After an age I give the door an easy shove, and it comes open. My stomach drops.

Slide my gloved hand along the edge of the door, feel around the central lock, my digits come away covered in gray powder. Gingerly I smell it . . . nitrates. Explosives.

Oh, Dos, goddamnit my brother. Pull out my CZ and chamber a bullet. Ease the door open with my shoulder, darkness within. Slide inside. No clue where the lights might be. I make my way around the big chamber, back to the wall, feeling for a switch.

The only illumination stems from the multiple screens, which I'm unable to see clearly from where I'm at, but show the street, the corner, and the downstairs "soundstage."

"Dos!" I call out, figuring fuck it. Everybody gone. Listen to nothing but the hum of the monitors.

I'm about a quarter of the way around the whole joint when I run into what I believe to be the mains. Deep breath and throw the switch.

There's far more to see but my eyes are naturally drawn to the two bodies, one of which is flat on its face in Cynacorp garb, closer to the main door. And the other of which is Dos Mac. He is cuffed to an Aeron chair and appears even at a distance to have been beaten.

Fuck, Dos.

I wait for a moment and absorb as much as possible given my compromised brain. The joint has been torn apart.

Move. Go to what remains of the Mac. Feel for a pulse. Nada. Man is dead, plain and simple, and it's not a pretty picture cause they got to fucking him up bad. Body cooling, but not yet cold. I spin him around. He's shirtless, revealing a beautifully rendered stylization of his subway map across his back. Turn him front again. Lacerations around his neck and chest. Burn marks, some from cigarettes and a few look more like taser trauma. Familiar stuff. We're old buddies, torture and I, having done it to others, and having had it done to me.

Dos Mac was a friend. I brought this horror here. My man. I meditate on the Mac, sitting down here with his righteous works, and me with mine up in Midtown. We were cut from the same sheet of leather, no doubt. Damn shame we never really got it together.

Cruise over to the Cyna-corp soldier. Kick the body over. Knock off the helmet. Another corpse, this a muscular black dude with shaved eyebrows, sightless peepers. Put the helmet back on. Consider shooting him up, airing him out, but I doubt if that would improve my mood.

Back to Dos. Need to suss this fast. Gotta look deeper. I inspect his mouth. Feel around his scalp. Then, there, right there on his left hand . . . in blue ink, scrawled: D! 116.

I stand upright. 116. Is that an address? An indication of time?

No. Dos knows me pretty well. Go to his books, mostly reference tomes on subjects like *Systems Theory*, *Thermodynamics*, *Mass Movement: A Comparison of Indian and Chinese Transport Infrastructure* . . . these I jump over, come on, come on . . .

The number 116 in the Decimal classification system is "Change." Usually in a metaphysical sense.

There are two books that are not textbooks as such. One is the Robert Moses biography, and the other is a worn edition of the *I Ching*.

The Book of Change. Snatch the slight volume off the shelf, flip it open fast. Two coins hit the floor. Scrawled on the title page is: *FALSE BOTTOM LOWER DRAWER*.

Back to the desk, two metal filing cabinets supporting a plank of wood, jerk open the lowest drawer on the left, full of sketches and papers, dump this stuff. Feel around . . . spot a kitchen knife. Grab that and pry at the edges, the thin metal bottom comes away.

A pile of dude-on-dude porno, a labelmaker, my hard drives, DVDs. On top a neat-looking folder marked *ANALYSIS + FINDINGS*, with today's date.

Quick work. I sit down with this in my lap, lighting a cigarette. In Dos's neat tiny handwriting:

SUPERFICIAL FINDINGS

1) Discrepancies and deliberately misleading information found in digital audio on DVD marked "Four Seasons 6/27." Audio data when opened in ProTools program was seen to be heavily edited and in some instances entire phrases attributed to a Senator Howard were constructed entirely of syllables taken from elsewhere. CONCLUSION: In comparison to unedited material, very different conversation emerges in which the men ID'd as an "ATF agent" and "Nic Deluccia" seem to be attempting to convince Howard of the wisdom of "disappearing" or murdering an individual, it is implied to be the senator's girlfriend. The senator has a lot to say on the subject but is slippery, and ultimately he refuses the proposal outright. From the evidence it seems that an attempt is being made via tampering/deception to portray sen as initiator of hit on said g-friend.

2) Pretty lady singing karaoke on DVD marked with Korean characters has lovely voice. Not a K-Pop fan but enjoyed listening.

3) Dismayed to view surveillance video on hard drive (Glyph manufacture) marked NYPL RRR CAM 3, dated yesterday (Monday, November 9), as it appears to show destruction of

*library books via flamethrower by individual known to me as
the "Librarian," a.k.a. Dewey Decimal . . .*

I dry heave into my mouth. Bring my wounded hand
to my lips, the dirty gauze . . . this . . . must be a mistake.
Dos must've not seen things clearly, these cameras are . . .
it's impossible.

Drag myself back to the Mac's report, vision dimming a
notch, my gorge barely under control:

*. . . in what appears to be the Rose Reading Room in the New
York Public Library, beginning at 15:16, and terminating
around 15:25. CONCLUSION: If this is not thought to have
taken place as described, it is suggested the "Librarian," a.k.a.
Dewey Decimal, himself view this footage and look for indica-
tions of digital tampering or image falsification as this analyst
could find none.*

END INITIAL REPORT, TUES 10th NOV

H ands trembling. Insert the DVD with the Korean words for *Cabin Four, 3/12/94* into the iMac's disc drive. Pixelated view of the now familiar karaoke cabin.

I light another smoke off the butt-end of the one I'm just finishing. Chaining it.

The video starts without preamble. There is a seated woman on the couch. Even with the pixelation and poor quality I can see that she is classically beautiful. I believe I recognize her to be Song Ji-Wong.

She wears a tight black or dark-colored (the footage is in black-and-white) reflective dress, looks like silk. She wears her hair in a single long braid thrown over her left shoulder, which hangs down below her left breast. On the table are two martini glasses, two smaller bowls, a pack of cigarettes, an ashtray, and a dark cordless microphone.

Song sits quite still, in silence, though faint laughter and music is audible, probably coming from surrounding rooms. She seems occupied with her nails. At one point she looks at her watch, sighs, glances around the room. She returns to her nails.

I cannot explain it, but I am entranced. Could easily spend the rest of my natural life watching her on that couch. Observe for about ten minutes, during which time Song hardly moves. Her posture is extremely proper.

Then she starts, as if having nearly fallen asleep. Picks up the microphone. Moves to what must be the karaoke machine and fiddles with it for a moment. She then returns to her spot. She wears rather high heels, which she now removes. Climbs daintily up on the glass table. Her stockinged feet. Closes her eyes.

Music starts. It's clearly a ballad, the sounds are cheesy and wack, the chord progression simple and sad. Behind her a video commences on a recessed or flat-screen monitor, showing a '80s-looking couple milling around.

Song is focused, eyes remain closed. She then opens them and looks directly into the camera. The hair on my arms and the back of my neck stands straight the fuck up, it's unsettling and inexplicably thrilling.

Song ignores the video behind her, which starts scrolling the lyrics in Korean characters, and begins to sing in English:

> *On the floating, shapeless oceans*
> *I did all my best to smile*

Her voice is crystalline, with smoke at the edges. It soothes and it disturbs. She's an earthbound angel and/or demon. A sorceress. She does not shift her eyes from the camera, not for an instant. Something's off, and I realize it might be the fact that she does not blink. It's a physical impossibility and I chalk it up to the video quality. She slides into the next verse:

> *Did I dream you dreamed about me?*
> *Were you here when I was full sail?*

She pauses again for the reintro. I am with her. To describe this as sexual would be missing the depth of the experience.

Something soft grazes my neck—

Spin around, gun aloft, a shift in air pressure, the memory of movement behind me, but there's nothing save two dead men and a lot of trashed machinery. On the tape Song moves to the third verse:

Should I stand amid the breakers?
Or shall I lie with death my bride?

I still have my gun out. My hand is shivering. I am positive I did not just imagine that. It could be . . . it could be military. Who knows what kind of technology Cyna-corp has at its disposal? I don't rule out . . . but I have to turn and watch Song. Have to do it, no choice in the matter.

Hear me sing: "Swim to me, swim to me, let me enfold you.
Here I am. Here I am, waiting to hold you."

The music shimmers to a close. Song drops her gaze, and with that the intensity is broken, like a telephone connection. It's abrupt and physical and I wobble slightly, unsteady. On the tape she gets off the table and busies herself with putting her shoes back on. Then she returns to her nails.

I turn and look at the dead men. Dig the ransacked shelving.

What the fuck just happened?

Stand stock-still in the middle of the room for a few moments, listening. Kill the audio on the DVD. I do not breathe. Keep listening. A leak somewhere, steady trickle of rain on concrete. Otherwise nothing at all, nothing.

My smoke singes the gauze. Toss the cigarette aside,

break the quiet with a hissed "Fuck." Think I hear something shift, something nearby. Knot in throat, I croak, "Hey."

And get silence in return.

Spooked. I eject the CD, which is so hot I nearly drop it. A magical thing, a talisman. One has to be careful with this shit.

Realize I gotta cut out, gotta dip but fast. With much effort I consider the hard drive, the one with the library surveillance. Does it matter? That's the question. Does it matter what I might see on there? Who does it affect, besides myself?

No one, no one at all.

I believe Dos. I believe that's what he saw. Or was manipulated to see. I can't know that if I watched this material I wouldn't be manipulated in exactly the same way. How can I know that?

All right. Perhaps, just perhaps, it was neither Nic nor the senator, nor Nic's people at either of these men's bidding, who destroyed my stock back home. I can accept that.

And if I accept that, then whatever might be on this hard drive, it simply doesn't matter.

Relevant: based on Dos's analysis, Nic is/was leaning on the senator. Not the DA. It's been Nic all along. Take that a degree further, and I like Nic for having had Song and the baby whacked. Whacked and hacked. *Dismembered.* Limbs, head removed . . .

Drop the hard drive on the floor and crush it with my heel. Grind it in there good. Time, time. Get to fucking work, Decimal.

Lean over the computer. Open up this freaking Skype

program. This much I can do, I'm not a total troglodyte, motherfuckers. List of past callers, check it. Scroll . . . there. I click on *BOOGIE_OOGIE_OOGIE_MAN_2.*

Peck out a message, gut saying go, go, go:

NEW MEETUP, NIC + NEW VIBE. I HAVE DOCUMEN-TATION REGARDING SEN. HOWARD U WILL WANT 2 HAVE IF U WISH 2 CONTINUE BLACKMAILING TH MAN. IN EXCHNGE FOR THIS MATERIAL, AND FOR A LIVING KATHLEEN KOCH, I WANT ROSE HEE, AND I WANT U PEOPLE OFF MY ASS AND OUT OF MY WORLD 4EVER. MEETUP TOMORROW (WEDS) MORNING, 4:45AM, BROOKLYN BRIDGE TOWER, MANHATTAN SIDE. I WANT TO SEE YOU, ROSE, AND SEN. HOWARD. NO GUNS AND NO ENTOURAGE. ANY DEVIATION AND KATHY DIES.
BEST,
DD

Never said I was a poet, habibi. I just like books.

Hit *Enter*. There's the cartoon blip.

Collect the rest of my material, throw it in my new bag. Hit the good Purell™. Kiss my man Dos on the top of his head. Through the surgical mask, natch.

Whisper: "I loved you, brother. See you on the flip."

Toss back a pill, shaky. And with that I dust.

Ghosts pursue me up the FDR, shrieking and raging. Ghosts increasing in number, in ferocity. I flee them at a gallop. Drilling it, hit Harlem River Drive.

Major Deegan, exit 13.

Flash through blighted neighborhoods, long ago emptied of anything organic.

Stand before the Gun Hill Houses. Behold the architectural cruelty of American public housing. Behold the banality of economic segregation, of slow genocide.

Observe the empty playground, and the singularly ghetto debris strewn here and there: forty-ounce bottles of Olde English Malt Liquor, Doritos bags, chicken bones, a stray toddler-size Rocawear sneaker. Et-fucking-cetera.

Note all of this. Disregard it. Move.

Enter the building. All surfaces are subway-car metallic, imperious to graffiti.

Enter the elevator, which is functioning tonight, and a cloud of old piss and beer. Push the correct button with my elbow.

Exit the elevator; follow the hallway to the correct door. Shift the bag of dried octopus and the jerky to the other hand. Two bottled waters in my bag.

Take out the key.

Key in lock.

Listen at the door.

Weapon out. Just in case.

Open the door.

The rain ceased about two o'clock in the morning, replaced by yet more dense cloud cover.

Naturally, I did not close my eyes even once, lest Senator Kathleen Koch slit my throat with her manicured talons. Restraints notwithstanding. Though it seemed as if she had given up.

Kathy ate a bite or two of the food I brought, drank a bit of water, and had nothing to say that made sense. For Kathleen Koch she spoke very little whatsoever. Kept talking hazily about a migraine, and I do believe the woman did indeed have a serious headache. So much the better. Call me weak-willed but I fed her a couple Percocet. Added value: further sedation.

Gagged the girl again, once she seemed ready to sleep.

Disappointed in Kathleen Koch. Was expecting a more formidable mind, if totally bonkers, but in the end it seems she's no more than a vacant mask, containing nothing.

Sat and smoked cigarette after cigarette. Lighting one off the butt of the last.

Approximately four fifteen a.m. finds me propelling the Volt southward. Koch is spread out on the backseat, secured and compliant.

I am alone with my city in that ungodly hour, the hour of the wolf, when even an all-but-abandoned metropolis takes on yet another dimension of strangeness.

Fucking ghosts hound me all the way downtown,

howling, making demands I do not understand. I'm reeling, spinning. Pedal fully depressed, and I don't dare look back, not for an instant.

Despite having not slept, or perhaps because of it, and despite the urgency of it all, I possess a certain tranquility, and I honor the System by choosing the correct routing: Bronx River Parkway to the Bruckner Expressway, exit to Bruckner Boulevard, cross the Third Avenue Bridge and onto the FDR Drive, which will carry us to the Brooklyn Bridge.

Mindful travel. I force a peaceful kickoff to a day that will very likely plunge me into some fresh abyss.

I wear my unremarkable gray suit, as if headed to an office job. Shoulder holster under my jacket with my freshly cleaned CZ-99, a fresh fifteen-round magazine. At my belt I carry the diver's knife. Ankle holster with the P290, six rounds in the clip. On the front passenger's seat I have my bag with the senator's file, retrieved from the air vent, and all accompanying digital media.

Meditate on the transient nature of corporeal existence. On the impermanence of our institutions, our monuments to ourselves. Certainly, I have seen a great many of these massive shrines to our ambition fall, dissolve, be reduced to ash.

After the rickety UN underpass and at about 39th Street, I look west at the lights of the Chrysler Building, and I experience a profound rush of sadness, accompanied by the realization that, as the Buddha teaches, a denial of one's true nature and clutching at perishable and changeable things can only result in acute suffering.

Y'all think I don't suffer? Oh I suffer, acutely, and shower this anguish on all who come near me.

Spiritual reconstructive surgery is required, should I survive the next few hours. My next big to-do, on my extremely short to-do list, which at the moment looks a little something like this:

1) ORGANIZE BOOKS AT LIBRARY ACCORDING TO DECIMAL SYSTEM
1A) DON'T DIE
2) TBD

But fuck such musings. Can't afford waxing philosophical now. I gotta stay good, I gotta stay gold.

Spark a smoke and keep tight on the road. The ghosts hang back, perhaps sensing my resolve. Headlights hit the sign for exit 2: *Brooklyn Bridge/Manhattan Civic Center.*It is necessary that we pass this up, and come back around, in order to avoid violating the no-left-turn edict of my System.

Attain the on-ramp. Screetch-slide the Volt to a sideways halt, at the head of the bridge. Above what I know to be the appropriately named Rose Street.

Let's do this thing and get it done. Move. Lean over, grab Howard's papers. Hop out, toss my cig, smooth my suit, quick-check my tie. With the file under one arm, I jerk open the rear door, produce the diver's knife. Kathleen bug-eyed like I'm gonna slash her. Stuff the file halfway down my pants.

"Senator Koch, just behave or I'll cut you," I say, slicing her legs free and hefting the woman out of the car. "We're going to meet your husband. If you stay cool we should all be going home this morning, and I promise you you'll never have to see my fucked-up face again. Understand?"

Kathleen affirms this, hair a modernist sculpture, all

that spray holding it fast in a gravity-defying shape. Her soul-windows unfocused, but black with . . . what? Loathing? That would, at least, make the woman human.

I leave the duct tape on her hands and mouth in place. Don't need her crazy lip.

With my back to 100 Centre Street, where but a few days ago this action jumped off. Picture myself on the nineteenth floor that day, with a pair of vintage binoculars, observing my progression now, lugging Senator Kathleen Koch. One of her heels has broken, so the both of us hobble like a pair of gimps up the wooden walkway of the great bridge.

As we draw nearer to the Gothic tower, I admire afresh the symmetry of the structure. Dual traffic portals like a pair of colossal bullets. The structure is lit up from behind by an unseen source. Two relatively new American flags hang from the top of each portal.

Ahead, beneath the central column, I can make out several figures.

Set it off.

"Pardon me, Senator Koch." Stow the knife, pull the CZ, cock the hammer, and place it against her temple. Correct my breathing; easy, circular.

A stairwell connects the promenade with the Manhattan-bound roadway, where I observe a parked limousine. Beyond the massive structure, I note a helicopter, engines off, positioned on the walkway, with a large spotlight directed skyward, illuminating the immediate area. Parking the chopper any further out would prove dangerous, as it's unlikely the wounded bridge would provide needed support.

Can't see faces, but I make out figures I assume to be Nic, Senator Howard, and Rose, who wears the orange jumpsuit I saw her in earlier. Nic and Howard sport wool overcoats, the senator leaning his large frame on his famous cane.

Check the spires and lattices, structurally compromised as they are, for signs of snipers or hidden gunmen. There: I note one solo soldier, crouching on the very same cable upon which I observed the potential jumper. He or she cradles a rifle of some kind. Motherfuck. Make that two, there's a second shooter on the opposite side.

I can also assume we have personnel in either the limo, the chopper, or both. Despite this I proceed, pound forth, gripping Kathleen. Wanna end this.

"Godawful time of day, son," calls Nic. "Had to set an alarm—"

"Did you misunderstand me, fuckwad?" I lift my damaged shoulder in the direction of the shooters in the latticework. "I said no extras."

Flash on Rose, who looks scared but okay.

Nic spreads his arms, makes a what-are-you-gonna-do gesture, indicates the senator, who speaks now.

"Son, I take responsibility for the security. I found your conditions to be unacceptable. I apologize if this is disturbing to you and I hope you will consider that these measures are for all of our protection. Understand that you have the advantage, and please forgive the liberties I've taken."

I stopped about thirty feet from the trio and re-up my hold on Kathleen. Shift the pistol to the right of her eyeball. She makes murmuring sounds.

"Senator Howard, sir, you gotta understand that if I detect more bullshit I'm gonna shoot your loony-ass wife, no problem. Be doing the world a fucking favor. That's my promise to you. Can you dig me?"

The senator has placating paws out. "I believe you, son,

and indeed I have strong faith that we, all of us, given our differing views and perspectives, are honorable people, and can find light in the darkness here, which will lead us to greener pastures. Now, may I speak with my wife?"

"Tell your shooters to back up on out of here."

The senator offers me a tight smile. "I can't do that, son. Now, I ask you kindly, might I have a word with my wife?

"No sir," I say. Proceeding gradually closer. "What happens first is you all release Rose. Once Rose is with me, you and your lady can slide back to your Sugar Hill crib and burn miniature crosses and spew crazy at each other as y'all see fit. Deal?"

Nic watches all of this, tense. His eyes flicker back to me.

I am close enough now to make eye contact with Rose. Once-over my girl . . . handcuffed, hands front, but otherwise unbound. She starts blinking rapidly . . . dig a pattern . . . short-long-short, Morse code? I crinkle my brow, are you okay? She seems to get this, bobs her head subtly.

"Son," begins the senator, "as Galatians tells us . . ."

Nic wades in: "I think what Senator Howard is trying to say here—" interrupts himself with a smoker's cough. I size up Deluccia, the man is as nervous as a stray dog in Hanoi. Him knowing I know. Me thinking: I got you, motherfucker.

An eyelid spasms on the old man, him saying, ". . . is that he needs a show of good faith coming from your side, you know—and hell, only way to make your . . . commitment to a peaceful resolution here is to just let Kathleen go now, that's the way I see it, son."

I shift my grasp on Kathleen. Tighten it. "Both of you

all best stop calling me *son*. It's irritating. You cut Rose loose, you get Kathy. Simple like that."

The older black and white men make reassuring noises, though nothing about our configuration changes. Senator saying, "Of course, of course . . ." like anything else would be unimaginable.

Which is to say: bitches running a game on me.

"Am I failing to e-nunciate proper? Did you all not savvy the fucking deal? Last time. Rose goes first, she comes to *me*, Kathy goes to *you*. Done, now do it!"

Nic saying, "Let's just dial it back a couple notches. Simmer down. We're gonna," throws an eyeball at the senator, the gunmen above. "We're gonna talk this thing through."

That zinger makes me smile ugly. "Oh, we gonna *talk*. Let's talk about *this* then, Nic. Just so everybody is clear with each other from the jump." I'm enjoying the man's clear discomfort. "I assume you've come clean with the good senator here?"

Senator Howard looks slowly over at Deluccia, with interest. Nic grimaces.

"Not totally sure what you're referring to there, young man," answers Nic, his upper lip nearly writhing off his face.

If I was shooting in the dark a bit prior to this moment, I see all the affirmation I need in the man's twitchy mouth. Me saying, "Oh, so perhaps this is something y'all would prefer to discuss in private then. Talking about blackmail, some shit like extortion being a serious matter and all . . ."

Kathleen's head slowly comes up at the word *extortion*, and she watches her husband. The senator's ears are perked, and he looks over the older white man as if for the first time.

"What would this gentleman be making reference to, Nicholas?" posits the senator flatly, brows arched.

Nic is grinning unsteadily at everybody. Looking from face to face. Figuring he's fucked. Then he looks back out at the river.

"Aw jeez . . ." he starts, as if it's a damn shame, and makes the move I'd make in his position. Producing an automatic he draws Rose to his chest, places the gun at her neck. Planting the girl between the two of us. "Ya know . . ." he says, grinning again, "I never did trust you black motherfuckers. Oh, I *worked* with you. All these years . . ."

Rose has her face set, looking resigned. She closes her eyes. Fuck me. I'm doing the math, counting all the guns. Press mine firm against Kathy's skull, saying, "Nic, man. Happy to kill the good Missus Senator here, kindly unhand—"

Howard cuts me off, attention locked on Deluccia. "Nicholas."

"Okay," says Nic, bobbing his head. "Black motherfuckers. I regret having just said that. I spoke in anger. My point being . . . you people think you've had it tough? I'm from *Staten Island*, goddamnit. My pa gets kicked off the force for being a drunk bastard, goes to work at *Fresh Kills*, for Christ's sake. I come from *garbage*. From hunger. Kill myself getting out of it. Had to prove my worth every goddamn day, but I did it, hell if I didn't do it. You all think you're the only ones had to climb that fucking ladder?"

The senator shifts his weight, taps the cane on the ground. Looking disgusted with Deluccia, with the world, deeply inconvenienced.

"Nicholas," he says, "that is neither here nor there."

"Every goddamn day on the force, I had to listen to the

crap, this *racial quota* stuff. Sensitivity training. Endless crap I gotta listen to, you think I never dug a goddamn hole?"

Cry me a fucking river. Count two shooters up in the railings. Think, Decimal. Saying lightly, "Does anybody, anybody at all, give a shit about this here white lady?"

"Nicholas," the senator intones, holding up a hand to me, getting more Southern-fried church-ified. "Friend, are you going to address this young man's assertions or are you going to have yourself a prideful pity party over there, talking nonsense and putting both of these women in harm's way like a damned coward?"

Nic doesn't look at the senator. Peering down a tunnel at me. "Everybody know who that young man is right there? What he is? Murderous ghetto trash. A stone killer. I *saved* you, son. Nobody ever did that for me, oh no. I picked you up out of the gutter, boy. You weren't on anybody's radar. Woulda been dead or in the joint serving twenty-to-life like the rest of your buddies."

It cuts, I won't lie. Coming from Nic. He can still burn me like that, and it's a fucking drag to acknowledge this. Mouth open, primed for snappy comeback, but generating zilcho.

Nic carries on: "I gave you every possible tool you needed to rise above your shit-assed station, and this is the kind of thanks I get in return? This is the *respect* I deserve?"

"The way I hear it," pipes in Rose, her voice rough but steady, "you'd've never made chief had this boy not broke that child-killer case for you back in the—"

Rose with the tight research. Nic pulls her closer and places the gun across her lips. I tense even further. If I paste Kathleen . . . but then I got nothing . . .

"Keep your fucking buckethead mouth closed, miss.

You're in enough trouble as it is, and you should be smart enough to not talk such nonsense."

Clarence's mouth spreads into a grimace. "Well, there's some truth in there somewhere, Nic. But let's not dwell on such matters."

I keep my split lips zipped. Nic is wild-eyed, unhinged. Letting dude bury himself, flecks of spittle popping out his mouth.

"With my bare hands, Clarence. I built everything. And now I gotta stand here and be insulted by you fucking—"

The senator smacks his cane on the wood of the walkway. "You will at the very least curb your language, in the presence of the ladies!"

"Clarence." Nic is coming apart, pleading with his friend. "Listen now. As much as I owe you, my pal, you owe me twice over. I broke this city in half for you and your people. Hell, Clarence, we cleared out tremendous populations, *nations*, for your fucking lawyers, your people to come in and do your—"

Senator Howard waves his paws like he's battling wasps. "Nicholas, that is enough, you will stop your blathering this instant! You benefited more than any man on God's earth from these arrangements, and don't you dare say different! That is enough, sir!" booms the big man.

Me straining, digging the snipers, thinking one shot there, one shot here . . . it's doable.

Nic spins his head my way, shifts gears. "And that devil," he snaps, thrusting his jaw at me, "did things in my employ that no other man I've known would *contemplate*. No hesitation." Nic speaks faster and faster. "He's a goddamn psychotic, is what he is, plain and simple. And what's more, the bastard has all manner of unholy . . . med-

ical enhancements that make him that much more dangerous, and that much more *unpredictable*."

Unbidden, it's the DA again: "*Decimal. Your file. The stuff
they did . . .*"

The stuff they did . . . shake it off, stay now, soldier. Don't
be played. Let the haters hate.

We inch forward, my coiffed hostage and I. My priority
here is Rose Hee.

And the girl is looking at me, to me . . . With great
fucking effort I maintain my multiple foci, Kathleen, Nic,
snipers ahoy. Does the tiny machine in my neck squirm a
little? Brain playing with itself . . .

Saint Nic is now officially on a rant: ". . . good reason
to believe this bastard is completely and utterly insane. He
comes out of the goddamn woodwork and you are going
to take his word over mine? After all these years? Two-time
Purple Heart? Medal of Honor?"

"Nicholas!" bellows the senator. "I will not listen to
you debase yourself further! We are all aware of your service to the New York Police Department, and the government of the United States—"

"I AM the goddamn government, Clarence!" Nic snarls.
He knocks Rose aside and moves in the senator's direction.
"I AM the goddamn United States! We OWN this country,
Clarence, together, as a unified body! Let's not pretend . . ."

Nic closing in on Howard, lifting his arms as if for an
embrace. Me thinking: unwise, Deluccia.

"That's enough. Take him down," says the senator
quietly.

There's a faint *thwipp* from overhead, Nic Deluccia puts
his hands over his throat, head bobbing, blank-faced, he
sways in our direction, spins back toward Howard, nod-

ding, and collapses facedown, blood pooling out the bullet hole in his neck.

Howard steps forward, stands over him. Shakes his head gravely. Looks like he's getting misty. Or is suppressing a yawn, hard to tell which.

I tense, getting ready to grab Rose. Clarence indicates Nic's deflating corpse and says, "He was a great American patriot. Let us never forget that. Let us remember him as he was." Howard pauses, smiling crookedly, many levels to that smile, looks sideways at Deluccia's body as it bleeds out. "A great . . ." This is the first time I've heard the senator hesitate. "A great patriot," he finishes. Looks toward me. "Kathleen. Let her come to me now."

Contemplate the two shooters, thinking it remains possible I could take them out and still be prepared for whatever might pop out of the chopper . . . or come from below. No. Suicide jag.

Fuck it.

Wordlessly, I nudge Kathleen toward her husband, and thus 50 percent of my leverage. Howard's file sticking out of my pants. The other 50. But it's Rose, nobody else, who I've got a constant eye on. Frantic for an opening.

As Kathleen wanders forward, an Aryan Secret Service agent is coming up the stairs from the motorway, presumably having been in the limo.

His wife comes into range and Clarence air-kisses a smudgy rouged cheek, making no effort to remove the duct tape from her mouth. Kathleen appears catatonic, gives no visible reaction to being released, to the presence of her husband. It's an empty moment, a loveless exchange of zero.

"Tom," Howard addresses the agent, tilts his head in the direction of the waiting limo.

Tom guides Kathleen across the walkway and down the stairs. She's staring at a point in the middle distance, zombified, and disappears below deck, still gagged and bound, as if simply transferred to another hostile agency.

Two Cyna-corp soldiers in full regalia float around the main pillar and move to collect Nic's corpse. Howard looks off toward the Statue of Liberty, as if it's just another day at the office. Or out of discretion. Or whatever.

Must be getting simple cause I just cannot fathom how any of these motherfuckers are behaving. Plenty of time to ponder this later, as my only objective now if to snag Rose and get her off this bridge alive, second priority to do the same for myself. Primed to blaze, but Rose has her own plans, stepping forward to . . .

Woman spits on Deluccia's body, the back of his head. A big hocker. "Piece of shit," she hisses.

The soldiers point their visors toward Howard for guidance, but the senator is leaning on his cane and studying southern Manhattan island. One of them glances at the other and shrugs. The drones commence scooping up Deluccia, a leaky bag of fluid and fat in an overcoat.

Do this, Decimal. As if in a stop-motion nightmare, I'm trying to close the distance between myself and Rose, still just too far away to touch . . . calculating the odds of surviving a swan dive into the East River from this height . . .

Hobble barely two steps and the senator barks, "Move no further lest you be struck down. Fire on my say so."

A red point of light, so small and tremulous, appears above Rose's heart. Spiky shivers down my back, me saying, "Senator, we don't need to get all agitated, right? You got Kathleen, right? Let's put a fork in this one, everybody go home. How about it, Howard?"

Clarence is unresponsive. Lock on Rose Hee, voice lowered, steady now.

"That's all right. That's all right, Rose. Almost over."

But Rose, icy cool, doesn't seem to need reassurance.

"Drop that gun, son," Clarence says to me. "Kick it over the side there."

What can I fucking do, but do like I'm told. Bye-bye, 99.

"Emotional," mumbles Howard. "I get emotional, Lord knows. It's my nature . . ." His back to us. The man has not turned during this entire exchange.

Nobody saying shit as the chopper comes to life, lifts off, and banks away, taking with it the body of a man I once knew, and the spotlight that had allowed us to see properly.

Now the prick of red is even brighter, wavering over Rose's breast. In the half dark, she begins to speak.

I was fifteen," says Rose to nobody in particular. "Song was, oh I don't know, maybe three or four years older, probably eighteen or nineteen, but of course at that age it's a big deal, you know. The gap is huge."

Shifts in my direction, the dot shifting with her.

"Mister Decimal, listen. Song was like my big sister and I loved her. I want you to know that. I am telling *you* this. I am not talking to him."

By which I assume she means the senator. Who is still showing us his back, seemingly fascinated by the view, and seemingly uninterested.

"I loved her," Rose continues. "I would sit up at night and do my makeup like her and get in bed and sing to myself like she did. But I was so goddamn jealous too, in that way you are at fifteen, it all seemed so easy for her, despite her problems with the language, having just come over and all. And this extremely dangerous job, you know. But she kept it pretty clean. I mean, there was some coke and shit but this was just kid's stuff. She was intensely Catholic too, in this twisted way, but on Song it made sense."

The wind flares up for a moment, causing the flags overhead to whip angrily.

"Always had men around, of course." Rose makes no attempt to free her hands and scarcely adjusts her position. "I mean, you should have seen her, real grown-up men, some of them pretty scary, the kind of men you're drawn to, though, at a certain point in your life, you know?

Always taking her to restaurants, white places with fancy white-people names like Pravda or Le Cirque. Flashy cars and all. My dad did everything he could to keep me away from her, said she was a bad influence, and she probably was. But what I couldn't explain then is that none of it seemed dark to her. She was so totally alive, open, always laughing. Singing. Otherworldly. She was like a fairy, or an angel. I know how that sounds. And she really listened. You could feel her listening, and just that she would listen to me and my stupid shitty fifteen-year-old problems made me feel very special. It wasn't just that she was beautiful either. It was . . . the Kanji word is *myokon*. Life-force, prana, you get me?"

I nod. All this I saw on the videotape, plus.

"And her voice. Her presence. I don't know what she thought she was doing but she could have easily been . . . a pop star, oh that sounds so fucking cheap, or run her own business, any kind of business. Be important. Whatever she wanted."

"And enter Nic Deluccia," I say, gently now, because Rose is crying in that honest way grown-ups cry. The laser doing a happy little dance on her breast. I'm thinking if I rush and tackle her, we just go off the side like a pair of doves . . .

She rallies, takes a couple deep breaths. Says, "Well, no Nic yet. Song told me about one man in particular. He was a black man." She sniffs, casts a glance at Howard. "She'd been with other black men before, which, well, we're all adults here, was considered not acceptable, but she was dating one of the Knicks, so I assumed it was another athlete. But at one point she said no, he was some kind of very powerful person, a politician, and she told me they had this chemistry and this almost . . . religious kind of connection. She never used the word *love*. They would have this intense sex and then intense prayer session. I didn't get it, but it was clear he was different than her usual guys. Said his name was Howard. Said he was famous."

The senator leans on his cane, still focused in the opposite direction. Me thinking we just run for it, get clear of the tower . . . but no, we wouldn't make it five feet without getting straight ventilated. Best to hold steady, wrack my deeply compromised brain for angles.

"So." Shows me a cheerless smile. "Nic Deluccia. I mean, come on, I'm fifteen and this is a fucking NYPD police chief. He was famous too, I'd see him on TV and my dad would turn it off. I'd ask why he turned it off and my dad wouldn't answer. So Nic is smart as hell, as you well know, Mister X, just picks me up off the street, very official-seeming and scary. You know, a squad car on the way home from school kind of thing. Like I'd done something wrong. But he was extremely kind as well. I mean, that was how he got to me."

Maybe it's just a passing breeze, but I get a wave of chills. I know all about Nic Deluccia's brand of kindness. Dig. His manner with kids.

"Kind but clear about what he wanted to happen; I was to feed him information on this Howard as it came in from Song. Simple. I was to do this or . . ." Rose falters, looks over at the senator. Returns her eyes to me as they well up. She lifts her cuffed hands and presses her thumbs there. And I am reminded that I just met her the other day, which now seems deep in the distant past.

"Rose, you don't have to—" I begin, but am cut off as she says, "Or he'd take away my father. Destroy him. Had everything he needed to do it. I didn't want to know about some of the stuff he claims my father did, I still don't, but remember I'm fucking fifteen, he says my dad will get life, just gone forever. He even talked about the death penalty, which hadn't been tossed in New York yet . . . told me about lethal injection, described death row, told me what it would be like for my dad. I . . . it was just so unreal."

"So you did what you had to do." What she needs to hear. "Protect your family, shit, you did your best, sweetheart. How you did that, it doesn't matter anymore."

The lady nods. "What else was there? I didn't see an option. Chief Del . . . Nic, he told me he'd kill my mother if I told anybody. Said he'd know immediately, he had people watching. At school, everywhere. Oh sure, he didn't want to do it. And he knew he wouldn't have to, cause I was such a good, smart girl."

"Yeah," I say quietly, "I know how the motherfucker did."

Rose takes me in. "So you know I didn't feel like I had a choice."

Think about a fifteen-year-old child, wrestling to wrap her brain around these terrifying uniforms, this sense of complete helplessness, these softly expressed threats. I've seen that movie.

"Yeah," I say. "Let it go. You had no choice, Rose." It's what she needs to believe.

Gratitude is creeping into her grim smile now. Fresh tears, but she appears at least partially released. Cleansed.

"No, Rose. No indeed, dear," says Clarence.

Senator Howard speaks at the river, then pivots and saunters our way, slowly, head lowered. I cannot see his eyes. Start moving too, wanna get between them.

"He was not a perfect man," says the senator, his voice liquid sugar. Fat finger my direction. "Stay where you are, son, that'll do."

Crimson dots doing a jig, one on me and one on my girl. Fuck.

Rose snorts and pulls her shoulders up. "Nic Deluccia was an ruthless, evil fuck. Stepped on everybody in his life, acted like he was doing them a favor. He was a user, a parasite."

Tell myself if the senator comes closer, I'll go for my other gun, shoot him dead, sniper or no.

"He ordered a human being be killed and cut to pieces," says Rose. She looks swiftly at the senator. "A woman you claim to have loved."

"And an infant. Your own goddamn child, sir," I add through my teeth, everybody always forgetting about the baby, which to me is perhaps the most demonic aspect of this whole crime.

The senator is wagging his head slowly. "The kind of decision-making Nic Deluccia engaged in," says the man, soothing, "is part and parcel of being a success. No other way to go about it, dear."

He lifts his mug. The edges of his lips arch slightly heavenward.

"And of course he had your help. Even if you only provided him information. Did he not?"

Rose is now studying her feet, looking childlike and entirely vulnerable. "But he . . . lied to me," she says, simply.

The senator, the complexity of his face, he wears an approximation of compassion but snakes churn beneath that veneer. Don't like it one fucking bit. Think about my ankle holster.

Fuck. Still aware of the snipers.

"That's far enough sir," I say, my voice not resonating authority in the way I might have hoped. "You stay put, hear?"

Howard neither looks at me nor modulates his tone, saying, "Bradley, just a warning for the gentleman."

Red blip near my foot, small pop and there's a quarter-size hole in the walkway. Watch the blip zip up my leg and land in the middle of my chest.

Sure it gives me pause, but motherfucker. Senator still approaching my girl, saying, "Rose. Child of God. You must forgive yourself. That's the first step. Here."

Gunmen with laser sights notwithstanding, don't like this one bit, say fuck it and lurch quick and sloppy to block his progression . . . Howard ducks me with speed befitting a much younger man, Rose steps backward . . . and within a rat's heartbeat he is standing before the girl, hand on her cheek, tender.

Rose, her eyes are on me. Color them confused, but unsurprised.

"Mister X, I think . . ." whispers Rose.

Half kneel and jerk the Sig off my ankle, the gun is up and pressed into the back of the senator's head, getting in tight so the folks overhead might not want to risk a shot . . . I'm shouting something, Howard knocks me back with a simple sweep of his heavy forearm, and it's as if I'm watching a slo-mo replay of an action that's already occurred.

In which:

Senator Howard steps to one side and withdraws the tip of his cane, a long thin stiletto blade, slowly from Rose's solar plexus. *Twisting* as he does so.

Me grabbing at the motherfucker, as close as I can get,

dragging the much larger man backward and down . . .

The front of Rose's orange torso is already saturated with dark. She watches me, not the senator, not the knife that killed her. Her mouth opens, and she says one last thing that I do not hear over the wind. Rose lifts her shoulder, and dies, folding like a dropped marionette, her head smacking the wooden walkway with a hollow thunk.

I want to step to her but I know she's gone.

So I prepare to do the senator, thick ball in my throat, get him in an unsteady choke hold, gun shoved so hard against his head it's like I wanna push the fucking thing though him and out the other side. If the gunmen above get any ideas both of us will eat a bullet, either theirs or mine, and this is clear to all present.

The big man maintains, Zen-master serene. His voice is slightly constricted by my elbow, but he speaks slowly and clearly.

"Consider your next set of actions with much care, son. I have only been the agent of divine retribution."

"Is that what you call it?" I say in his ear. "Cause I just saw you stab an unarmed woman in front of Jesus, Mary, Joseph, and everybody else."

"No. No, indeed. Stand down now, stand down."

I realize he's speaking into a microphone. Snap my head up and one of the snipers has me on lock. Looking up at the barrel, the scope, two perfect little circles, red all in my eye like I'm getting my vision checked.

"I suggest you take your hands off me, and we can talk properly. I want to speak to you, I need to express a few things."

Again I have little choice but to step back. Show the snipers my hands, trying to make eye contact but the one is completely cloaked in dark and the other hangs partially in shadows.

Fuck me. I want this man dead in a huge way. For the moment, however, I back off. Until I can come up with an angle to work, and I'm calculating fast and sloppy, my processing a big jumble, machinery looping on Rose is dead, Rose is dead . . .

I did not . . . I failed her. I have failed.

Senator Howard dusts off his coat. Clears his throat. As he's adjusting his tie, he begins to speak: "When I was robbed of the one woman in Creation who I truly have loved, robbed in such a . . . coarse, abrupt manner, my sorrow knew no end. I will mourn her into the grave."

"Grave I'm about to drop you in, pops," I rasp, but the senator is talking over me, and I'm gouged-out inside anyway, can only spew harmless venom.

"Oh, my union with Kathleen is a sham. Any fool can see that. It's a political expedience. Nothing more."

Howard pauses. Fingers the flag pin on his tie.

"And how about your child, Clarence?" I say, my mouth trembling. Everybody leaving out the child. Innocent blood. I am no better, bringer of death, magnet of mayhem. My chest tightens, need a pill, I manage, "Or is a child, is that immaterial to a big motherfucking man like you?"

The senator angles his chin at the ground, says, "Abraham faced the very same dilemma. It was not my choice to make, you see. Son, in the Book of Luke, Jesus tells us of a prostitute who came to Him. *She stood behind Him at his feet weeping, she began to wet His feet with her tears. Then she wiped them with her hair, kissed them, and poured perfume on them.*"

He moves his eyes to me, heavy lidded.

"You are perhaps a man who understands love, and in

this way you must understand loss. Deep loss. So in this act," shifts his gaze for a second to Rose, "I become unburdened. A great weight has been lifted from this heart of mine, son." Takes a breath, then: *"The righteous shall rejoice when he seeth the vengeance: he shall wash his feet in the blood of the wicked."*

Wicked like my black heart. Death is my escort, my bride.

Yes, I'm cognizant of the snipers; and yes, I'm gradually bringing my gun back up. There's a corner of Hell reserved for specialized worms like myself, so I might as well get some shit accomplished before they drop me there.

Say, "An eye for an eye makes the whole world blind, and other saggy-ass motherfucking clichés."

"The Word is the eternal Word. Impervious to the insults of men." Howard shows me his profile, aloof.

Jesus, the fucking nerve . . . that's it. Fuck a sniper. I've taken a bullet or two, I can take a couple more if need be.

I lean into the big man hard with my Sig, dig into his substantial gut. Dude has to savvy which nigger is in charge over here.

That's me. I'm running this motherfucker.

So why do I not feel like I'm in the pilot's seat?

Howard falls back casually, leans away from my pistol, appears generally unconcerned.

Cause I'm the one who's trembling. Manage: "Motherfuck your Good Book. This ain't church now. You're out here with me. Out here? This is the street, and you're just another citizen. About a minute you're just another floater headed down the river."

Howard's earpiece is almost vibrating off his head. "No, that's quite all right." Talking to the gunman overhead. "Stand down now, stand down."

I cannot believe . . . I reach up and jerk out the earpiece, get real close, and whisper: "Think I won't I'll kill you where you stand and walk away with a satisfied mind, you're thinking wrong."

The senator actually laughs. An easy laugh, as if we're discussing something amusing but ultimately unimportant. Says, "Yes, well, there's a lot of thinking going on, so you think on this, son. You've hit a wall. It's all slipping away, young brother. But along comes Clarence Howard, quite suddenly a man, a generous man, in need of assistance."

I kick him in the leg. "Goddamn right you're in need of assistance, about to get a bullet right through your crazy motherfucking head."

He stumbles, looks up, shaking his head rapidly at the unseen gunmen, signaling no, no, he pushes his rap forward: "A new security chief, perhaps, son. Something along those lines. The timing of this bodes well, as I am aware of an opening. Mr. Deluccia's men, they are a flock in need of a shepherd. You know this organization well, from within. Think on that and tell me it doesn't make good sense."

"I'd fucking shoot my own self before I'd work for a fat snake like you."

"Is that a fact? No, son, you're far smarter than that. And when it comes to snakes, you've kissed the ring of far more poisonous breeds than me. You'd be very much your own man anyhow. Very lucrative position, believe me. This is why I find this extortion business so surprising, why Nicholas would . . . he was certainly not wanting. Ah well, I suppose it's just as Proverbs would have it: *He who hath love for money shall never have money enough*."

I couldn't be pressing the barrel any harder to the side

of his face. See that I've actually broken skin. Though you wouldn't know it by the man's expression.

"Preacher, keep preaching fast. You're getting closer and closer to God by the fuckin moment." My tongue is basically in his ear.

Howard isn't bothered. The big man sighs. "One of the saddest things about you, son, is your illusion that you have any control whatsoever over the course of your relatively worthless life. Sadder still because you could be a man of accomplishment."

Try to speak but I am at a momentary loss.

"Son, I read this whole situation wrong, I afraid, and I am truly sorry if I spoke harshly to you at any point along the way. Apologies are due to you and our mutual friend, the late district attorney. No, it was my own house that was not in order. Well. Let me make amends with the modest means at my disposal."

The senator simply lifts his hand, and gently nudges my pistol out of his face. I'm so fucking shocked I let him do it. I stand back reflexively, and realize that I've relinquished control to him. That he was always steering this ship.

He lifts his cane, indicates the lights of the Empire State Building. Even at this hour, helicopters orbit the top, casting lights here and there. That there is ongoing activity is clear.

"We're doing great work here, son. Rebuilding the Kingdom of God. You understand so very little of what has been set in motion. And yet you were part of it once." He gestures in the direction of Midtown. "I don't expect you to understand. You're a foot soldier. But it's just as Christ had it in John 2:19: *Destroy this temple, and I will raise it again in three days*."

Pegged, frozen. The universe demands I execute this loathsome man. What stops me?

He then slides his attention back toward me, looks down, and very deliberately, the senator begins to clean the blade at the head of his cane on my pant leg.

"In my generosity, I offer you a renewed opportunity to participate in this new great American experiment, and in a greater capacity. I do so because for all your . . . erratic ways, you have solid *bones*. Do you know what I mean? You're raw, but in possession of all the makings of a leader. Capable of much."

He presses the top of his cane and the knife disappears. Indicates my pant leg, now decorated with Rose's blood.

"Gonna need to dry-clean that, son. Send my office the bill, no problem at all."

Trying to speak. Chest empty, constricted.

"Well. That's about the long and short of it, son. I will leave you to your private thoughts, and be on my way."

Find some air, saying, "Wrong, boss. Another step, you meet your cocksucking Jehovah in person."

Howard lifts his brow, and offers up a sympathetic look. "I am," he replies, not unkindly, "walking away now son. My chariot awaits."

He steps around me. I let him pass. I do not know why.

Turn with him, my gun still raised. Open my yap, close it. Open it again. "Three seconds," I blurt, just chin-wagging, "and I start shooting. One."

Senator pauses, rotates back in my direction. "Oh, I do hope I haven't done anything unwelcome, but upon your return to your library you will find certain . . . repairs and restorations have been made there. Consider this an advance on your first payment, and furthermore a gift of the U.S. Congress for which I proudly serve."

"Shit on your gift, I don't do fucking bribery, Uncle Tom."

Clarence chuckles. "Well, let's just see about that, now." He claps his hands, raises them skyward. "Yessir!" The exclamation makes me jump and I almost inadvertently pull the trigger.

His face is beatific, rapturous. His insanity profound and rare. Specific. It occurs to me that all men and women of power have varying degrees of this sickness within them.

"What a fine morning." He takes a moment, his true thoughts utterly unknown to me. "Does the Lord not work in unfathomably mysterious ways?"

Nods his head. Digs on the view. The very first light is just visible, spreading diffuse over the surface of the river, the southern islands. Morning creeping in.

My left hand is getting tired, and I'm still just a touch away from shooting this man.

Slaps his forehead. "Yes," he says. "I believe you have some paperwork for me?" As if discussing a dental chart or a W-2.

I think about that. And then I withdraw the file, hand it to him. He takes it, hefts it. Says nothing. Glances at me, lifts his eyebrows yet again, as if impressed by its weight.

Gun still trained on him, we stand there in silence for a bit, the senator looking out over the water. Humming a tune. Something secular. I recognize it, having only recently heard that track in a twenty-year-old video, it's fresh in my mind.

Finally he taps his cane to his hat.

"So, now. Goodness. The question at hand is: are you

interested in the future, my boy? Cause if not, well . . ." Lets that dangle. Then, "Get in touch at your leisure, and enjoy what promises to be a beautiful day, young man."

Senator Clarence Howard ducks down the flight of stairs and into the limo with a backward wave. The black thing rolls off in the direction of Manhattan.

And it's not until I see its taillights swing right on to the exit ramp for the FDR that I lower my gun.

Returning home, to the library. It's as if nobody's been here at all. Superficially.

Reckon they'll be waiting here, to kill me on my own turf. The balance in that arrangement, that's how I would do it.

I mount the stairs, my little gun drawn. Longing to shoot it at somebody, anybody. But I'm let down in this respect, as it's as empty as it ever was. Thus far.

Took Rose's body back to her people in Koreatown. They absorbed it without a word, and that world closed its doors in my face, with softness and finality.

On a concentrated inhale, I enter the Reading Room. Any sign of violence is absent. Neatly, symmetrically, a staggering number of books line the wall where my shabby piles, my work, had once stood.

A quick swivel left and right with the gun. I am alone.

I set down the weapon. Slide my mask down far enough to jam a cigarette between my busted-up lips, and light up.

Approach the new stock. Read the spine of one volume, then another. Check the adjacent row.

I kneel. This is a precise replica of my work. More than a replica, a restock. Decimal classes 000–004. Copies of common periodicals and books one might easily find, and, I can see, copies of rarities I had not thought existent anymore.

Standing, I clock a blue leather binder, with the congressional seal emblazoned on the cover, and the words *Library of Congress* in gold leaf.

Flip it open. It's a catalog of the books, printed neatly on thick, expensive paper. The title page is coated with a congressional watermark. It's printed on Senator Howard's office letterhead.

> *Dear Sir,*
>
> *Please accept this gift, with compliments of the 114th Congressional Body, to be considered a permanent loan from this date onward. I very much look forward to working together in the near future, and wish you all the best.*
>
> *May the Lord God be your guide, and may God bless the United States of America.*
>
> *With warmest regards,*
> *Sen. Clarence Howard*

Throw that motherfucking binder across the big room. It bounces off a deco metal railing, and comes to rest beneath one of the long wooden tables.

Touch the back of my neck.

Pop a pill, hands twitching.

Reach for the Purell™, and find that plastic bottle empty.

Also available from Akashic Books

THE DEWEY DECIMAL SYSTEM
a Dewey Decimal novel by Nathan Larson
252 pages, trade paperback original, $15.95

"A nameless investigator dogs New York streets made even meaner by a series of near-future calamities. [Larson's] dystopia is bound to win fans . . ."
—*Kirkus Reviews*

"*The Dewey Decimal System* is a winningly tight, concise and high-impact book, a violent, exhilarating odyssey that pitches its protagonist through a gratuitously detailed future New York."
—*New York Press*

CURSE THE NAMES
a novel by Robert Arellano
192 pages, trade paperback original, $15.95
*Edgar-award finalist for *Havana Lunar*

"In this unsettling mix of noir and paranormal obsession . . . Arellano displays a sly, Hitchcockian touch."
—*Publishers Weekly*

"Arellano pulls off the not-inconsiderable feat of making the disintegration of his hero more compelling than the end of the world as we know it."
—*Kirkus Reviews*

BLACK ORCHID BLUES
a novel by Persia Walker
272 pages, trade paperback original, $15.95

"The best kind of historical mystery: great history, great mystery, all wrapped up in a voice so authentic you feel it has come out of the past to whisper in your ear."
—Lee Child, author of *Worth Dying For*

"A remarkable achievement; imagine the richly provocative atmosphere of Walter Mosley or James Ellroy's best period work, and a savvy, truly likable heroine, and you have *Black Orchid Blues*. Persia Walker is a rising superstar in the mystery genre."
—Jason Starr, best-selling author of *The Pack*

OFFICE GIRL
a novel by Joe Meno
296 pages, hardcover, $23.95, trade paperback, $14.95

"Fresh and sharply observed, *Office Girl* is a love story on bicycles, capturing the beauty of individual moments and the magic hidden in everyday objects and people. Joe Meno will make you stop and notice the world. And he will make you wonder."
—Hannah Tinti, author of *The Good Thief*

MANHATTAN NOIR
edited by Lawrence Block
264 pages, trade paperback original, $15.95

Brand-new stories by: Jeffery Deaver, Xu Xi, Robert Knightly, Lawrence Block, Liz Martínez, Thomas H. Cook, S.J. Rozan, Justin Scott, John Lutz, Maan Meyers, Charles Ardai, and others.

"A pleasing variety of Manhattan neighborhoods come to life in Block's solid anthology . . . the writing is of a high order and a nice mix of styles."
—*Publishers Weekly*

BROOKLYN NOIR
edited by Tim McLoughlin
350 pages, trade paperback original, $15.95
*Winner of Shamus, Anthony, and Robert L. Fish Memorial awards; finalist for an Edgar Award and a Pushcart Prize

Brand-new stories by: Pete Hamill, Chris Niles, Arthur Nersesian, Maggie Estep, Nelson George, Sidney Offit, Ken Bruen, and others.

"*Brooklyn Noir* is such a stunningly perfect combination that you can't believe you haven't read an anthology like this before. But trust me—you haven't. Story after story is a revelation, filled with the requisite sense of place, but also the perfect twists that crime stories demand. The writing is flat-out superb, filled with lines that will sing in your head for a long time to come."
—Laura Lippman, winner of the Edgar, Agatha, and Shamus awards